GIANT SPECIAL EDITION!

Twice The Action And Adventure On America's Untamed Frontier—In One Big Volume!

DEADLY AIM

Having made up his mind, Nate faced around and began hiking. From the position of the sun he knew the day was only four hours old, so there was plenty of time for him to find the river before nightfall. His stomach rumbled, reminding him it had been almost a full day since last he ate, but he was not about to stop to eat until he learned the fate of his family and Shakespeare.

Suddenly the drum of hoofbeats shattered Nate's reverie and he turned to find nine warriors galloping toward him with shafts notched to bows and lances upraised. By their hair he knew they belonged to the same tribe as the man he'd seen in the trees. He was lifting a hand to make the sign for friend when the foremost brave took aim and let an arrow fly.

The *Wilderness* series published by *Leisure Books*:
1: KING OF THE MOUNTAIN
2: LURE OF THE WILD
3: SAVAGE RENDEZVOUS
4: BLOOD FURY
5: TOMAHAWK REVENGE
6: BLACK POWDER JUSTICE
7: VENGEANCE TRAIL
8: DEATH HUNT
9: MOUNTAIN DEVIL
#10: BLACKFOOT MASSACRE
#11: NORTHWEST PASSAGE
#12: APACHE BLOOD
#13: MOUNTAIN MANHUNT
#14: TENDERFOOT
#15: WINTERKILL
#16: BLOOD TRUCE
#17: TRAPPER'S BLOOD
#18: MOUNTAIN CAT
#19: IRON WARRIOR

GIANT SPECIAL EDITIONS:
HAWKEN FURY
SEASON OF THE WARRIOR

WILDERNESS

PRAIRIE BLOOD

David Thompson

LEISURE BOOKS **NEW YORK CITY**

To Judy, Joshua, and Shane.
And to all the good folks we meet on our travels
through Nebraska, Kansas, Montana, Wyoming,
and the Dakotas.

A LEISURE BOOK®

October 1994

Published by

Dorchester Publishing Co., Inc.
276 Fifth Avenue
New York, NY 10001

Copyright © 1994 by David L. Robbins

Printed in the United States of America.

AUTHOR'S NOTE

For the benefit of those who will wonder, four clarifications are in order.

The account of Nathaniel King's experience (and you'll know which one when you get there) is derived from contemporary records of a man who survived a similar ordeal.

Yes, the names of the various warriors are based on historical sources. The particular name that will either make you blink, laugh, or brand me as vulgar (you'll know which one when you get there) was in fact the name of a prominent Minneconjou.

The Pawnees did indeed practice the rite mentioned (you'll know it when....) until the early nineteenth century.

And, finally, please forgive the liberties I have taken with sign language in the interests of dramatic license.

Chapter One

The four riders were strung out in single file, riding along the south bank of the meandering Yellowstone River. They rode alertly, their rifles across their thighs, their eyes trained to the north.

"I'll sure be glad when we're past this stretch, Pa," said the youngest of the four, a lanky boy who hardly appeared old enough to handle the long Kentucky in his lap.

"I don't blame you, Zach," replied the father, Nate King. "Those Blackfeet get right riled when they find whites near their territory."

Nate was a big, powerfully built man clad in garb typical of those who made their living as free trappers: buckskins, moccasins, and a beaver hat. Angled across his broad chest were a powder horn and ammo pouch on one side and his possibles bag on the other. On his right hip nestled a tomahawk, on his left a large butcher knife. Wedged under the front of his wide leather belt were two matching flintlocks.

No sooner had Nate made his comment than from behind them came a hearty chuckle. "The Lord preserve us! I never met such a bunch of worriers in all my born days. If I had a dollar for every time you fret over nothing, I'd never have to raise another beaver for as long as I live."

Twisting in the Indian saddle he straddled, Nate gave the speaker a critical look. "You don't think the Blackfeet are worth worrying about, Shakespeare? With all the trappers they've rubbed out?"

Shakespeare McNair gazed at the sluggish Yellowstone and grinned. In his style of dress he was the spitting image of the other man, and like Nate he carried a Hawken. But where Nate's hair and beard were as dark as coal, Shakespeare's were as white as driven snow. And where Nate's green eyes were usually somber, Shakespeare's sea-blue eyes danced with playfulness. "You see any Blackfeet out yonder right this minute?"

"No," Nate admitted.

"Then I reckon we don't need to fret ourselves silly, do we?" Shakespeare asked. He adopted the tone of an orator on a stage and quoted the playwright to whom he was passionately devoted. "A man may, if he were of a fearful heart, stagger in this attempt. For here we have no temple but the wood, no assembly but hornbeasts. But what, though?" Shakespeare paused to give Nate a meaningful glance. "Courage!"

Young Zach shook his head. "Pa, why is it I can never figure out what he's saying when he goes on like that?"

"Don't feel bad, son," Nate said. "Half the time, he doesn't have the foggiest notion what the dickens he's talking about himself."

Shakespeare made a noise reminiscent of a bull buffalo on a rampage and looked over his shoulder at the lovely Shoshone woman bringing up the rear. "Did you hear what your husband said, Winona?" He launched into another quote. "An honest fellow enough, and one that loves quails. But he has not so much brain as ear-wax."

Winona laughed and said in flawless English, "Do not try to involve me in your petty arguments."

"Petty!" Shakespeare cried. "You've wounded me to the quick, fair maiden. Here I am trying my best to educate your husband in the ways of the wild, and you say I'm being petty?"

It was Nate who answered. "Yell a bit louder, why don't you? Maybe the Blackfeet haven't heard you yet."

"Ungrateful pups," Shakespeare muttered.

Nate King grinned and faced front. The brief diversion had taken his mind off the problems of the moment, but there was no denying them for long. He had two big worries eating at his innards, and no matter what his mentor Shakespeare said, they were legitimate.

Nate's first worry concerned the Blackfeet. His small party was on its way back to the Rockies after a visit to a Mandan village on the eastern plains. To reach the mountains, they had two choices. They could either follow the Yellowstone, which was the southern boundary of Blackfoot country, or they could strike out straight across the prairie, which would put them in the heart of Sioux territory. Neither prospect was all that appealing, and he had opted for the lesser of the two evils. By sticking to the Yellowstone, they might get through without seeing either Blackfeet or Sioux.

Nate's second worry revolved around his wife. Winona was over eight months pregnant, and he keenly desired to get her safely back to their remote cabin high in the Rockies before she gave birth. Although she was holding up well, he'd noticed she tired easier than she normally would, and the long hours on horseback were causing her pain in her lower back.

At that very moment the object of Nate's concern was touching her spine and grimacing. For the ninth or tenth time that day Winona had felt a sharp twinge. She was mildly upset that the sensations were becoming more and more frequent as time went on, but she did not relay her anxiety to her husband. She knew how he would react; he'd demand that they stop and rest for a day or two, delaying their homecoming even longer.

And, truth to tell, Winona sorely yearned to be home. She chided herself, as she had repeatedly the past few weeks, for talking Nate into taking the trip east when she'd known they would be hard-pressed to make it back before the delivery. What had she been thinking of?

Winona glanced at Nate to be sure he had not seen her flinch, then she straightened and pushed back her waist-length raven hair. Attired in a beaded buckskin dress that was loose fitting enough to partially hide her condition, she was as comfortable as she could be under the circumstances. She would not disgrace herself by showing weakness. She would endure whatever came along without complaint.

Just then young Zach looked at her. "You all right, Ma?"

"Fit as a flapjack," Winona said, deliberately mangling the figure of speech.

Zach cackled and slapped his thigh. "That's fit as a fiddle, Ma. This heat must be getting to you."

"It is hot," Winona allowed.

The boy nodded and squinted up at the blazing sun. He could remember only one other time when the temperature had been so high, the year his family journeyed to Santa Fe and wound up tangling with a band of Apaches. Wiping the back of a hand across his brow, he licked his dry lips and gazed longingly at the river. If it had been up to him, he would have stopped and run over to gulp the Yellowstone dry. But his pa had warned him about drinking too much, saying it would make him so sick he couldn't sit in the saddle, and from hard experience Zach had learned that his pa had an uncanny knack for being right about such things.

Humming softly, Zach stared at the expanse of buffalo grass to the south and wondered whether they would stumble on any of the shaggy brutes. The thought caused his mouth to water and his stomach to rumble. Buffalo meat was his favorite food in all the world, next to blackberries, of course.

Zach felt the breeze pick up and tilted his face to take advantage of its cool touch. He saw his Uncle Shakespeare do the same and hoped the breeze would last a while so it would cool them down.

Had the boy been able to see Shakespeare's face and not just his back, he would have observed how Shakespeare focused on the western horizon, studying dark gray clouds that had appeared. The grizzled mountain man pursed his lips, then sniffed a few times. Was that moisture he smelled? he asked himself. Or was imagination playing tricks on him?

Shakespeare adjusted his beaver hat, then stifled a yawn. He reluctantly had to admit he wasn't as spry as he used to be, and the long journey was gradually taking its toll on his stamina. When he got back, he aimed to sleep for a month.

Shakespeare thought of his beloved wife, Blue Water Woman, and pictured her attractive features in his mind's eye. He couldn't wait to see her again, to have her snuggle against him under a heavy buffalo robe, to know the thrill of her knowing touch. Stamina or no stamina, there were some things a man just couldn't give up.

The thought sparked a smile. Shakespeare idly gazed at the river, and at the undergrowth bordering its shore. A hint of tawny movement riveted his attention and he immediately called out, "Hold up !"

The other three complied. Nate turned his sorrel sideways and asked, "What's the matter?"

"This coon saw something, Horatio," Shakespeare said, with a nod at the brush.

"What?"

"Couldn't be sure. Painter, maybe."

Nate raised his Hawken and probed the vegetation. As he well knew, panthers were notoriously unreliable. Nine times out of ten they would go out of their way to avoid humans. But there was that one instance in ten when a rogue cat would stalk a man as it would a deer, and only quick wits and a steady trigger finger could bring it down. "Stay put," he said. "I'll take a look-see."

"Can I come, Pa?" Zach asked eagerly. He had never killed a panther before, and the prospect of tangling with one set his blood to racing.

"You keep close to your mother, son," Nate said. "Protect her if the critter gets past me." Nudging the chestnut with his knees, he slowly moved forward.

"If you get a shot, take it," Shakespeare urged. "No meat shines like painter meat."

Nate bobbed his head. Most trappers relished a juicy cut of panther tender loin now and then, but he'd never met anyone so almighty fond of the tasty meat as his friend. Cocking the heavy Hawken, he angled between a pair of saplings and scoured a thicket in his path. By now the cat was probably long gone, but he had to make certain. If it attacked, it might bring down one of their mounts before they dropped it, and at this stage of their journey they couldn't afford the loss of a single horse.

The cool wind was now blowing so hard the brush rustled and crackled as if alive. Nate wouldn't be able to hear the cougar, as some of the trapper fraternity had taken to calling the beasts, until it was almost upon him. He continually swiveled his head, checking in all directions, his whipcord body tensed for action.

Nate covered twenty yards, but saw neither hide nor hair of a panther. He rode nearer the river, where the going was easier, and drew rein on spying a set of fresh tracks in the soft soil. They were huge panther prints, as clear as could be. His finger resting lightly on the trigger of his rifle, he ventured westward, following the tracks.

The panther had paralleled the river for a dozen yards, then veered into a cluster of cottonwoods. Nate scoured the trees from end to end and saw nothing to suggest the cat was lurking in wait. He started to turn the sorrel, to go back and report they could go on, when a hint of motion out of the corner of an eye proved him wrong.

Nate had made a critical mistake. He'd been raking the growth at ground level, assuming the panther would come at him from out of the brush. He should have remembered that panthers liked the high ground, that they preferred to pounce on their quarry from boulders or trees when such were handy. And this particular cat was no exception.

The panther was perched on the branch of a cottonwood, its long tail flicking like a thick whip. Venting a feral shriek, it leaped, its front legs outstretched, its curved claws unsheathed.

Nate barely had time to bring the Hawken up. He stroked the trigger just as the cat slammed into him. The impact deflected the barrel upward even as it knocked him from the saddle. He landed hard on his shoulders and promptly rolled to his knees, expecting the panther to be on him in a flash. And he was right.

The cougar paid no attention to the sorrel as the horse whinnied in fright and bolted. It closed on the two-legged prey, its thin lips pulled back to reveal its tapered fangs.

Nate reacted instinctively, throwing the Hawken at the panther to buy him the precious seconds he needed to draw the flintlocks. But the big cat merely leaped over the rifle and swooped down intent for the kill.

Frantically Nate threw himself to the right, rolled once, and pushed upright, clearing a pistol as he rose. He hastily pointed the .55-caliber smoothbore and fired. The ball ripped into the panther's right shoulder, spinning the big cat completely around.

Snarling lustily, heedless of the blood pouring from its wound, the enraged panther coiled and sprang.

Nate was in the act of drawing his second flintlock. The cougar was on him before he could and he clubbed at its head as it bowled him over. Stinging pain lanced his forearm and he felt razor claws tear into his thigh. When he hit, he lost his grip on the second flintlock and it fell.

In desperation Nate shoved, pushing the animal from him. He got to one knee, dropped the spent pistol, and whipped out his tomahawk and butcher knife at the selfsame second the cat charged again. A deft swing caught the cougar flush on the skull and sent it tumbling, but it was up again in the blink of an eye and coming at him in a tawny blur.

Nate cleaved the air with his tomahawk, but missed. The cat rammed into him and they went down locked in a struggling flurry of limbs and steel. He stabbed once, twice, three times, and nearly cried out when fangs sank into his shoulder.

Suddenly Nate found himself flat on his back, pinned under the cat's great weight. The panther hissed and lunged at his exposed throat. He began to swing the tomahawk, aware it was too little, too late, and braced for the sensation of having his jugular ripped from his body. Instead, he heard the loud crack of a rifle and the panther went flying, tumbling end over end for a good ten feet.

Surging up, Nate crouched and waited for the next onslaught. There would be none, though. The panther was wheezing its last as gore and brains seeped from a cavity in the side of its head. Exhaling in relief, Nate glanced over his shoulder.

"Can't you do anything right, Horatio?" Shakespeare quipped, already in the process of reloading his Hawken. "The idea was for you to kill the varmint so we could have it for supper, not for you to wrestle the danged thing."

The close shave had rattled Nate. His heart was beating so fast, his temples were pounding. He sank to his knees and sucked air into his lungs, grateful to be alive.

"You all right?" Shakespeare asked as he tugged on the ramrod to extract it from its housing under the Hawken's barrel.

"Just dandy," Nate said.

"You look a mite cut up to me. I'll fetch Winona and have her tend you."

"It's just a few nicks and scratches, is all," Nate insisted, looking down at the blood flowing from his shoulder. A wave of dizziness assailed him and he fought the sensation. What kind of man was he, he mused, that he fell all to pieces after a little tussle with an oversized kitty?

Shakespeare was wheeling his black stallion.

"Hey," Nate said.

"What?"

"Thanks."

"Don't thank me. Thank your ladylove. She's the one sent me to check on you."

"She didn't think I could handle myself?" Nate asked, slightly annoyed that his wife would think so little of his ability to protect his family.

"Not that, so much."

"Then why?"

Shakespeare smiled. "She knows as well as I do that you have this natural knack for getting yourself into more trouble than ten men put together."

"I do not."

"Oh?" Shakespeare nodded at the still panther. "Most times a painter will leave a man alone, but not if one sees you. It attacks." He

17

gave a low snicker and went on. "Most times a bear will go the other way if it sees a man, but if one sees you it tries to rip you apart. Most times wolves will head for the hills if they so much as catch a whiff of human scent, but if they smell yours they figure you're their next meal. Most times—"

"I get the point," Nate cut McNair off. "There's no need to belabor it."

"There must be something about you that draws the beasties like rancid meat draws flies," Shakespeare commented thoughtfully.

"I like your comparison."

"Now don't get all cantankerous on me."

"I'm never cantankerous," Nate grumbled.

The mountain man studied his young companion a moment. "I've got it! Maybe it's your scent."

"What are you raving about now?"

"Your scent! It must set the animals off, sort of drive
 them into a frenzy the way catnip does cats."

Despite himself, Nate broke into a grin and shook his head in amusement. "I swear. The older you get, the crazier you get."

"Though this be madness, yet there is method in it."

"*Hamlet* again?"

"Good memory," Shakespeare said. "God's bodykins, man, much better."

"Weren't you fixing to fetch my wife before I bled to death?"

Shakespeare stiffened in mock indignation. "My pulse, as yours, doth temperately keep time, and makes as healthful music." He jabbed his heels into his mount and dashed off through the woods, the grin he wore belying the fear he felt on recalling how very close Nate had come to meeting his Maker. Had he not shown up just when he did, Nate would now be dead and Shakespeare would have two grieving souls on his hands.

Sometimes Shakespeare worried greatly about his impetuous friend. Nate was too head-strong for his own good. And the only thing that kept Shakespeare from taking Nate to task was the fact that Shakespeare remembered being the exact same way when he was in his mid-twenties.

Winona and Zach were anxiously waiting. Shakespeare noted their worried looks and promptly relieved their anxiety by announcing as he reined up, "He's sliced up some, but it's not serious."

"Take us to him," Winona directed.

"You really should have a talk with that man of yours," Shakespeare said, turning his horse and falling into step beside hers. "He should have let me tag along instead of riding off to face the painter himself."

"He wanted you to be able to look after us if something happened."

Shakespeare smirked. "Figured that out, did you?"

"I know how his mind works. He is always ready to sacrifice his life for ours, whether we want him to or not." Winona's eyes sparkled with pride. "It is yet another reason why I love him so deeply."

"He's a lucky man."

"As are you. Blue Water Woman is a wonderful woman."

Nodding, Shakespeare gazed at the western horizon and was taken aback to find a roiling bank of ominous black clouds had replaced the gray ones. He also realized the wind had gained even more strength, and there was no longer any doubt about the moisture in the air. "We're in for a storm," he remarked.

"Yes. We must tend to Nate, then find somewhere to take shelter," Winona said.

Little Zach, who had been listening to their conversation, now spoke up, "I like storms, Ma. All that thunder and lightning is exciting."

"Not if our horses get spooked and run off and we wind up afoot," Shakespeare said. "It would take us half a year or better to reach the Rockies."

Winona placed a hand on her huge belly. Bothered by the thought, she hurried on until she came to where Nate was kneeling by the river, naked from the waist, washing his wounds. She slid down, removed her medicine bag from a parfleche, and ran to him.

Nate stood, grinning self-consciously, held out his arms, and embraced her. "Got nicked up a bit, but at least we have fresh meat for supper."

"I see the panther almost made fresh meat out of you," Winona said, gingerly touching the fang marks in his shoulder. They were inches from his throat. Her heart fluttered and she gave him a tight squeeze. "Please be more careful in the future."

"You know me."

"Which is why I want you to be more careful."

While Winona prepared an herbal poultice for her husband's wounds, Zach rode off to find Nate's mount and Shakespeare pulled out his butcher knife and went to work carving up the panther. In short order he had the hide off and the best cuts of meat wrapped inside it.

The whole time Shakespeare kept one eye on the western sky and did not like what he saw. A massive wall of black blotted the heavens, creeping steadily nearer like a gargantuan ethereal monster. Occasionally the inky curtain was rent by vivid bolts that briefly illuminated the churning belly of the building tempest.

Shakespeare had lived through his share of fierce storms in his time, but this one promised to be the granddaddy of them all. He mentioned as much as he lashed the painter meat to the back of his horse.

Nate strode over, fully dressed, Winona at his side. "I'm ready to go." He glanced around, his brow knitting. "But where's Zach? Hasn't he returned yet?"

The three adults exchanged shocked looks. They had been so involved in their own tasks that they had completely overlooked the boy's absence. Together they shouted Zach's name over and over, but there was no answer.

In the distance, faint rumbles of thunder pealed.

Chapter Two

Fifteen minutes earlier Zachary King had been tracking his father's sorrel westward along the south shore of the sluggish Yellowstone River. He was thrilled at having been asked to fetch the horse. Like many his age, he was eager to show his father that he could be trusted to handle such chores. In his view, all too often his folks and other adults tended to treat him as if he was still a child of seven or eight instead of a grown boy of ten.

The chestnut had fled at a full gallop for over a mile, then slowed to a trot. Zach had no problem finding tracks in the soft soil. He came to a spot where the horse had stopped to drink, and from the depth of the prints he knew the animal had stood there a while gazing at the opposite shore.

"You wouldn't, you dunderhead," Zach muttered and forged on. Presently, though, he discovered that the sorrel had indeed waded into the river at a narrow point and forded to the north shore.

"Blackfoot country," Zach said aloud. He had the habit of talking to himself when alone, a quirk shared by his father and many other mountain men.

"Now what do I do?" Zach wondered. The fierce reputation of the Blackfeet was well known to him, a reputation reinforced by the several occasions the Blackfeet had attacked his family. If he ventured across the Yellowstone, he ran a very real risk of running into a band of the most dreaded warriors west of the Mississippi.

Flicking the reins of his bay, Zach plunged into the river and felt the water rise up around his knees. His father wouldn't think too highly of him if he shirked his duty. He had a job to do, and by thunder he was going to do it, come what may.

The water rose an inch higher, leading Zach to worry the river was deeper than expected. Thankfully, in short order the level dropped, and within another minute he was safe on a gravel bar projecting from the far bank.

Here Zach found more tracks. The sorrel had left the Yellowstone and gone straight through the bordering strip of trees and brush to the open prairie.

Zach reined up and searched the grassland. Far to the northwest a single creature could be seen running off, and although the distance was too great to make identification possible,

Zach knew it had to be the chestnut and he immediately gave chase.

It was fun to give the bay its head, to feel the wind whipping his hair and tugging at his beaver hat. Zach held his Kentucky in his left hand and pumped his legs to urge the bay on. With a little luck, he figured he could catch the sorrel and be back with his folks inside of half an hour.

Not much time had gone by, however, when Zach realized the sorrel was faster than his bay. Much faster. He fell farther and farther behind, and at length the sorrel was no more than a speck barely visible in the gloom from the approaching storm.

The dark clouds didn't worry Zach at all. Nate had taught him well. The boy knew that a lone rider on the open plain was an inviting target for lightning, so if he was caught in the storm, he'd simply dismount, force the bay to lie down, then lie beside her until the bad weather passed. He'd get soaked, but otherwise he'd be fine.

Besides, as Zach had mentioned earlier, he'd always loved thunderstorms. He liked to sit at the window of the King cabin high in the Rockies and watch crackling bolts dance around the towering ramparts. And he liked high winds, the way they shrieked through the trees, bending the stoutest of limbs. To his way of thinking, being caught in a thunderstorm would be a lark.

So on and on the boy rode, paying little attention to the massive black curtain descending on the stark landscape All that mattered to Zach was the sorrel. Eventually he lost sight of it but he didn't stop and go back. He had a job to do.

The wind had increased steadily. At first, Zach was tickled and turned his face to the west to feel the full brunt of the chill blast. Then the wind grew so strong it threatened to tear his hat from his head, and when he faced westward he had a hard time taking breaths. He heard thunder in the distance and guessed the rain would soon commence.

Zach slowed and glanced behind him to see how far he had traveled from the Yellowstone. He was mildly shocked on finding the river nowhere to be seen.

A large drop of rain struck the boy on the temple, and when he tilted his head to check the sky more splattered on his face. Except for a pale band to the east, black clouds now dominated the heavens.

To the southwest a vivid streak of sawtooth light shot to the ground. Seconds later thunder boomed. The bay fidgeted nervously, and Zach had to speak softly and pat her neck before she calmed down.

Breaking into a gallop, Zach sought to out-flank the storm. He figured if he could ride far enough north, the worst of the weather would be behind him and he could concentrate on locating the sorrel.

It soon became apparent the plan was founded on false hope. There was no end to the clouds, and more and more rain fell every minute. The lightning now lit up the atmosphere without letup, several of the bolts coming so close the

25

bay nearly panicked and bolted.

Zach finally drew rein, slid off, and tried to get the horse to lie down. He'd taught the trick to his own mount over a year ago, but his horse was being tended by Shoshone kin in the Rockies. This was a Mandan animal given to their party by a grateful chief named Mato-tope, and it balked. Tugging on the reins, he pushed against its front leg and shouted, "Down, girl! Down!"

The bay snorted, jerking back, her head bobbing. Zach grabbed her mane for extra leverage and hung from her neck, thinking his weight would do the trick. It only served to agitate her more and she began running with him clinging on for dear life. "Whoa!" he cried. "Stop!"

Suddenly the bay came to a gully. She took the slope too fast, slipped on the slick grass, and fell. Zach saw the ground rushing up to meet him and let go, pushing off from the bay's neck to keep from being crushed underneath her. His shoulder smacked the earth, something slammed into the small of his back, and he hurtled end over end.

The rifle flew from Zach's hand. A gut-wrenching impact brought him up short, dazed and winded. He heard the bay whinny, heard the drum of her hoofs. Alarmed, he struggled to sit up and glimpsed the horse as she disappeared over the top of the gully, heading to the northwest.

"No!" Zach shouted, his yell drowned out by a clap of thunder. He pushed to his feet and managed to take a few halting steps. Then a bolt of lightning struck so close that it lit up the landscape as bright as day, followed instantly by a deafening thunderclap. His hair stood on end, and he felt as if a million tiny needles were pricking his flesh. An acrid odor assailed his nostrils as his knees buckled and he slid to the bottom of the gully.

Zach hugged the grass and listened to the storm rage on all sides. Going after the bay might well get him killed so he decided to wait out Nature's tantrum. It wouldn't be long, he told himself, and he'd be on his way.

The rain now fell in torrents. Thunder roared without cease. Zach was certain the ground trembled from some of the blasts and he put his hands over his ears to shut out the din. Water dribbling down over his cheeks caused him to realize his hat had flown off somewhere along the line. He reminded himself to look for both his hat and the Kentucky once the downpour ended.

Time passed, the seconds becoming minutes, the minutes, hours. But the deluge showed no indication of letting up. Zach was drenched to the skin and took to shivering uncontrollably every so often. The continual barrage of lightning and thunder numbed his senses.

In due course the boy heard a new sound, a strange noise that he didn't recognize at first. Lifting his dripping head, he listened to a loud gurgling hiss. It made him think of a nasty incident involving a rattlesnake and he looked all around in panic although he knew full well no snake could be so loud. And he was right.

Visible up the gully was a writhing sheet of white water that swept toward him with all the power of a rampaging juggernaut. Zach's breath caught in his throat when he saw it. Leaping up, he bolted, fleeing up the south side of the gully, attempting to get high enough to escape.

Flash floods were the scourge of the mountains and the plains. All it took was an extremely heavy rain to transform dry washes and gulches into frothing maelstroms of rampaging current. Many times Nate had warned Zach to stay out of such places when it rained. Now the boy was learning his lesson the hard way.

Zach was still a yard shy of the rim when the flood hissed down upon him and coiled him within its liquid grasp. He tried to keep his footing but was plucked from the slope as he might pluck a strand of straw. An invisible clammy fist enclosed him within its wet grasp and he was yanked under.

At the last second Zach was able to take a deep breath. He felt cold water seep into his ears, into his nose. Flailing his arms, he fought to regain the surface, but his strength was as nothing compared to the might of the current. He began to sink, despair welling up in his young heart as it occurred to him that he might die.

Then there was a bend in the gully, and as the flash flood swept around it, the seething water catapulted him against the earth bank. For a fleeting moment he was able to dig in his heels, but it was enough to add to his momentum and propel him upward.

Zach's face broke into the clear and he gratefully gulped fresh air. He was still helpless to resist the surging flow, but by paddling he could keep his head up.

There seemed to be no end in sight. On a serpentine coursed the boy was hurtled farther and farther into the night. Gradually Zach's limbs tired. He began having a hard time pumping his arms as he should and no amount of mental prodding would get them to cooperate.

Without warning, the gully took another turn, the sharpest of all. Zach was close to the north side, and as the flood swept him around the bend he was tumbled along like a helpless tumbleweed, his battered body smacking the bank again and again.

A dark object loomed in Zach's path. He saw a tree trunk and low-hung limbs and instinctively lunged upward. His desperate fingers closed on a branch and clamped fast. The current tried to rip him loose but he was able to hold on and slowly, painfully, claw his way higher. In his ears the water hissed angrily, threatening to plunge him into its depths if he failed.

Gritting his teeth in determination, Zach climbed until his moccasins pulled free. He relaxed for just a second and nearly sealed his doom as his weary fingers began to give way entirely. With one last effort he hauled himself up onto the limb and sat with his back to the trunk, staring at the flood waters in an exhausted stupor.

Unexpectedly the tree itself gave a sharp lurch. Jolted, Zach looked down and was horrified to see the bank under the tree being rapidly washed out, exposing its root system. With a sinking feeling in his heart he realized the tree could not stand for long. Shoving up, he scrambled around the trunk, seeking another limb that would lower him safely to the ground.

The tree lurched again, tilting steeply toward the gully. Zach threw caution to the wind, tensed his legs, and leaped just as the roots parted with a tremendous crunch and the tree toppled into the water.

There was a scary moment when Zach thought he would do the same. But his soles smacked down on firm earth and he immediately ran, putting as much distance as he could between himself and the gully.

A lancing bolt out of the sky reminded Zach of other perils. Convinced he had gone far enough, he flattened and cringed as the storm continued to pummel the prairie. How long? he asked himself. How much longer?

The answer to that was all night.

Pink tendrils graced the eastern sky when the last of the pelting rain stopped and the somber clouds began to break up. Much to Zach's amazement, he had dozed off in the wee hours of the morning, only to be awakened by the chirp of a bird.

Sitting up, the boy stretched and winced as his sore body protested the movement. His clothes clung to him like wet rags, and he was cold clear to the marrow. Rising unsteadily, he gazed around in awe at the flattened grass that stretched for mile upon mile.

"Where am I?" Zach asked himself. He gazed to the south but did not spot the Yellowstone. By his reckoning, though, he should be within a few miles of the river and south of the spot where he had last seen his ma and pa.

Zach had a decision to make: Should he head on back or go after the horses? Since they were probably many miles away and he had no way of catching them, his best bet was to rejoin his parents and report what had happened.

There was only one problem. The water in the gully had not gone down, not enough, anyway. It contained about half as much as before, yet the current appeared twice as strong. Zach didn't dare try to cross for fear of suffering a repeat of his nighttime ordeal.

Turning westward, the boy paralleled the gully, seeking a narrow or shallow point where crossing would be easy. He was so tired his eyelids drooped, and his once boundless energy had dwindled to next to nothing.

When the sun finally broke through the clouds, the heat invigorated Zach. His teeth had started chattering, and no matter how he rubbed himself he was unable to keep warm. The flood waters had dropped a little more but still not enough to satisfy him.

By midmorning the boy had covered over a mile. He was trudging along, his head bowed, his soul heavy with gnawing worry, when he smelled the faint but unmistakable odor of burnt flesh.

Glancing up, Zach beheld a once-in-a-lifetime sight. Yards off lay the scattered remains of a horse. The animal had been blasted to pieces, torn asunder by a devastating force that had left the charred head lying twenty feet from the ruptured hindquarters and the front legs jutting from the ground as if they had been hammered into the earth. Grisly chunks of flesh dotted the grass. To one side was a torn parfleche. Elsewhere the blackened saddle was a total ruin.

Zach gaped and gulped. He realized what had happened to the bay as it fled, a fate he would have shared had he still been on it. Stunned, he skirted the remains to the left and stared down into the gully. There was no trace of the Kentucky and there never would be. The flood had swept the long gun away.

Depressed, Zach sat and took stock. He was stranded afoot in the middle of nowhere, a fate many trappers considered certain death. He had a butcher knife and a tomahawk, which would serve him in good stead, and a powder horn and ammo pouch, which would not unless he found another gun in the same caliber. His possibles bag contained odds and ends for starting fires and sharpening blades and such, but no food.

The thought made the boy's stomach rumble, reminding him he had not eaten since the day before. He gazed out over the plain, seeking game, but there was none to be found. Then his eyes settled on the charred pieces of the bay and an idea cropped into his head that made him shake it and declare, "No! Never!"

Zach's belly growled louder. He thought about the Apaches, who ate horse flesh as a matter of course, and some of the other tribes who would eat it when times were lean. Even his Uncle Shakespeare had eaten horse a few times and claimed the meat was quite tasty.

As yet no flies had gathered. If Zach was going to do the deed, he had to do it soon.

Scrunching up his face, he walked to a tempting morsel and squatted. The chunk was warm to the touch, and greasy. He turned it over in his hands, saw a stringy piece hanging down, and took a tentative nibble.

The meat had a distinctive flavor all its own. When his first few swallows didn't make him gag, Zach bit into a juicy part and chewed lustily. It couldn't compare to venison or elk steak, but it would do, and do right fine.

Over the next half an hour Zach gorged himself on as much as he could eat. He didn't know when he'd have his next meal, and he had to stay strong if he was to have any hope of finding his folks again.

Here was another matter that had to be mulled over. Zach figured his parents would come looking for him, and that notion was encouraging until he realized they had no idea which way he had gone. Worse, the storm would have erased every track he'd made. His parents would be unable to pick up his trail.

The boy knew his father and mother were devoted to him, knew they wouldn't give up until they had scoured the countryside for miles around. He also knew they would concentrate their search on the south side of the Yellowstone since that was where they'd last seen him. They probably wouldn't even cross to the north side.

As Zach saw it, he had to hike to the river and find a way across. Maybe he'd be lucky and spot his folks. If not—well, he'd cross that bridge when he came to it.

Selecting a sizable portion of crispy meat,

Zach crammed it into his possibles bag and stepped to the gully. The water had gone down a little further but not enough for him to safely reach the other side.

Thinking there must be a better spot elsewhere, Zach tramped westward. He wasn't a good judge of distance so he couldn't say if it was half a mile along or three quarters of a mile farther that he came to a severe bend where the opposite sides were only a couple of yards apart.

The boy stood close to the edge, gnawing uncertainly on his lower lip. He might be able to make it in one long jump, but what if he slipped? To his amazement the current was still too strong, and he couldn't understand where all the water was coming from.

Turning, Zach went a dozen feet, then faced the gully. He flexed his legs, wriggled his fingers, and breathed deeply. He could hear the water gurgling and he shut the sound from his mind.

Exploding into action, Zach ran for all he was worth, sprinting to the very brink and hurling himself into the air.

He looked straight ahead, not down, his arms and legs whipping wildly, and squawked in surprise when he landed safely and tumbled.

Jumping up, the boy laughed in triumph at the barrier, wheeled, and trudged to the south. Despite all the activity and the meal he was still cold, so he often rubbed his arms as he might on a winter's night. It didn't seem to help much.

Zach had no idea how far he had ridden the day before. But he was confident he would shortly spy the ribbon of vegetation bordering the river, and he stayed confident for the first hour, and the second. By the third he was having doubts, so much so that he had been hanging his head in sorrow over his plight for some time when he idly glanced up and saw the river not a quarter of a mile distant.

Beaming, the boy ran, his young heart soaring at the idea of soon being reunited with his family. But as he neared the Yellowstone it became apparent the reunion would not take place any time soon.

So much rain had fallen to the west as the storm raced eastward that the usually languid river was at flood stage. Surging water had overflowed both banks by a dozen yards, more in some places.

Zach stood and forlornly watched logs, brush, and dead animals being swept down the river at a dizzying speed. For him to try to reach the far side would be foolhardy.

Still, the boy had hope. Just a glimpse of his parents was was all he asked. He walked back and forth, scouring the south shore. No smoke from a friendly campfire curled skyward, no movement could be seen. He guessed they were searching farther west and he started to go westward when he noticed a very strange thing.

For a long way in both directions along the south shore, all the trees and undergrowth had disappeared. Zach looked, blinked, and blinked again. It was impossible for trees and brush to up and vanish, yet that was exactly what had happened.

There had to be a logical reason, Zach told himself, and the first idea that popped into his head was that the wind had blown the trees and bushes over just as it had done to the grass. He squinted against the glare on the water, trying to spot downed trunks and busted branches, but there were neither.

Now here was a mystery of no common occurrence, and the boy forgot all about his parents, for a while at least, as he tried to make sense of the barren shoreline. The flood waters couldn't be responsible because where the banks had overflowed, the trees and undergrowth still stood, only partially submerged. Nor could the heavy rain have been the culprit.

Finally Zach had to admit defeat. He couldn't explain the mystery. But it should work in his favor, he decided. If his parents were close to the river, he'd see them.

Encouraged, Zach continued to the west, seldom taking his eyes off that far side. He didn't realize he had been hiking for hours until the long shadows warned him the entire day was nearly gone. Shocked, he stopped under a cottonwood. His body was still sore, his legs ached terribly, and the chill had worsened. As if that wasn't enough, soon the sun sank in a blaze of red and yellow and night claimed the countryside.

Zach King sat with his slender back to a tree, listening to a growing chorus of howling wolves and yipping coyotes, and wondered if he would ever see his folks again.

Chapter Three

The evening before, at the same time that Zachary King was galloping to the northwest in pursuit of the sorrel, Nate and Winona King were following his tracks westward along the south shore of the Yellowstone River. Or they were trying to, because by now the sky had grown so dark they could barely see the grass at their feet. To aggravate their fears, it had started to rain, and Nate voiced the thought on both their minds, "The prints will be washed out."

"Would a torch help?" Winona asked.

For an answer Nate pointed at the nearby trees which were being bent nearly in half by the blustery winds. He was walking in front of Winona's mare, stooped over as he tried to read sign. Straightening, he stared at the river where small waves lapped the shore, then at the rapidly worsening storm. "Damn!" he snapped.

"We will find him," Winona said with her customary confidence. "He can't have gone far."

Nate cupped his hands to his mouth as he had done twenty times already and bellowed at the top of his lungs, "Zach ! Where are you?"

The only reply came from the shrieking wind.

"I shouldn't have let him go after the horse alone," Nate scolded himself. "One of us should have gone with him."

"He is old enough to handle such chores alone, husband. Wise are the parents who know when to keep their young ones close to the nest and when to let the young ones stretch their wings. Fewer feathers are ruffled that way."

Nate couldn't resist a grin. "Another one of your Shoshone sayings?"

"More or less."

Swiveling, Nate gazed toward the prairie to the south. Thanks to the Stygian murk, all he could see were a few sable patches of grass off through the waving trees. "Maybe's he's out in the open somewhere. Luck might smile on us and we'd spot him from a ways off."

"Want me to look?"

A crack of lightning and a blast of thunder made Nate's decision an easy one. "All right. But if you don't see him, hurry on back and we'll go tell Shakespeare." He paused, his apprehension obvious. "I didn't like leaving him behind, but he had to stay in case Zach showed while we were gone."

"You are doing all you can," Winona said. Leaning down as best she was able given her condition, she kissed him on his upturned lips, then jabbed her heels into the mare and trotted toward the open plain.

Nate watched her go with a sense of sinister foreboding in his heart. He shrugged the feeling off as a case of bad nerves and devoted himself to finding tracks.

For several minutes Nate pushed on with his nose inches from the damp ground, fighting the wind every step of the way and ignoring the barrage of huge raindrops. The tracks took him close to the Yellowstone, which was covered with whitecaps. He wondered if maybe, just maybe, his son had crossed to the opposite shore, then dismissed the notion as ridiculous. Zach knew better than to go into Blackfoot country by himself.

The next instant the heavens unleashed a hellish torrent. Raindrops the size of walnuts stung Nate like liquid hail. Shielding his eyes with one hand, he faced to the south, thinking of Winona out on the prairie in her state, unprotected. Should he go after her or continue after Zach?

There could only be one answer. As much as Nate loved his son—and he loved the boy as dearly as any man living had ever loved his offspring—his wife claimed first priority. Tucking his chin to his chest, he hastened through the trees, the brutal gale pounding him every step of the way.

It was now so dark that Nate couldn't see his hand six inches in front of his face. He shouted

Winona's name several times but received no response. Without warning there was a rending snap and a limb hurtled at his face from out of the gloom. He saw the branch and ducked, losing his hat but not any flesh.

The wind, incredibly, became stronger. Nate had to bow into the brunt of the storm to keep his footing. He made tortuous progress, losing a foot for every yard he gained. At last the trees fell behind him and he knew he was at the edge of the prairie.

All Nate saw was a wall of rain falling against a backdrop of near solid black which was illuminated every few seconds by thunderbolts. In the light of the flashes he sought Winona and thought he spotted her far, far out on the plain.

"Winona!" Nate shouted so stridently he hurt his throat. He coughed, tried again. Whatever was out there came no closer, and it occurred to him that he had lost both his wife and son in the midst of the worst tempest he had ever experienced.

What else could go wrong? Nate bitterly asked himself as he took several strides. That was when he heard the new noise, the oddest noise he had ever heard, a noise that raised the short hairs at the nape of his neck and sent his heart to racing even though he had no idea what it might be.

In the distance, to the west, there arose a strange howling roar, a sound not unlike that of a wolf in its death throes only a thousand times louder. No, a million times louder.

Nate faced around, his head cocked, trying to hear better above the squalling wind and the driving rain. It seemed as if the roar was getting closer and closer with each passing second. He had never heard anything like it, although he had a nagging feeling that he should know what it was.

Suddenly the sky changed. It moved of its own accord, seeming to shift and swirl and expand as if imbued with dark life of its own.

Nate squinted, trying to make sense of the motion. In his confused frame of mind he had the impression a huge section of the heavens had detached itself from the rest and was bearing down on him like some supernatural behemoth. The rain slackened slightly, permitting him to see the source of the roar more clearly, and the sight he beheld caused his breath to catch in his throat and his blood to run cold.

A colossal grayish funnel over half a mile wide and thousands of feet high was tearing across the grassland, ripping up the earth at its wide base and sucking trees, grass, and other debris into its maw. A monumental engine of destruction, irresistible in its awesome grandeur, it screeched like a demented banshee as it bore steadily eastward.

Nate looked on the aerial leviathan and was riveted in place with unbridled shock. A single word blared in his brain, over and over again: Whirlwind! It towered above him as high as a mountain, twisting and dancing like a snake about to strike, the mushroom shaped crown rearing so high up Nate had to tilt his head back to see it.

The spell broke, and Nate spun and ran even though he knew the futility of trying to flee.

He was directly in the tornado's path. He had nowhere to go.

To Nate's rear the ground churned and was ground to dust or ripped into the air and sent whirling. Sprinting as he had never sprinted before, Nate flinched as the howl blistered his eardrums. He tensed for the doom poised to claim him, his only consolation the fact Winona was far enough south to be spared. About Zach he had no idea, but he hoped the boy *had* crossed the Yellowstone so the whirlwind hadn't swept him up.

Nate thought of Shakespeare, waiting at their camp, and wished there was some way of warning his longtime friend and mentor. They had been through so much together, shared so many good times that——

Nate was thrown violently forward. It felt as if a giant hand had slapped against his back, and he only kept his footing with the utmost effort. He ran on, the shriek of the wind so piercing it sent goosebumps shooting down his body.

Again was Nate's back pummeled, and this time he was driven to his knees. He began to shove erect, glancing over his shoulder to see how much of a lead he had on the whirlwind. He had none. The tornado hung in the air above him, its sides spinning round and round and round.

Nate stared straight up at the flared top, so far overhead it appeared to be on a distant planet. He instinctively clutched the Hawken to him, and the next moment he was engulfed in a wall of whirling wind. Like a feather in a gale he was lifted bodily and streaked high into the air.

Now everything happened so fast that Nate had only fleeting impressions of the next few minutes. His senses swam as he tumbled out of control. He had trouble breathing but managed to take labored breaths, and his skin felt as if it was being blasted by stinging sand.

Dimly, Nate was conscious of moving in a great circle over and over again at an incredible rate of speed. He became slightly dizzy and felt his stomach churn. Something bumped into his shoulder, and when he twisted his head he was shocked to behold an entire tree sailing along beside him. He blinked, and the tree was gone.

Suddenly Nate became aware of a quiet pocket of space to one side. He looked and promptly wished he hadn't, because he seemed to be perched hundreds of feet in the air next to the inner edge of a mammoth shaft. Inside the shaft miniature blue lightning bolts danced in eerie silence. At the very bottom was a circular path of ground, stripped of all vegetation. As Nate watched, the shaft moved, and he realized with a start that he was gazing upon the bowels of the monster that had claimed him.

A hard object rapped Nate's skull and his vision blurred. Vaguely he realized he was spinning steadily lower, and he wondered if he would be smashed to bits on the earth. Then his whole body was flung outward and cold air struck his face, reviving him.

Nate could hear the whirlwind off to one side. He tried to turn but couldn't. Gravity had him in its unyielding grip and he knew he was falling. He mentally pictured every last bone in his body being shattered on impact, and braced himself.

Seconds later Nate hit. To his amazement, there was no bone-wrenching jolt, no crack of bones and cartilage. His shoulder bounced once, then he was sliding over slick grass, sliding for yards and yards, and just as he started to slow he hurtled over the lip of a precipice and plummeted,

The next impact was brutal. Nate involuntarily cried out. He tumbled end over end and ultimately smashed into something with such force he was left barely conscious, his chest in agony.

Gritting his teeth, Nate tried to stand. He had to insure Winona was safe and check on Shakespeare. He put a hand under him and shoved, but instead of pushing away from the ground, the ground leaped up to strike him in the face. An indigo cloud formed out of nowhere, enclosing his mind, and he collapsed.

It was warmth that brought Nate around, the welcome warmth of sunshine on his cheek. Dazed, he sat up and blinked in confusion, trying to recollect exactly what had happened to him and why he was sitting at the bottom of what appeared to be an earthen cliff.

Nate touched a hand to his head and winced. His entire body was sore and battered and there was dried blood on his temple. He gazed skyward, saw a puffy pillow of a cloud, and suddenly remembered everything.

Pushing upright, Nate licked his dry lips and took stock. He was in a wide, barren ravine. A trickle of water that barely qualified as a stream flowed past on his left. He wagged his arms, shook his legs, and found no broken bones.

Nate saw a game trail leading to the top. Before ascending, he hunted for his Hawken and failed to find it. One of his pistols was also missing. He still had the other pistol, though, and the knife and tomahawk.

As Nate climbed he tried to make sense of what had happened. The whirlwind had picked him up and cast him down again. That much was certain. Miraculously, he had survived. But where was he? He remembered tall tales he'd heard of men being sucked into tornadoes and carried to far-off lands, and while he had always doubted such stories were true, a finger of fear gnawed at his innards, fear that it just might have happened to him.

Eagerly Nate scaled the final few feet and stepped onto the upper rim. In all directions stretched the vast rolling prairie with which he was so familiar. So much for the tall tales! But when he pivoted on a heel, scanning the far horizon, he was flabbergasted to find no trace of the Yellowstone River, nor a vestige of vegetation other than the ever present buffalo grass.

"Where the blazes is it?" Nate asked aloud, bewildered. The river should be in sight, had to be in sight! On the open plain the strip of trees bordering it was visible from miles off.

Nate took a few steps, pondering. Since he couldn't see the Yellowstone, that meant he had to be at least five miles away. Had the whirlwind carried him that far? Surely not. He moved along the rim, totally confused.

Suddenly the quiet was shattered by a low, wavering groan.

Nate stiffened, his hand dropping to his pistol. He spun toward the source and was stunned to discover a figure sprawled on the opposite rim, forty feet away. High weeds prevented him from seeing more than a buckskin-clad outline.

"Winona!" Nate cried. She must have been caught in the whirlwind too and deposited at the same time! Spinning, he dashed to the game trail and went down it at a reckless pace, nearly falling twice. Once on the bottom he searched for a trail up the other earthen wall but there was none. Exasperated, he stood directly under the figure and studied a cleft to his left. Could he do it?

The crack was wide enough for Nate to brace his back against one side, his feet against the other. Pressing his hands flat behind him, he slowly worked his way upward. The groaning had ceased, and he worried that his beloved had breathed her last.

The ravine was only twenty-five feet high but to Nate the climb seemed to take forever. He ached to be on top, to be holding his wife in his arms. Near the rim he felt the dirt behind him give way and heard clods rattle down the cleft. Freezing, he waited for the slide to stop, then cautiously resumed, placing each hand and foot carefully. A fall from that height might seriously injure him.

The thought brought a grin. Nate glanced at the deep blue sky, thinking of his fall from the tornado. Compared to that, a tumble down the cleft would be like nothing.

At last Nate was able to reach up, grip the rim, and pull. Inch by inch he lifted himself higher and finally rolled out onto the grass. Rising, he ran to the unconscious figure, a warm smile curling his mouth, his heart singing for joy. Then he saw the face of the one he had assumed was Winona, and he stopped dead in his tracks.

It was a man, a warrior with hawkish features and hair cropped in a style Nate had never seen before; the head had been shaved bare except for a strip running from the forehead to the nape of the neck. Red paint had been smeared on the warrior's brow and both cheeks. And on the front of his buckskin shirt had been painted the likeness of a gigantic bear, again in red.

Nate racked his brain, trying to identify the tribe the man belonged to. No two tribes dressed the same or wore their hair the same way so it was possible for an experienced mountaineer to tell the members of each apart at a glance. But this style was new to him.

Placing a hand on the flintlock, Nate knelt and searched for evidence of a wound or blood. There was neither. He rolled the warrior onto his back and felt the man's wrist to gauge the strength of the pulse. As he did, the warrior's dark eyes unexpectedly snapped wide.

Nate smiled to show his friendly intentions and opened his mouth to speak, but before he

could utter a word the Indian's features contorted in stark terror and the warrior yanked
his wrist loose and jumped to his feet. Aston-
ished, Nate gaped as the man spun and fled
down the slope of a hill flanking the ravine,
fleeing as if his very life depended on it.

"Wait!" Nate yelled, to no effect.

The warrior glanced back once, his face still
reflecting abject fright. At the bottom of the hill
stood a stand of trees, and into this he plunged
at full speed and was soon lost from view.

Scratching his head, Nate stood. He'd never
seen any Indian react in such a bizarre fashion
and he didn't know what to make of the man's
behavior. The only explanation he could think
of was that the warrior had never set eyes on a
white man before. Even so, it hardly accounted
for the extreme terror the man had shown.

From this side of the ravine Nate enjoyed a
sweeping vista of seemingly limitless prairie
to the southwest. There were a few scattered
stands of trees, fewer hills, and grass everywhere else. He detected movement to the southeast and spotted several buffalo.

Nate debated his next move. By his reckoning
the Yellowstone River should be to the north,
so if he walked long enough in that direction
eventually he would find it. But what if he was
wrong? What if the whirlwind had carried him
much farther than he suspected?

There was one person who knew exactly
where Nate was, and with that in mind Nate
ventured down the slope to the edge of the trees.
He listened intently but heard no sounds other
than the sighing wind and the rustle of leaves.

Harsh experience had taught Nate the value of caution. Instead of entering the vegetation and risking attack, he skirted the perimeter, probing the shadows in search of the warrior. He glimpsed a flash of buckskin racing away from him and called out, "Hold on! I'm not going to hurt you!" Realizing the man probably did not understand English, he switched to Shoshone and shouted, "Stop! I come in peace!"

No response was forthcoming.

Nate walked on, often squatting to peer into the undergrowth. He saw sparrows and a squirrel but no trace of the warrior. Nor were there any tracks, but that was to be expected. The condition of the grass, which had been flattened in spots and was damp close to the roots, testified to the severity of the storm the night before.

The stand covered over five acres. Nate had gone half the way around it when he finally caught sight of the warrior, and when he did he sank low so as not to be seen.

Twenty yards in was a small clearing. In the middle of it knelt the Indian. He had opened a leather bag and removed a number of peculiar items: sticks, bones, feathers, and such. As Nate looked on, the warrior picked up several small bones and cast them at the ground, then bent over them, studying their arrangement.

Nate had no idea what the man was doing. The Shoshones did not indulge in the practice, and neither, to his knowledge, did the Flatheads or the Nez Perce. He saw the warrior recoil in shock, then hold his arms aloft, close his eyes, and silently mouth words, apparently chanting to himself.

Figuring that it might have religious significance, Nate stayed were he was, reluctant to interrupt. After a while the man stopped chanting and collected the items into the bag. The warrior rose, turned to scan the trees, and slowly backed in Nate's direction.

Standing, Nate stayed still so as not to spook the man, and when the warrior was closer, spoke softly in Shoshone. "Please do not run away again, friend. I would talk to you."

At the first word the man jumped and whirled, his features betraying the same fear as before. Venting an inarticulate cry, he threw his hands in front of his face as if to ward off an assault, then he dashed into the brush, just like before.

"Wait!" Nate urged, and again met with disappointment. The warrior was soon out of sight. Had Nate not been so annoyed, he would have laughed at the man's comical antics.

Nate speculated. Could it be the Indian was touched in the head? He knew that various tribes sometimes banished crazy members, who lived in isolation far from any village. Maybe he had stumbled on one of them.

One thing was apparent. Nate would learn nothing from the red-faced Indian. He would be better off heading north and hope he was as close to the Yellowstone as he believed.

Having made up his mind, Nate faced around and began hiking. From the position of the sun he knew the day was only four hours old so there was plenty of time for him to find the river before nightfall. His stomach rumbled, reminding him it had been almost a full day since last he ate, but he was not about to stop to eat until he had learned the fate of his family and Shakespeare.

Thinking of them brought a frown. Nate sometimes fretted that he was doing the wrong thing by living in the wilderness where those he cared most about were subjected to constant danger. Whether from wild beasts, hostile Indians, or the weather, threats arose on almost a daily basis. They would be so much safer back in one of the settlements. There they could live to ripe old ages without fear of being scalped, mauled, or snatched up by errant whirlwinds.

But would they be happy there? That was the main question, and Nate knew the answer, a resounding no. In the settlements they would be confined to a small plot of land and have to live as others expected them to live. They would always have to conform to rules and laws set down by a bunch of elected officials who had nothing better to do with their time than to think up new ways of telling folks how they should spend every waking moment from the cradle to the grave.

Nate cherished his freedom too much to permit that, and Winona and Zach were the same way. They'd rather be free to do as they pleased when they pleased, and have to abide all the dangers being truly free entailed, than let themselves be lorded over by a bunch of power-seeking politicians.

Suddenly the drum of hoofbeats shattered Nate's reverie and he turned to find nine warriors galloping toward him with shafts notched to bows and lances upraised. By their hair he knew they belonged to the same tribe as the man in the trees. He was lifting a hand to make the sign for friend when the foremost brave took aim and let an arrow fly.

Chapter Four

Winona King knew she should not have left her husband a minute after she did so. Her back was aching again, so badly the pain made her temples throb. And the wind lashed her long hair so severely she could not keep it out of her eyes no matter how hard she tried.

But Winona refused to quit. Their son was missing, and she would do her part to help find him. Ducking under a low limb that clawed at her face, she skirted other trees until she came to the plain. Here the wind was worse, howling with a fury she had never before heard.

Cupping a hand to her mouth, Winona shouted for her son in Shoshone, using the name she had bestowed on him at birth. "Stalking Coyote! Answer me!"

In the hope the wind would carry her voice farther if she was away from the trees, Winona touched her heels to her mount and trotted into the thick of the storm. She hadn't gone ten feet when the wind increased dramatically. A gust nearly blew her from the saddle.

Winona bent low over her horse and held on with all her strength. This was hopeless, she told herself. She could not see more than a few feet and could hear nothing over the crashing thunder. Worse, the lightning was striking much too close for comfort. It would be wiser, she reasoned, to return to Nate, and once the storm passed they could renew their search.

About to tug on the reins, Winona paused when a new sound reached her ears, a strident howling that made her think all the coyotes in creation were yipping at once. It was new to her, and not a little frightening. She began to turn her mare when the horse stiffened and cocked its head high.

"Go!" Winona goaded, slapping her knees against its sides. The animal paid no heed and whinnied in fright. She worked the reins but the mare shied to the right, as if from an unseen attacker. Again she urged it on and let herself relax a bit when the mare at last obeyed.

But only for a moment. Winona was taken unawares by the violent motion of the mare whirling and racing off across the prairie. She had to grab its mane to keep from being thrown to the ground.

Fighting back rising panic, Winona grit her teeth and hauled on the reins with all her might. She might as well have been trying to stop an avalanche because the mare ignored her and flew into the driving rain like an animal gone berserk. Again and again she attempted to halt it, without success.

Winona flinched as a jarring spasm lanced her lower back. She checked a cry threatening to burst from her lips, then leaned forward again to reduce the torment. In that position, though, she was unable to pull back hard on the reins. She was forced to do as the mare wanted, forced to go along for the ride whether she liked it or not.

And what a ride it was. The mare galloped at breakneck speed, head bobbing, tail flying, sides slick with rain. Lightning and thunder had no effect, except perhaps to spur it to go faster.

Winona was trying to keep track of their direction of travel, a hopeless task. She thought they were bearing south but she couldn't be certain. Maybe it was southwest. Behind her the howling had risen to a crescendo and there was an odd scraping sound.

Soon the mare would tire, Winona reflected, and she would be able to go back to her husband. Or so she believed during the first few minutes. But when it became apparent the mare was in the grip of a fear so great the horse was not going to stop shy of total exhaustion, Winona sat up and tried once more to bring her mount to a halt. She had the same result as before.

A vivid bolt of light rent the heavens, and the earth to Winona's right exploded in a stinging shower of dirt and grass. She shielded her face with a hand as clods and small stones battered her from head to toe. One stone rapped her knuckles, leaving her hand numb for a bit.

Winona risked a glance back. The view was the same as in front: rain, rain, and more rain. With a subtle difference. It seemed to her as if something moved far to her rear, a thing so massive it bent the sheets of rain. Her eyes must be deceiving her, she figured. Nothing could be that enormous, that powerful.

Except the storm itself. The heavy drops peppered Winona without cease, stinging mercilessly. The wind tore at her hair, her dress, her very body, chilling her terribly. The cannonade of thunder pounded her eardrums. And whenever she straightened, her back flared, filling her with such anguish she feared she might pass out.

Finally Winona stopped trying to turn or stop the mare, stopped doing anything other than to hold on and hope her ordeal would soon end. She steeled her will against the torture, reminding herself that she was a Shoshone and Shoshones did not give in to hardships.

All sense of time was lost. Winona could not say how long she had been riding when the inevitable occurred and disaster struck.

A shift in the mare's center of balance alerted Winona to the fact the horse was going down a slope. She compensated by sliding her bottom several inches backward while pushing on the animal's neck. Suddenly the mare stumbled, almost pitching her off, but she clamped her legs tight and averted tragedy.

The mare came to a level stretch and resumed galloping in headlong terror. Winona, relieved, eased the tension in her legs and rose up to peer ahead. At that selfsame instant the mare must have stepped into a hole or a cleft because the horse stumbled and catapulted forward, tumbling in a disjointed whirl of limbs, mane, and tail.

Winona was hurled clear on the first spin. Her rifle sailed loose and she tried to grab it. Then her head hit something or something hit her head and the whole world changed from murky black to an empty black, so empty there was no movement or sound or life, not even her own.

Minutes passed, or so it seemed when Winona opened her eyes and gazed up at a pair of buzzards circling far above her in the daytime sky. She automatically sat up and nearly screamed as her lower back protested. Glancing around, she saw the remnants of the storm fading to the east where the sun was faintly visible through the clouds. She also saw something else.

The mare lay a dozen feet off, one front leg shattered at the knee, the bone protruding through the ruptured flesh. Its neck was bent at an unnatural angle, its tongue lolling in the wet grass.

Putting her hands flat, Winona pushed up, stopping suddenly when the baby kicked, aggravating her condition. She rubbed her stomach and said, "Not now, little one. If you ever hope to enter this world you must rest quietly until I rejoin your father."

Winona walked to the dead mare and squatted beside the saddle. The pair of parfleches were still there but one was pinned underneath and she had to wedge her feet against the mare's back to yank it out. Inside one of the beaded bags was jerked venison and pemmican, so at least she would not go hungry. The other contained assorted items which might prove useful later. Neither held a weapon. All she had was the hunting knife at her hip, which would prove a poor defense should she run into a roving grizzly.

Standing, Winona slung the parfleche over a shoulder and looked around for her rifle. She felt it couldn't be far, and she turned out to be right. A thorough search of a fifty-foot area around the mare rewarded her with the flint-lock, beaded with moisture and spotted with dirt but none the worse for wear.

Winona heeded her husband's warning about letting a gun get wet and made it her first order of business to reload. Nate had insisted that she learn how to use both rifles and pistols, saying the knowledge might one day save her life. Time and again circumstances had demonstrated his wisdom, and now, after countless hours of practice and experience, Winona was as skilled a shooter as any free trapper in the mountains. Nate believed she was better than most.

Removing a piece of jerky, Winona turned her footsteps northward and bit off a salty morsel. She chewed slowly but her thoughts raced. How far had she ridden? Would she reach the Yellowstone before noon? What had happened to her loved ones in her absence? Anxiety gnawed at her heart and she hardened herself against it.

Eventually the clouds dispersed and the sun broke through, revitalizing Winona with its warmth. She happened to gaze upward and was surprised to see the buzzards still circling her. On an impulse she raised the rifle to scare them off, then realized she must conserve her ammunition and powder.

Their stupidity made Winona laugh. She knew that sooner or later they would get it through their bony skulls she hadn't died and they would go elsewhere. And indeed, when next she looked, they were gone. She smiled and adjusted the parfleches, then felt a cold breeze fan her spine as behind her a horse whinnied.

Winona spun, leveling her rifle. Her heart leaped to her throat when she saw six warriors astride fine war horses. They were a stone's throw away, lined up in a row watching her. She marveled that they had been able to get so close without being detected even as she trained the flintlock on the man in the center.

The warriors appeared more puzzled than hostile. They talked quietly among themselves, gesturing often at her.

Of utmost importance to Winona was identifying the tribe to which they belonged. Blackfeet, Piegans, or Bloods might well slay her on the spot. Mandans would be friendly and help her rejoin her loved ones. But a close scrutiny revealed these men were neither her dreaded enemies or potential friends.

They all wore their hair parted in the middle and four of the six had theirs braided. Two wore silver disks on their braids, attached by leather bands. Two others wore bands of quills topped by a pair of feathers from which hung locks of horse hair. They were dressed and painted for war and held either lances or bows.

Only once before had Winona seen a warrior similarly dressed. That had been shortly before Zach's birth, when her husband had befriended an outcast Lakota named Red Hawk. The trappers had called Red Hawk's tribe the Sioux, which, Winona knew, was a shortened version of the name the French had once used, the *Nadowessioux*.

So these six warriors were Lakotas. The knowledge meant little since Winona's people, the Shoshones, had few dealings with them. She had no idea how they would treat her. Common sense told her to hope for the best but prepare for the worst, so she kept her rifle tucked to her shoulder as a tall warrior with a strapping physique came toward her.

The Lakota had a bow but he made no move to use it. His head cocked as he examined her, and he rode in a wide circle, grinning when she pivoted to keep him covered. He halted ten feet in front of her and addressed her in his tongue.

Winona did not understand a single word. She gazed beyond him at the others, who had not moved. Maybe they would go away and leave her in peace, she hoped, although deep down she knew that would never happen.

In a deft motion the Lakota slung his bow over an arm and raised both hands in front of him. "Question. Your tribe?" he asked in sign language.

Not about to lower her flintlock to answer, Winona did not move a muscle.

"Question. You know sign language?" the Lakota probed.

Winona did, but she held a bead on the warrior's chest.

"I am Thunder Horn," the man signed. "What is your name?"

Once again Winona offered no reply.

"You do not look as if your brain is in a whirl. Why do you not answer me?" Thunder Horn demanded.

Winona was unsure of what to do. So far none of the warriors had shown any inclination to harm her, and she wanted to keep things that way. But Thunder Horn was becoming angry. She reasoned that it would be in her best interests to respond in order to avoid a clash. Accordingly, taking a gamble, she stepped several paces backward and moved her rifle to the crook of an elbow to free her hands. "I do not want trouble," she signed emphatically.

Thunder Horn grunted. "That will be up to you." He raked her from head to toe with a frank, admiring look. "You are not Blackfoot. That much is obvious."

"I am Shoshone."

"Minneconjou," Thunder Horn said, tapping his barrel chest. "How are you called?"

"Winona." She remembered hearing that there were seven great branches of the Lakotas: the Oglala, the Minneconjou, the Brule, the Sans Arc, the Two Kettles, the Hunkpapas, and one other she could not recall.

"Where are your people?"

"I am alone."

The Minneconjou showed his skepticism. He surveyed the rolling prairie, then nodded westward. "I raided a Shoshone village once so I know that your people live far off in the mountains. They only come onto the plain to hunt buffalo, and when they do they come in large groups. So I ask you again. Where are your people?"

"I am alone," Winona insisted. To tell about her family and Shakespeare invited disaster. These Lakotas were on the war path, and they might not care whether they counted coup on Indians or whites.

Thunder Horn frowned. "We both know you are not telling the truth."

"All I know is that I would like to be left alone," Winona hedged.

The Minneconjou changed the subject. "We found a dead horse earlier. It was yours?"

"Yes."

"What happened?"

"There was a storm. It panicked," Winona said.

"And where are you going now, if not back to your people?"

Winona said nothing.

"You do not tell me because you do not want them coming to harm," Thunder Horn signed. "You are wise as well as beautiful. I like those qualities in a woman." He leaned forward. "You will hand over your gun and come with us."

"I will not."

"You do not have a choice." Thunder Horn twisted and shouted to his companions who promptly fanned out to surround Winona. As yet not one of them brought a weapon to bear but the threat was still there. "We can kill you any time we choose," Thunder Horn stressed after his friends were in place. "Would you rather die or live?"

Raising the flintlock, Winona aimed at Thunder Horn's face. "I will not die alone."

The Minneconjou did not flinch. "My brother has a rifle. I have watched him shoot it, so I know that yours can only fire once and then must be reloaded. Perhaps you will kill me, but you will be taken captive before you can shoot again and you will pay for being so foolish. That would be a waste."

There was no denying the inevitable. Winona knew all too well her fate if she harmed one of the Sioux. They would do the same to her that her own people would do if the situation were reversed.

Women weren't accorded special treatment in warfare. When one tribe raided another, women caught unprotected were either slain outright or taken back to become the unwilling wives of the raiders. On many occasions Shoshone women had been set upon while out picking roots or berries or while tending to some other chore, and the bodies of the older ones had been left to rot while the younger ones disappeared, never to be seen again.

"I will not wait forever for you to set down that gun," Thunder Horn signed.

Winona squared her shoulders and held her chin defiantly. "I cannot," she signed.

Thunder Horn seemed to idly gaze to his right, then coughed. "You would throw away your life?"

"I will not go with you," Winona signed. "I already have a husband, and I will be true to him."

The tall Minneconjou chuckled. "I will make you forget all about him. No Shoshone can match a Lakota man in his prime."

His boast caused Winona to laugh merrily despite her predicament. "Are all the Minneconjou so unduly proud of themselves?" she taunted. "And you are wrong in another respect, too, because my husband is not Shoshone." She paused to emphasize her next statement. "My husband is white."

The Minneconjous broke into excited talk, the subject of which had to be Winona's revelation. It mystified her immensely. Unions between trappers and Indian maidens were not all that common, but neither were they so rare as to spark astonishment. She knew of quite a few Flathead, Crow, and Nez Perce women who had given their hearts to whites. So far she was the only Shoshone who had done so.

Thunder Horn interrupted her reflection. "What is the name of this white man?"

"Grizzly Killer," Winona signed, her face shining with the intensity of her love.

"His white name."

As there were no sign symbols for it, Winona replied aloud in the perfect English she had mastered after much time and effort, "Nathaniel King."

An attempt by Thunder Horn to mimic the sounds was unsuccessful. He tried several times, then gave up with an irritated toss of his head. "Am I to take it that you speak the white tongue?"

"I do."

This prompted another excited exchange. In due course Thunder Horn signed, "His name is not important. That you took him as your husband is."

"In what way?"

"Do your people trade with the whites?"

"Yes," Winona answered honestly, unable to conceive of any importance the question might hold. "Many tribes do."

"And what do you trade them?"

"Beaver skins, buffalo hides, sometimes horses and food."

"What does your tribe get in return?"

"Rifles, pistols, powder, blankets, steel knives and tomahawks, traps, many things," Winona signed. Her bewilderment grew when for the third time in as many minutes the warriors commenced chatting like agitated squirrels. As Nate might say, she did not understand what all the fuss was about. She listened to their words and watched Thunder Horn carefully but was unable to glean a clue.

"It is a good day for the Minneconjou," the tall warrior signed after the discussion had ended. "This is even better than counting coup on Blackfeet, which is why we are in this territory."

"I do not understand," Winona confessed.

"In time you will." Thunder Horn rested a hand on the neck of his war horse and regarded her with renewed interest. "Tell me. Do you have children?"

"A fine son," Winona answered.

"This husband of yours. He beats you at times, and treats you like a dog?"

"Never!" Winona signed with such vigor her arms trembled. "Grizzly Killer is the kindest man I know. He treats me with respect, as an equal."

"How many grizzlies has this mighty hunter slain?" Thunder Horn signed with sarcasm lining his features.

"Too many to count."

Every last warrior burst out laughing.

"And you accused me of having too much pride!" Thunder Horn baited her. "No man has ever killed more than one or two of the fierce bears and lived to tell of it."

Winona had been trying to recall exactly how many Nate had rubbed out over the years. "My husband has killed more than six. He slays them as lesser men slay flies."

"Ho!" Thunder Horn said aloud before reverting to more sign language. "I would like to meet this giant among men!"

"Try to steal me and you will," Winona was swift to assure him. "Not only is he the best hunter alive, he is also the best tracker. He will find you no matter where you take me and he will punish you for your deed."

"I was wrong," Thunder Horn signed with a smirk. "You did not marry a giant. You married a spirit in human form who has the ability of a hundred men!"

Once again the men enjoyed a good laugh. And as Winona sat staring at those in front of her, she realized there was an odd quality to their mirth, as if they were forcing themselves to laugh harder than was called for. She wondered why they would behave so strangely. It was almost as if they were doing so for her benefit, but such an idea was ridiculous.

Too late Winona heard the scrape of a hoof close by her side. Too late she awoke to the fact the laughter had not been for her benefit, but for *theirs*, to cover the sounds made by a pair of warriors who had crept up on her from the rear while her attention was distracted.

Winona gripped the flintlock and tried to turn but she was seized under both arms and the rifle was torn from her grasp. She bit one of the hands holding her and was able to tear loose. As she twisted to bite the other hand, two other warriors appeared in front of her, both on foot. They grabbed her and held her fast while another brought a grass rope and tied her wrists. Before the shock had quite settled in, she was lifted bodily and forced to straddle the back of Thunder Horn's mount.

"Now you are mine!" the tall Minneconjou declared, and uttering a whoop, he wheeled his horse and led the rest of the war party southward at a trot.

Chapter Five

Shakespeare McNair was worried. His friends had been gone far too long and the storm was worsening by the minute. One hand firmly holding the reins to his skittish horse, he shielded his eyes from the cold, pelting rain with a flat palm and gazed at the turbulent heavens.

In all Shakespeare's years in the wilderness he had seen few storms to equal this one. Nature was throwing a fierce tantrum, and unless he found shelter soon he risked bodily harm. But he was loath to leave with the Kings unaccounted for. Young Zach might return at any time and someone had to be on hand.

Lightning speared the earth with uncanny frequency. Thunder drummed incessantly. Shakespeare was soaked to the skin but he paid the discomfort no heed. To one accustomed to the weather whims of the fickle Rockies, being wet was no more than a trifling inconvenience.

As the minutes labored past, Shakespeare's worry mounted. He knew it would be impossible for Nate to track the boy, that the rain must have washed out all tracks by now. Gnawing on his lower lip, he glanced at the Yellowstone, which was rapidly assuming the proportions of a raging torrent. Already the quicksilver current had overflowed the bank and begun devouring the vegetation.

A bristling bolt suddenly struck a tree thirty feet away. The blinding flash caused Shakespeare to avert his eyes. For a moment every hair on his body stood on end and an invisible hand slapped at him. He closed his eyes as brilliant white dots whirled everywhere.

Shakespeare's horse panicked, heaving mightily on the reins, and it was all he could do to hold on. "Calm down, you ornery cuss!" he declared, seizing the mane. "This isn't no time to be acting contrary."

The horse had no chance to comply. Another close blast of lightning to the south sent it racing pell-mell in the opposite direction, to the north—toward the river.

Looping the reins around a wrist, Shakespeare dug in both heels and threw all his weight into trying to stop the animal. He might as well have tried to stop a charging buffalo. In blind terror the horse bolted into the roaring water. It awoke to its mistake almost immediately but by then the river was halfway up to its shoulders. It tried to turn, stepped into a hole, and floundered.

Shakespeare realized he couldn't hope to pull the horse to safety by himself. And unless he moved quickly, the animal's stupidity would cost him his life. He lunged toward the bank and was brought up short by a tug at his wrist; in his haste he had forgotten to unwind the reins.

In order to accomplish that, Shakespeare had to transfer his Hawken from his left hand to his right. He was doing so when his legs were swept out from under him and the next instant he was sailing downriver beside the thrashing horse. Before he could lift a finger they were carried out toward the middle of the river where it was so deep he could not touch bottom.

Shakespeare was in dire straits. On either side the inky shoreline streaked past, but it would be the height of folly to try to reach land. His only recourse was to let the Yellowstone take him where it would and hope he survived.

Since the horse might sink and Shakespeare did not care to go under with it, he quickly unwound the reins and lightly placed one hand on top of the saddle. The animal had quieted somewhat but its eyes were wide with fright, its nostrils flared.

Over the tumult of the river rose a faint new sound. Shakespeare spat water and twisted. Against the backdrop of the night something gigantic moved, and it took several moments for his brain to register its dimensions and recognize the shape for what it was.

"Tarnation!" Shakespeare exclaimed. "Not that!"

A tornado of Cyclopean size was moving parallel to the river, chewing up the south shore, sucking trees and weeds and rocks into its writhing maw as if dining on the earth itself. Shakespeare could not see well enough to observe every detail, but he could tell that everything in the behemoth's path was being destroyed.

Shakespeare's first thoughts were for the Kings. No one caught by that twister would live to relate the experience, and it was plain the tornado had ravaged the very strip of land where they would have been. The thought jarred him to the depths of his soul. They were, after all, the closest thing to true family he had left in the world other than his wife, and he loved each and every one of them fervently.

He fought back a mad impulse to push off and swim for shore. There was nothing he could do except stay alive and go back to look for them once he managed to reach dry land, which promised to be a formidable chore in itself.

So far the current had done no more than sweep Shakespeare along, but that could change at any time. There were few waves, few eddies, and he was moving so fast that he hardly had to tread water at all.

Shakespeare shot around a bend, his body banging against the horse, his gaze still on the tornado. It was much closer to the river and soon might swing out over the water. The old saying about being caught between a rock and a hard place had never been more true. If the dancing funnel didn't get him, the murky depths of the Yellowstone would.

With a screeching wail the twister abruptly leaped into the air, spun off into the clouds to the southeast, and was gone. It happened in the time it would take Shakespeare to snap his fingers and left him blinking in surprise. He had never seen one do that before. He wondered where it had gone and whether it would set down again elsewhere.

The following minute the tornado was completely forgotten as Shakespeare rounded another bend and spied white froth ahead. He tucked his legs to his chest and kept both arms over the back of the horse, a precaution that proved prudent when they slewed into a stretch of rapids at dizzying speed.

A squeal of agony was torn from the horse as its legs slammed into a submerged boulder. Shakespeare felt the jolt in both arms and wished there was some way he could steer the animal to quieter water. It resumed thrashing, more wildly this time, bucking its head and neck. A second jolt drove it into an absolute frenzy.

Shakespeare clung onto the saddle, the Hawken wedged under his chest. He held his legs high enough to prevent the horse from kicking them but he still had to keep his eyes peeled for obstacles. A glistening mass materialized in front of him and slightly to the right so he shifted higher onto his mount and hooked his ankles on its back. It wasn't enough.

He absorbed the brunt of the blow. A million pinpoints of pain flared in his right thigh on impact, then they were off, swept along into another boulder, and yet another. These the horse struck with full force, driving the animal berserk. It wanted out of the river, and to that end it veered to the south, fighting the current but making scant headway.

Shakespeare was aware of the new danger even if the horse wasn't. He attempted to turn it back into the flow but had no more than grasped its mane when it rammed into another boulder so hard that the crack of its ribs was audible above the howling storm.

The horse whinnied, sagged, and kicked feebly as it was borne along in the current's irresistible grasp. Shakespeare couldn't determine how badly it was hurt but he suspected the injury was severe.

More jolts followed. The poor animal nickered pitiably, making Shakespeare wish he could put it out of its misery. He dared not let go to pull a pistol, though, not when surrounded by bubbling foam.

The harrowing ordeal lasted over a minute. Then the water calmed but the current did not slacken one bit. Rain continued to pour from the sky while the wind howled unabated.

Shakespeare tried to estimate how far he had traveled. Miles, probably. He felt the horse drift toward the north shore and kicked his legs in a vain bid to drive the animal in the opposite direction. The last time he saw the Kings they had been on the south side of the Yellowstone and if he wound up on the north he might not be able to rejoin them for days. Provided, of course, they were still alive.

The rapid current had a mind all its own. The harder Shakespeare fought, the faster it seemed to sweep him where he didn't care to go. Presently the eerie shapes of whipping trees silhouetted themselves against the backdrop of rain and somber heavens.

Shakespeare bowed to the inevitable. Pulling his legs high, he watched the shoreline rush out to meet him. The bottom of the horse hit, then his knees scraped lightly, but neither caught hold. He was carried farther, into another bend, only now he was so near land that he was propelled into a newly created shallow marsh adjacent to the roaring waterway.

With a lurch the horse slammed into a snag and stopped. Shakespeare lay on top a few moments, drinking in the cool air. He slid off into water up to his knees. Thunder and lightning united in a crescendo of unearthly proportions, the bolts brightening the landscape in intermittent flashes that enabled him to see the horse was dead, its blank upper eye fixed on the cold, drenched world that had so callously claimed its life.

"Alas, poor Yorick," Shakespeare quoted under his breath. He quickly stooped to strip off the sole parfleche still strapped to the animal. Both the painter meat and the other parfleche were gone, torn off by the demented Yellowstone.

Shakespeare sloshed onto solid ground and stood shivering in the downpour. He was damned lucky to be alive and knew it. He wondered, had the Kings fared equally well?

The far bank was lost to view in the murk, providing no clues.

Turning, the mountain man sought shelter. Among the trees the rain slackened slightly but the risk of being targeted by a bolt from above was much higher. He weighed the two on mental scales and huddled at the base of a thick trunk, deciding creature comfort outweighed personal danger.

Worry for the King family filled Shakespeare's breast. For himself he had no fears since he could live off the land anywhere, anytime. Hostiles and grizzlies would be his two main concerns, the former in particular since he was now on the Blackfoot side of the river and the tribe had been after his hair for longer than he cared to remember.

Shakespeare bent low over the parfleche and eased a hand up under the flap to check the contents. One had contained food, the other spare powder, lead balls, and other essential odds and ends. He hoped Fate had spared the powder and shot; instead he had the food.

Making do as best he was able, Shakespeare took a bite of jerky and sat listening to raindrops pelt leaves overhead. His buckskins and beaver hat were so soaked they offered no protection whatsoever from the elements. Every so often he experienced bouts of chills that quickly subsided.

Eventually, despite the conditions, Shakespeare dozed fitfully. Occasional thunderous peals would startle him to wakefulness and it was during one of these interludes that he saw an enormous creature. Bathed in the fading glow of lightning the beast moved through the water toward the horse.

Shakespeare could barely make out the thing's shape let alone any details but the little he distinguished was enough to apprise him of the creature's identity. He thought he heard a series of guttural grunts. The beast nosed around the horse, then opened wide a gaping maw and bit down. Soon the crunch of bones competed with the other sounds.

Keeping perfectly still, Shakespeare watched the grizzly eat and prayed it wouldn't catch his scent or stray into the trees and blunder onto him. The Hawken and the pistols were too waterlogged to function and he had not been able to reload yet. His butcher knife still hung from his waist but he would only use that as a last resort.

Staying awake now was no problem. Shakespeare inched backward around the tree until only his eyes and forehead were showing. The great humped bear was too engrossed in filling its belly to notice.

In due course the storm started to taper off. First the wind dropped to a whisper, then the lightning nearly ceased, and ultimately the rain tapered to a heavy drizzle.

The bear lingered. Oblivious to the rain and cold, it ate greedily, ripping off large chunks with a swipe of its tremendous jaws. Horse-flesh was a rarity it clearly savored.

Shakespeare's joints grew stiff, his head ached. He yearned to seek out a sheltered nook where he might get a fire going and dry his clothes and himself. Common sense dictated he lay low until the bear was done. But as more and more time went by and it became plain the grizzly had no intention of wandering off any time soon, he threw caution to the wind, tucked the parfleche under one arm, the Hawken under another, and backpedaled, keeping the tree between them.

A grizzly relied mainly on its keen sense of smell to detect prey and enemies. Its eyesight was average, its hearing sharper than a man's but not as sharp as a panther's or even a coyote's. Its nose, however, surpassed that of most other animals.

Shakespeare counted on the breeze not shifting in order to effect his escape. He covered a score of yards, the drizzle drowning out what little noise he made. The edge of the trees appeared. Beyond, a sea of partially flattened grass led into the distance.

Just as McNair emerged from the strip of woodland, the breeze changed. He felt it caress his face and instantly whirled, fleeing pell-mell across the prairie. Thirty more paces he covered, his anxious gaze fixed on the trees.

It was pure instinct that made Shakespeare flatten not five seconds before a bulky outline materialized near the plain. The grizzly had smelled him and come to investigate.

Being stalked was always a nerve-racking ordeal. Being stalked by a monster boasting a thousand pounds of sinew and razor teeth was a nightmare brought to life. Shakespeare hugged the slick grass, his heart beating wildly, and resolved to go down swinging if the grizzly found him.

The massive form paced back and forth, its slab of a head tilted upward to better read the air.

Go on! Shakespeare wanted to shout. Go finish your meal, damn your bones! He held a handful of stems in front of his face so the gleam of his skin wouldn't give him away. When, after a while, the grizzly lumbered back toward the river, he exhaled and rested his chin on his forearm.

Waiting another five minutes seemed a prudent move. In a crouch Shakespeare hastened to the northeast, paralleling the trees so he wouldn't stray far from the river. He intended to find a means across at first light.

A convenient gully offered the haven McNair needed. In the gully itself water six inches deep flowed, but part of the bank on the near side had eroded away long ago, exposing a portion of the underside of a pine tree. There a small spot had been shielded from the brunt of the downpour by the branches and roots.

Gratefully Shakespeare clambered down and sat with his back to the trunk. The temptation to close his eyes and sleep was almost too much to resist but he did. He gathered such kindling as was available, removed his fire steel and tinderbox from his possibles bag, and set about starting a fire. It took forever and made the tiny flame that crackled to life more precious for the effort. Once the first one had been produced, building a higher blaze was no problem. All he had to do was break off roots and add them as needed.

Outside Shakespeare's sanctuary rain continued to fall. He rigged a crude tripod over the flames, stripped off his buckskins, and hung them to dry, shivering despite the fire's warmth. Next he inspected his powder-horn and ammo pouch. His black powder was damp in spots but there were enough dry grains to enable him to reload the Hawken and both flintlocks.

Jerky filled his belly. To get a drink all he had to do was move a few feet and dip his mouth to the water flowing through the gully. He was feeling quite content when he resumed his post next to the fire and felt his shirts and leggings. They were still too damp to put on.

"Ahh, well," Shakespeare said aloud. "It's nothing to get all bothered about. I'm alive and that's all that counts." Leaning back, he gave voice to the bard. "I have neither the scholar's melancholy, which is emulation, nor the musician's, which is fantastical, nor the courtier's, which is proud, nor the soldier's, which is ambitious, nor the lawyer's, which is politic, nor the lady's, which is nice, nor the lover's, which is all these. But it is a melancholy of mine own, compounded of many simples, extracted from many objects. And indeed the sundry contemplation of my travels, in which my constant rumination wraps me in a most humorous sadness."

Chuckling, Shakespeare went to poke a root into the fire when a battering ram of total shock slammed into his mind with all the force of a runaway wagon and he jerked as if struck. "My Lord!" he exclaimed in sheer horror. "Old William S.!"

Not caring whether his clothes were dry or not, Shakespeare hastily donned them, slid the pistols under his belt, and grabbed the rifle. "Bear or no bear, I have to go see if I can find it," he declared. A lingering look at the comforting fire hardly slowed his climb to the open plain. Pulling his hat low against the drizzle, he jogged toward the Yellowstone.

Shakespeare knew he was violating every rule of common sense he had ever learned throughout his long, full life. He was being headstrong, rash, careless, and childish. In short, just plain stupid. But he couldn't help himself if he wanted to and he had no desire to curb his hasty impulse. Not where *this* was concerned.

"Please," Shakespeare addressed the empty air. "Please!" Presently he gained the strip of trees and ventured to the water's edge. Thanks to the overcast sky visibility was reduced to a few yards. Beyond that all was a blur, as he well knew. Still, he could not give up, not if there was the slightest of chances he'd locate his most precious possession.

The Yellowstone River still raged in full flood. Hazy objects shot past: logs, branches, other things.

Shakespeare turned to his left. Here and there floating objects had drifted into shore, fueling his fervent hope, a hope that was feeble at best because he had to concede that in all likelihood his cherished book had sunk to the bottom the moment the bundle in which it was wrapped came loose from the saddle.

Hiking eastward, Shakespeare probed the shallows, ignoring all else in his frantic hunt. Several times he plunged a hand into matted clumps of grass or weeds which he mistook for a bundled, partially submerged blanket. He tried assuring himself that if he had lost it, the loss was not that great, but he could not deceive himself if he tried.

Books were rare in the Rockies. Consequently they were highly valued, especially during the long winter months when trappers had little to do but gather wood, kill game when the snow permitted, and entertain themselves as best they were able. Reading was a favorite pastime. The works of Byron and Scott were highly regarded, as was the Bible and commentaries on it.

Many folks back in the States would have been surprised to learn such was the case since they regarded mountaineers as illiterate backwoodsmen whose only diversions were Indian women and wrestling matches. Few realized that quite a few of the young men who went west were highly intelligent, innately curious souls thirsting for adventure, drawn by the lure of the unknown to challenge Nature on Nature's terms and wrest a living from the unforgiving wilderness.

Shakespeare had been just such a young explorer when he crossed the wide Mississippi for the first time. Like his peers he had spent many a cold winter's day with his nose to the pages of the latest volume being circulated. And then he had found a copy of the collected works of William Shakespeare and he hadn't been the same since.

There had been an indefinable quality about the bard's works that had attracted McNair like a flame attracts a moth. He had devoured play after play, sonnet after sonnet, and craved more. On learning there were no more he had reread everything, not once or twice or even three times but again and again over the years until he could quote lengthy passages as easily as most quoted from the Good Book. And somewhere along the line someone had given him the nickname that would stick with him the rest of his born days.

Shakespeare had lugged old William S. over hill and down dale, across mountain ranges clear to the Pacific Ocean and from Mexico to Canada. A few pages had discolored and the spine had weakened but otherwise the volume had miraculously remained intact.

Call it silly, call it childish, but McNair regarded that book as he might a good friend, a boon companion who had stuck with him through thick and thin. He'd entertained second thoughts about taking it all the way to the Mandan village but had done so simply because he could not bear to part with it for any long period. He needed his daily dose of William S. just like other men needed their daily dose of coffee or tobacco or whatever their personal vice might be.

Now, barreling along the surging Yellowstone, Shakespeare searched high and low, single-mindedly focused on the job of finding that book no matter how long it took. He forgot all about the warm fire at the gully. He forgot all about the Kings and his anxiety over their well-being. And, most crucial of all, he forgot all about the grizzly that had made a supper out of his horse. This last oversight was remedied moments later when, on stepping over a log and skirting a thicket, he heard a rumbling growl and glanced up to discover the enormous predator fifteen feet away.

Chapter Six

Dawn broke chill and damp on the prairie. Bright sunshine warmed young Zachary King's eyelids, rousing him from a sleep of utter exhaustion. Blinking in the sunlight, he yawned and stretched, then surveyed the plain and the river, searching for sign of hostiles or predators. His pa had taught him to always be on his guard when in the wilderness and he had learned his lessons well.

Damp grass greeted the boy's anxious gaze on one hand, the swollen Yellowstone on the other. Except for sparrows and a robin or two there was no wildlife in sight.

Zach stood and arched his back to relieve the kinks produced by a night of leaning against the rough tree trunk. His tummy rumbled, as it always did first thing in the morning. For a few seconds he thought he must go hungry until he remembered the meat he had crammed into his possibles bag the day before.

Opening the flap, Zach reached in, grabbed the sticky chunk, and pulled it out. His nose scrunched up at the awful odor and he feared the portion had spoiled. Closer inspection revealed the meat was not likely to be served in any of the finer restaurants in New Orleans but would do for his breakfast.

Zach sank his fine white teeth into the piece and bit down. Somehow the consistency had changed to a rubbery mass he found hard to bite off and chew. He forced himself to eat it, though, since he had no idea when he would next enjoy a meal and his pa had taught him that a man alone in the wild took each day as it came, eating when he could and going hungry when he had no other choice.

Hiking to the river, Zach sank to one knee and drank a handful. The water was muddy, the taste flat. He wondered if it would be smart to boil some before drinking any more, then grinned at his silliness since he had nothing to boil the water in.

A close scrutiny of the opposite shore turned up no trace of his folks or Shakespeare McNair. The river was twice as wide as it should have been, the current still too strong for him to attempt to swim to the other shore. Nature had trapped him on the north side and he would have to make the best of things for the time being.

Zach saw a small stand of slender saplings and went over. He selected one the right size and used his tomahawk to chop it down, his knife to trim the thin limbs and leaves. Deftly he whittled at the thick end until he had a tapered point.

Makeshift lance in hand, Zach felt a little better. He could defend himself now, although his puny weapon would do little good against the likes of a raging grizzly or a hungry panther.

Hoping to find game, Zach hunted among the weeds and brush. Several rabbits were spooked into bounding off into the grass but they moved so fast he was unable to bring them down. A noisy squirrel interested him until it climbed to a lofty perch beyond his reach and chattered irately down at him.

Then Zach saw the deer. He was rounding a cottonwood and there not twenty feet away stood a small white-tail doe, grazing. Her back was to him. Tingling with excitement, he hefted the lance, took a few swift strides, and let fly with all his might.

The doe heard his footsteps and glanced around before the lance left his fingers. She was airborne the same moment as his weapon. And she was long gone, lost in the undergrowth, before the sharp point imbedded itself in the soft soil.

Frustrated, Zach reclaimed his spear. It seemed he would never have fresh meat. Thinking he might have better luck going after fish, the boy strolled to the Yellowstone and haunted the shallows. Other than a solitary frog that leaped far out into the murky water and disappeared, he saw no aquatic life.

By midmorning Zach was too depressed to hunt so he stopped to rest on a boulder. He thought he knew how to live off the land but he was learning there was more to it than he had imagined. Always before his father had been there to help him, except once in the middle of the winter when they had been caught in an avalanche. That time he'd had a rifle, and until this very moment he hadn't truly appreciated how much of a difference a gun made.

A rifle enabled a trapper to confront Nature on equal terms, to eat when hungry, to defend himself against anyone or anything that would take his life.

And there was more to owning a gun than simple survival. Much more. Many was the time his pa had impressed on him that owning a firearm was so important a right it was guaranteed in the Constitution of the United States of America. The men who gathered for the Constitutional Convention had seen firsthand the evil that resulted when government got too big for its britches. As his pa had put it, "arming average citizens was the only way to prevent that from ever happening here."

A sudden gust of wind fanned Zach's hair and brought to his ears the faint whinny of a horse. Sliding to the ground, he crouched and moved toward the prairie. He hoped against hope he would spy a party of trappers or perhaps friendly Shoshones or Crows. But since he was in Blackfoot country, he doubted he'd be so fortunate.

From the last rank of trees the boy spotted five riders far off, heading in his general direction. Scooting into dense cover, Zach dropped flat and placed his lance in front of him, ready for immediate use.

The horsemen approached at a leisurely pace. They had the complexions and high cheek bones of all Indians. Their long black hair was parted in the middle and braided from the ears down, a common style. But their features, their buckskins, and in particular their moccasins, were distinctive.

Zach swallowed hard and wriggled as if trying to worm his way into the ground. They were Blackfeet all right, and if they caught him he was a goner for certain. From their relaxed manner he knew they had no idea he was there, but that could all change if their horses were at all like Shoshone mounts.

As luck would have it, the Blackfeet were on a line of travel that brought them within twenty feet of Zachary's hiding place. He noted the bows and rifles they carried and tried to make sense of their conversation, but their tongue was utterly alien. One of the men caught his eye, a tall warrior astride a fine white stallion. The man reminded him of a Shoshone chief he knew in that the Blackfoot sat straight and proud as the chief always did.

Four of the five riders had gone past when the fifth man's horse abruptly bobbed its head and nickered loud and long. The entire band promptly reined up.

Zach held his breath, dread seizing him. The fifth horse was looking right at the thicket, nostrils flaring. Startled, Zach realized the fickle breeze had shifted slightly and was bearing his scent right to them.

The tall warrior said something to the last brave who kneed his animal closer to the thicket and notched an arrow to his bowstring.

A horrifying mental picture of that shaft tearing into his body was all the impetus Zach needed to shove to his feet, whirl, and flee. The Blackfoot would have discovered him in a few seconds anyway and he had to get out of there before they surrounded him. There were surprised shouts to his rear mingled with the thud of hoofs moving rapidly.

A glance back showed the warriors in pursuit. Already they had fanned out, three going to the north to cut him off from the prairie while the tall warrior and one other bore to the south to cut him off from the river.

Zach was desperate. He couldn't hope to outrun horses. Nor could he fight the Blackfeet off without a gun. In order to escape he had to do the unthinkable: dart toward the river, throw himself into the water, and swim for his life. He was almost there when a firm hand fell on his back and he was plucked high into the air and dangled in front of the tall warrior.

"Let me go!" Zach screeched, taking a wild swing with his lance. The Blackfoot easily jerked aside, grinned, and let go, tumbling Zach into a patch of weeds.

A gust of laughter greeted the boy as he shoved to his feet. Mad as a wet bobcat, he leveled his spear and glared at the warriors who now encircled him. "I'm not afraid of you!" Zach blustered. "Do your worst! You'll see that the King men know how to die!"

Louder laughter was the response. A pudgy Blackfoot jabbed a finger at Zach and said something while mimicking Zach's expression. Another warrior acted as if he was so afraid he would fall off his war horse.

"Poke fun at me, will you!" Zach fumed, charging. He drove his lance at the leg of the one imitating him but the brave flicked his reins and moved out of harm's way. Spinning, Zach pointed his weapon at each of them in turn, waiting for the moment when they would converge and slay him. He gulped, longing to see his folks just one more time, then straightened his slender shoulders and announced, "I'm ready!"

The Blackfeet were in earnest discussion, all except the tall warrior who merely stared thoughtfully at the small fury.

"What are you waiting for?" Zach demanded, unable to bear the suspense. He debated whether to try and dash between their mounts to gain the river and knew he'd never make it.

The pudgy Blackfoot drew a knife, then leaned down to wag it near the boy's head. He yipped fiercely, a mock scowl contorting his features.

Zach swung, his lance swatting the blade aside. He backed up a step, remembered there were more behind him, and shifted, striving to keep them all in sight at once.

A single word from the tall warrior ended the laughter. He addressed the pudgy brave who reluctantly sheathed his knife. Lowering the fusee he held to his lap, the tall warrior moved his hands in the universal tongue of the plains, sign language. "Question, boy. You know Indian sign language?"

Loath to answer since he must lower his lance to do so, Zach hesitated.

"Answer me," the Blackfoot motioned as would someone accustomed to being obeyed.

Casting a nervous glance at the others, Zach tucked his spear under an arm and signed, "Yes, I speak sign. The son of Grizzly Killer has been taught many things. Harm him and Grizzly Killer will track you down and kill you."

The pudgy man snickered until he received a stern look from the tall warrior. "Question. You called?"

There were no sign symbols for Zachary King so the boy gave his Shoshone name. "Stalking Coyote."

"I am Bird Rattler," the Blackfoot disclosed. "Why are you here alone? Where is this father we should fear?"

Suspecting he was being mocked again, Zach was all set to give the warrior a piece of his mind when he realized the man wasn't smirking like the rest. "My father has gone off a little way to hunt and will come back at any time," he fibbed, inspired to trick the band into leaving. "There are twenty white men with him and they have many long guns."

Bird Rattler cocked his head. "Does Stalking Coyote speak with one tongue or two?"

Zach began to move his hands, to say he was being truthful, but a pang of conscience gave him pause. His parents had taught him to always be honest. Always, without exception.

And they had made no allowances for special circumstances.

"Did you understand the question, Stalking Coyote?"

"I spoke with two tongues."

"There are not twenty whites with many guns?"

"No."

"Your father is alone?"

"No."

"How many are with him then?"

Here Zach balked. He could not bring himself to lie but that did not mean he had to reveal everything the Blackfeet wanted to know. It abruptly occurred to him that if the warriors knew about his folks and Shakespeare the band might attempt to hunt them down. So he stood still, refusing to answer.

"I think you are lost, little one," Bird Rattler signed. "I think you are all alone with no one to look after you."

The pudgy Indian joined in. "I see you have a powder horn. Where is your rifle?"

"I lost it," Zach admitted.

"What sort of boy are you that you lose something so valuable?"

"The storm," Zach signed, and stopped, seeing no need to explain himself to men who were going to lift his hair at any minute. Gripping his lance, he pointed the tip at the pudgy Blackfoot and waited.

"What are you doing, boy?" asked that worthy.

The tall warrior smiled. "He is going to give his life dearly, Cream Bear."

"His life?" Cream Bear snorted like his namesake. "We do not kill children."

"He has heard differently."

A heated exchange broke out in the Blackfoot tongue and all Zach could do was stand still, listening. He got the impression two others were arguing with Bird Rattler but had no idea why. After a while the pair fell silent although they were mightily displeased.

Bird Rattler bent low. "Climb on, Stalking Coyote. You will go with us." He offered his brawny hand.

Zach lowered his lance to respond, "I will not."

"You cannot wander the prairie by yourself. A bear might find you. We saw sign of one not far from this very spot."

"Do not worry about me. I can take care of myself."

"Very well. If such is your wish." Bird Rattler straightened and signaled the others, then applied his heels to his horse and began to swing around to the west. In a masterly display of horsemanship he suddenly wheeled inward, hung by one arm, and scooped Zach into the other. So swiftly did he pounce, the shocked boy was held firmly in place before he quite awakened to his capture.

"No!" Zach bellowed, twisting to jab his spear at Bird Rattler's chest. A hand flashed in and Cream Buffalo tore the lance from his grasp. He grabbed for his tomahawk but a third Blackfoot took it, the fourth his knife. They had stripped him of his weapons but not his resolve. Kicking and punching he sought to break free but his blows were as those of a tiny reed on solid rock; they had no effect. The Blackfeet laughed, enjoying his frustration, and this time Bird Rattler joined in.

Zach's anger mounted. Without thinking he drove the rigid fingers of his right hand into Bird Rattler's face, straight into the warrior's eyes. Bird Rattler yelped and raised his hands to protect himself, and in so doing he released the reins. Zach caught them, rammed his shoulder into the blinded warrior, then heaved with every ounce of strength he could muster. No one was more shocked than he was when Bird Rattler toppled off the horse, the rifle falling with him.

A jab of the knees was enough to goad the brown stallion into motion. Zach bent low to evade Cream Buffalo's clawed fingers, then he was in the clear and galloping for the prairie. Angry yells were hurled after him. He heard some of them give chase but did not lose precious moments looking back. Legs flapping madly, he lashed the reins as he guided his mount through the cottonwoods and willows.

The stallion was a superb animal, bred for speed and endurance. As with many Indian mounts, it had a wild streak and loved nothing more than to run free with the wind in its mane. Now, on being given its head by the boy on its back, the stallion flowed over the ground in a literal blur, proving in the first minute that Bird Rattler knew how to pick horseflesh. It handily outdistanced its pursuers and would not slow no matter how much they shouted.

Zach was tickled pink. He was getting away! Soon he'd have enough of a lead over the Blackfeet they'd never catch him! There was only one small problem.

The stallion was a big animal, sixteen hands high if it was an inch. Zach could barely straddle its broad back with his legs stretched to their limit. And guiding the horse took his full stock of horsemanship. He had to tug extra hard on the reins to persuade the stallion to heed his wishes.

For the first mile all went well. By the end of the second, Zach glanced around and giggled on seeing the warriors so far behind they were the size of black dots. He pulled on the reins to slow the stallion but the animal raced on at a breakneck gallop. Annoyed, he tried once more with the same result.

Zach straightened and heaved backwards, throwing his entire weight into the movement. He might as well have been striving to stop a plummeting boulder for all the good it did him. The horse ran on, unimpressed.

"Whoa, darn you!" Zach cried, pulling and jerking.

Head bowed, legs drumming, the stallion ignored him.

"I said whoa!" Zach reiterated, wrapping the reins around his wrists for better leverage. Another attempt was equally unavailing. The horse had no desire to stop. Either he jumped off, which might earn him a busted backbone or worse, or he hung on until the stallion tired. It wasn't much of a choice.

Clinging fast, Zach settled down for a long ride. If the animal's rippling muscles were any indication, it possessed stamina to match its speed.

He wished he had been able to grab Bird Rattler's rifle as it fell. His pa had spent many an hour instructing him in a flintlock's use and he could hit man-sized targets consistently at long range. With a rifle he could keep the Blackfeet at bay if by some miracle they overtook him.

But, as Zach had learned the hard way, only a simpleton cried over spilt milk. He had to make the best of the situation. Adapt and live, as his pa would say. It was interesting how he thought of his folks when things got rough and tried to imagine how they would handle the same situation.

The stallion galloped on and on. Zach guessed they were five or six miles from the Yellowstone, probably more. He wondered if the horse had a special destination in mind and he peered ahead for some indication of where they were headed. Minutes later he had his answer.

Pale spots appeared on the prairie, arranged in a large circular pattern. Having lived among the Shoshones on many occasions Zach identified those spots for what they were: scores of lodges, an entire Blackfoot village! The fool horse was taking him straight home!

Zach had to think fast. In another few moments someone in the village might notice them. Girding himself, he put both palms flat on the stallion's shoulders, slid his legs up under his buttocks, and, on seeing thick grass to his right, he vaulted off. Air brushed his face, then he hit on his shoulder, the grass cushioning the worst of the impact. He rolled and rolled until his momentum was spent and sat up to take stock. To his amazement nothing was broken.

The stallion kept on going, tail flying.

Zach congratulated himself on his narrow escape and rose into a crouch. He had to get out of there before he was discovered. To that end, he moved stealthily eastward. Going south would take him directly back to the Yellowstone but it also might bring him face to face with Bird Rattler's band, so he figured on swinging in a wide loop until he regained the river.

By elevating his head high enough for a look-see, Zach spied figures moving about in the village. As yet there was no outcry over the horse but that could soon change. He snaked among the tall stems, parting them with his hands, trying to move the grass as little as possible just in case there were Blackfeet nearer than he suspected.

Zach had gone a quarter of a mile when the grass thinned and in front of him appeared a gully that ran from north to south. Excited at finding the ideal hiding place, he made a dash for the near slope and went over the crest without bothering to see what lay below. It was a grievous mistake.

Strolling along the bottom of the gully were two Blackfeet. Blackfeet boys, that was, neither older than Zach by the looks of them. Both glanced up on hearing his footsteps. Both gaped in blatant astonishment.

Zach tried to dig in his heels to stop, lost his balance, and catapulted down the eight-foot incline. By sheer accident his fall brought him down on top of the boys, bowling them over. He was first on his feet, bruised but otherwise fine. Whirling, he sprinted southward, rounding a bend just as the Blackfeet found their voices and cried out at the top of their lungs.

Zach thought they were calling for help and grinned at their foolishness since the village was out of earshot. On negotiating another bend he learned he was wrong. For in front of him was a third boy, this one armed with a bow and arrow. As Zach appeared, the Blackfoot lifted the bow and took aim.

There was nowhere to run, nowhere to take cover, nothing to do but keep on running. Zach rammed his arm into the young Indian as the Blackfoot loosed his shaft. The boy stumbled to one side and the arrow streaked into the left-hand slope, imbedding with a thud.

Zach never slowed. More bends promised refuge if he could only stay ahead of the Blackfeet. He took the first one and an arrow nipped at his heels. Pouring on the speed, he crossed a straight stretch and slowed for a fraction of an instant to check on his enemies.

All three boys were furiously trying to overhaul him.

Zach uttered a taunting laugh and went around the next corner. His taunt had been premature, as the two Blackfeet in front of him made clear. These boys were slightly older and held lances. They had heard the uproar and were ready, their weapons leveled.

Stopping so abruptly he almost tripped over his own feet, Zach eyed both of them, seeking an opening so he could get by. Before he could take a single step, though, the other three charged up and stopped a few yards off.

Zach was trapped.

Chapter Seven

As the nine warriors bore down on Nate King and one of them let fly with a glittering shaft, he was raising an arm to make the hand sign for "friend." He had no time to react, no chance to leap aside. For a heartbeat he thought he was a goner, then the arrow whizzed under his forearm, missing him by a hair but clipping off several whangs.

Since Nate couldn't hope to outrun the band and there was nowhere to seek cover, he grabbed for his flintlock, determined not to submit meekly.

The warriors were fanning out, several taking deliberate aim. Chances were slim they would miss a second time.

Just then a newcomer arrived on the scene in a flurry of dust. Yelling, frantically waving his arms, he rode between Nate and the band and reined up.

Nate recognized the same Indian he had run into earlier, the strange man he had found at the top of the ravine. To his amazement the warrior seemed intent on having the others lower their bows and lances. In an unknown tongue the strange one went on at some length, often pointing at Nate for emphasis. Several of the others spoke up and were harshly rebuked. Finally they obeyed and the newcomer wheeled his horse, then jumped down and warily approached.

Nate straightened, keeping his flintlock leveled. He had no idea what to expect, no inkling of why this Indian should save his life when previously the man had acted as if he were the Devil incarnate.

The Indian halted. He nervously fingered his leather bag while examining Nate closely. Suddenly, sinking to his knees, he touched his forehead to the ground and said several words.

Bewildered by the man's behavior, Nate replied in Shoshone, "I do not understand." He repeated the same statement in the Flathead language. Neither garnered a reply.

The Indian glanced up and showed his teeth in what could only be described as a fearful smile. Slowly rising, he resorted to sign language.

A few of the symbols the man used were different than those Nate was accustomed to, but he was able to get the general drift by piecing those he knew together.

"Greetings, mighty one. Your medicine is more powerful than any ever known. We mean you no harm. We welcome you to our country and offer you a place to stay during your visit here."

Puzzled, Nate responded with, "I thank you for your kindness. How are you known?"

"Forgive my manners," the Indian signed. "I thought you would know all things." He tapped his chest. "I am White Calf, medicine man of the Pawnee."

Nate's stomach muscles tightened. He'd never had personal dealings with the Pawnees but from what he'd heard they were a treacherous tribe. Rumor had it that they would welcome large parties of whites to their villages in peace but lone trappers were frequently slain for their belongings and their scalps. Suspicious of a trick, he asked, "Why did you act as you did before?"

White Calf answered without hesitation, "I was afraid of your power, great one. I did not want to be consumed by fire or turned to stone."

Assuming the Pawnee to be joking, Nate smiled. Yet the man seemed wholly sincere, which added to Nate's confusion. "Why would I do such a thing?" he demanded.

"I was where I should not have been," White Calf signed without apparent guile, adding quickly, "I did not mean to be in your way. Believe me, had I known you were coming I would have been elsewhere."

Nate did not have the slightest idea what the man was talking about. Many of the warriors were regarding him oddly, contributing to his unease. He decided to pass on the invite and signed, "I do not hold it against you. One day we will smoke a pipe together but now I must be on my way."

Shock lined White Calf's face. "Have we offended you that you leave us so soon? Please, come to our village. Our people will rejoice to have you among us. We will sing your praises as our ancestors did, and all that you wish will be done."

Nate had heard false flattery before but nothing to equal this. He wanted to be on his way. At the same time he hoped to avoid antagonizing the Pawnees if at all possible.

The medicine man took advantage of Nate's hesitation and dashed to his mount. Head bowed, arm extended, he brought the animal over. "Here. Take my horse unless you would rather fly. I will ride with another."

As if on cue the other warriors closed in.

Resisting a tide of panic, Nate debated whether to make a fight of it or to run. He was convinced the Pawnees were playing him for a fool and intended to rub him out later. Perhaps if he went along with them, he'd get the chance to escape first. In any event, he'd be better able to elude them astride a horse. "I accept your offer," he signed, taking the reins.

White Calf beamed as if given his heart's desire. "This is a great day for my people."

A lean warrior rode up to offer a hand and the medicine man swung up behind him. The rest formed a circle around Nate, effectively preventing him from fleeing. With the pair riding double in the lead, the band headed southward at a trot.

Nate had one consolation. So far the Pawnees had not thought to strip him of his weapons. He might be able to shoot and slash his way out if they let down their guard at just the right time. He became conscious of being studied on the sly and wondered why they appeared to find him so fascinating when he was no differently dressed than other trappers would be.

Two hours of hard riding brought them to a shaded grove where they stopped at a signal from White Calf. Nate contrived to be the last one to dismount so he could dash off once they had all climbed down but the medicine man spoiled his scheme by walking over and taking casual hold of his animal's bridle.

Outsmarted again, Nate slid off and brushed dust from his buckskins.

"If it pleases you, great one," White Calf signed, "we would like to prepare for our return. There is a spring here where you can wash and slake your thirst, if indeed you need to drink as we do."

Nate was growing irritated by the sport the Pawnees were having at his expense. "Of course I need to drink and eat," he signed with angry gestures. "I have a body just like you. I hunger, I thirst."

White Calf swallowed hard and responded, "My apology for not seeing that which is right in front of me. My experience with your kind is limited."

More mad than ever, Nate strode off to burn off steam. None of the warriors tried to stop him. Rounding a cottonwood he discovered the spring and knelt. He dipped a hand in the cool water, then heard footsteps and spun, his hand flashing to his flintlock.

Several warriors halted in surprise but made no move to employ their weapons.

Rising, Nate backed off. Once on the other side of the spring he turned on his heel and entered the brush, resolved to lose the Pawnees at all costs. Swiftly he wound along until the undergrowth ended. The edge of the grove was in front of him, the open prairie beckoning. There might be a gully or a ravine out there in which he could hide. He dashed to the last tree and paused to scan the terrain.

In the distance buffalo roamed. Closer, a great hawk spun in majestic circles seeking prey. Insects buzzed, birds chirped.

Nate took a step, bearing to the northwest, when the crack of a twig warned him that he had been followed. And who else would it be but White Calf.

"Here you are, Sky Walker!" the medicine man signed. "I brought you this to make amends. From now on, when you are hungry you have only to let me know and you will have all the food you can eat." Over his shoulder was slung a parfleche into which he dipped a hand to produce pemmican.

Nate took the piece without comment. An impulse to pound the Pawnee senseless had to be checked because two other warriors trailed him. Munching halfheartedly, he gazed longingly at the prairie, so close yet in a sense so far. He had almost made it.

"We will leave when you are ready, Sky Walker, not before," White Calf signed.

Sticking the pemmican in his mouth, Nate responded, "Why do you keep calling me by that name?"

"What else would we call one who strides the sky as you do?"

Not having the slightest idea what the Pawnee referred to, Nate finished his morsel before replying, "The Shoshones know me as Grizzly Killer."

White Calf blinked in surprise. "You have visited the Shoshones first? What did they do to earn your favor that we did not do? Are our ceremonies done incorrectly? Do we dance poorly? Have our sacrifices been in vain?"

The wavering note of desperation in the medicine man's voice startled Nate. For the life of him he could not fathom the Pawnee's behavior. "They know me because I met them before I met you," he explained.

The medicine man considered this. "Will you go to other tribes as well?" he inquired.

"In time I will meet many," Nate predicted.

"So you did not come just to visit my people?"

"No," Nate signed, and was puzzled by the pained expression his response caused. "My people go where they wish, seeing who they please."

"How many of you are there?"

"More than the buffalo."

The astonishment lining White Calf's features was almost comical. He placed a hand over his mouth and gaped heavenward for a while, then regained his composure and moved his hands to say, "Truly there is much I have to learn. I thought there would be few of you. To support so many your land must be much bigger than we have imagined it to be."

Fond memories of his uncle's farm in upstate New York made Nate's voice husky. "Our land is not only big but thick with deer and fish. It rains more often so the ground is rich and there are many trees. The Blood Moon is not as hot, the Snow Moon is not as cold. And the people live in peace with one another."

"Truly you live in paradise," White Calf signed. "Do you need lodges or do you live in the open?"

Nate thought the question quaint. "We live in lodges, like you do, but ours are much different. Many are made with moist clay hardened by heat or with stone."

White Calf clapped a hand to his cheek. "How can this be?" he then asked. "Surely the stone is too heavy and falls?"

"Do your lodges fall down?"

"Sometimes when the wind is very strong."

"We make ours too strong for the wind," Nate detailed, "and as high as the tops of these trees."

"Your country is beyond words," the Pawnee said, gawking at the nearest treetop. "That you should leave so wonderful a place to come here is a mystery. What can we possibly have that would interest you?"

"We like to travel, to see new places, new faces," Nate said. He thought of Winona and expressed a compliment, "And some of us think your women are the most beautiful women anywhere."

The light of comprehension dawned in White Calf's restless eyes. "This, at last, I understand. Men have always admired the beauty of women and needed women as companions. Why should it be true for us and not for you?" He paused as if uncertain whether to continue. "But what do your own women think of this?"

"There are those who think badly of us. There are those who let us do as we please."

"Women are the same everywhere," the medicine man stated with a knowing grin. "Whether high or low many feel they must put us on the straight path because we are too stupid to find the path ourselves."

"Question. You have a wife?" Nate asked.

"I did," White Calf revealed. "The Blackfeet rubbed her out." He glanced up, abruptly excited. "This is something I have never understood. Why does your kind let the Blackfeet and the Bloods live? They are good for nothing other than stripping wives of husbands, children of fathers. Your people should kill them, kill them all!" Rabid anger transformed the Pawnee into a livid avenger.

More amused by the outburst than anything else, Nate signed, "My people do not go on the war path against other people unless those others attack us first."

"Then you must never go on the warpath. You are out of reach, safe in your stone lodges." White Calf sighed. "I wish we could say the same. My wife would be alive today." Hefting the parfleche, he brightened and wondered, "Do you want more pemmican?"

"No," Nate said, beginning to relax a little. The

Pawnee's friendliness had relieved some of his anxiety but not all. He debated whether to come right out and ask that they go their separate ways so he could resume his search for Winona.

"Would you have us leave?"

The unexpected query delighted Nate. "Yes," he signed eagerly. "I very much would."

A yell from the medicine man brought the rest of the band at a trot. Nate's elation was short-lived as his horse was led right up to him and the reins handed over. Discouraged, he climbed on and made no protest as the Pawnees trotted southward. They were not about to let him go, he realized, so he had better keep his eyes skinned for another chance to get away. "This coon isn't going under without taking a few with him," he vowed under his breath. Perhaps one day Shakespeare or another Mountainee Man would hear of the trapper who went down under a pile of Pawnees and recognize him from the description given. At least then Winona and Zach and his child yet unborn would learn of his fate.

For the remainder of the day the band pushed hard, riding their animals to the point of exhaustion. They clearly wanted to reach a certain destination before nightfall, and Nate had no difficulty guessing it. Nor was his guess wrong. Along about sunset they passed through rolling hills and reined up on one overlooking a tranquil river bordered by a large village.

"Our people," White Calf signed proudly.

Smoke curled from scores of campfires. Children scampered playfully about as they did in every Indian village, while the women were busily tending to supper. Lookouts spotted the new arrivals and yipped to alert everyone else.

"You will not regret coming," the medicine man assured Nate as they wound down to a lush strip of land where tilled fields of corn, beans, and squash grew in abundance.

These were the first crops Nate had seen in ages. His adopted people, the Shoshones, and most other Western tribes, disdained cultivating the soil. They were hunters first and foremost, although to add variety to their diet the women gathered berries, roots, and certain plants in season.

Having had experience on a farm when younger, Nate could tell that these crops were expertly tended. They were arranged in neat rows and any weeds had been diligently pulled out. No one had ever told him that the Pawnees farmed so extensively; his opinion of them rose several notches.

Once past the fields Nate received another surprise. The lodges of this tribe were not at all like those of the Shoshones, Flathead, and Crows. In place of the typical buffalo hide teepees, the Pawnees preferred odd affairs made from logs, dirt, and grass. He saw one under construction and marveled at its simple yet effective design. The log frame came first, then layers of grass and dirt were added for as much insulation as the builders desired. In the summer the interiors would be cool, in the winter comfortably warm.

White Calf led the band into the heart of the village. He rode with his back straight, his chin jutting proudly, drinking in the attention lavished on him because of the stranger he had brought back.

From all directions the Pawnees converged. Men, women, and children stopped whatever they were doing to investigate the commotion.

Nate found himself completely surrounded by a thick throng of humanity, the warriors at the forefront, many with bows and lances in hand. There was no hope of escape. Should the Pawnees decide to take his life he would be bristling with wooden quills before he could lift a finger to defend himself.

In front of a lodge much bigger than the rest White Calf drew rein. A gray-haired warrior whose stately features bespoke inherent nobility emerged and regarded the party somberly. His features were seamed with age yet his eyes were sparkling beacons crackling with vitality that belied his years.

Nate guessed that here was a chief. The man studied him intently, making Nate feel as if he was under a microscope. Other warriors joined the elderly man but respectfully stood either behind him or to one side.

The members of White Calf's band had formed a ring around Nate but at a distance. Nate didn't know if they had done it to hem him in or to protect him from the inquisitive throng, which milled steadily closer. Women tittered and pointed. Children gawked and giggled. The men, on the other hand, were gravely serious, and not a few displayed outright hostility.

Softly spoken words issued from the chief. White Calf responded at length, with frequent grand gestures, often indicating Nate. The chief

listened without expression but the same could
not be said of his people.

Nate was stunned to see the reaction rippling among the Pawnees. First there was
mild surprise, then stark astonishment, then
undeniable awe. Children hid behind the legs
of parents and peeked out at him in blatant
fear. Women backed away or averted their
faces when his gaze fell on them. Warriors
nervously wagged their weapons, some fingering their bow strings as if inclined to put arrows
into him.

What the devil was White Calf telling them?
Nate wondered irritably. He didn't trust White
Calf as far as he could heave a bull buffalo,
and something told him the medicine man was
bringing a heap of trouble down on his head.
He wanted to interrupt, to address the chief
directly, but such rudeness was only tolerated
in white society.

A tall warrior standing beside the chief
abruptly grunted and walked toward Nate. His
bearing marked him as a man of importance.
His face marked him as a man of courage. He
scrutinized Nate while circling Nate's mount
and when he was done he made a statement
that brought derisive smiles to many faces.

Nate glanced at the man and their eyes locked.
He smiled to show his friendly intentions but
the smile had an odd effect; the warrior backed
up a stride and fingered his knife. To confirm
his intentions, Nate used sign to say, "I come
in peace. You need not fear."

Instead of being pacified, the tall warrior
glowered and started to draw his blade. A

shriek from an attractive woman in the crowd stopped him.

White Calf turned. The chief advanced and addressed the tall warrior in his quiet voice. When the tall warrior answered, White Calf became angry and spoke sharply, again motioning a lot at Nate. Strangely, he pointed at the sky almost as much.

Thoroughly confounded, Nate impatiently waited for the parley to end so he could make it plain that he meant them no harm. The very notion was ridiculous, outnumbered as he was a hundred to one.

Suddenly White Calf and the tall warrior began arguing, the tall brave raising his voice and shaking a fist at the medicine man who merely smiled like a cat about to devour a canary. Another warrior, young enough to be the tall man's son, ran up to him and whispered in his ear. The tall one subsided but he was obviously displeased and simmering with resentment.

Here was the moment Nate wanted. No one was talking so he went to address them in sign. To his dismay, White Calf barked orders and several of the band closed in on his horse and led him toward a lodge nearer the river. Nate looked back and saw the tall warrior stalking off, the young one dutifully following. White Calf and the chief were in earnest conversation.

Damn it all! Nate fumed in frustration. Now he must bide his time until morning and then plead his plight. The chief had impressed him as an honorable man, and he felt sure that if he could only explain he might be permitted to leave, perhaps given a horse and enough jerky or pemmican to last him until he reached the Yellowstone River. He suspected White Calf had deliberately spirited him away but he couldn't imagine why. Nothing made sense.

At the lodge the warriors hung back, gesturing for Nate to go in. Sliding off, Nate stepped to the darkened doorway and scrunched up his nose in disgust at the awful odor that assailed his nostrils. Hand on the flintlock, he slowly entered. It took a minute for his eyes to adjust.

Parfleches and packs hung from walls or were stacked in corners. Charred embers formed a black circle at the center of the lodge. Blankets were rolled up nearby. To the left was an open space. To the right lay the source of the smell, a collection of several animal carcasses partially butchered. From the stench and the state of the putrid meat, Nate estimated the carcasses had lain there for at least a week.

Nate stomached as much of the smell as he could. Then, backing up, he went to leave. He was nearly to the entrance when his left heel came down on a large smooth object that rolled out from under his foot, causing him to lose his balance. His arm shot out and he gripped the wall for support to keep from falling.

Looking down, Nate sought the object and found it looking back up at him. In a manner of speaking, anyway. For the smooth thing that had made him trip was a human skull.

Chapter Eight

The Minneconjou encampment lay nestled in a verdant valley bordering a winding waterway in the middle of the vast plain. It had taken two days to get there, two days of hard riding that had taken their toll on Winona. Never once, though, did she let on about her condition, which her baggy dress hid so well, because she did not want Thunder Horn to know. Her effort proved for naught, however, since she collapsed from exhaustion shortly after arriving and was closely examined by an elderly woman.

Now, the day after, Winona lay on a blanket in a cool teepee, her hands pressed to her over-sized belly, listening to the many and varied sounds of village life. Twice the size of her own, it teemed with laughing children, roving dogs, and too many adults to count.

A shadow flitted across the entrance and Thunder Horn appeared, pausing long enough to let his eyes adjust to the dim light before he ventured inside. He came over and gave her a probing stare. "Question," he signed. "How are you this day?"

"Better," Winona signed. "The pains have almost stopped."

"Had I known you were with child we would not have treated you so roughly."

The sincerity on the warrior's face was self-evident. Winona pushed herself off the blanket, sitting with difficulty. "Prove your words are not so much empty air. Give me a horse and allow me to go find my family."

"I cannot," Thunder Horn responded.

Winona sniffed and signed, "I thought as much. And I tell you again that I will be true to my husband no matter what." She stressed that part. "No matter what."

The warrior squatted and said nothing for a while. He merely drew random shapes in the dirt with a finger, his brow puckered. When he looked up, he looked troubled. "I have only known you a short time and already I like you very much. I envy this Grizzly Killer of yours. He has found a rare woman."

Winona kept her features impassive, steeling herself against the flattery.

"I have made it plain to you that I want to take you for my own," Thunder Horn said. She started to lift her hands and he went on, "Yes, I know you would fight me. But that would make no difference. I would like you to fight me." He grinned at the pleasant thought. "But

116

old Butterfly tells me there is a chance you might be hurt inside and we do not want you to die."

"We?"

"Others have a stake in your welfare."

"Who?" Winona wondered, puzzled.

"The entire tribe."

Had he not signed the words with a somber face, Winona would have judged the statement to be a strange joke. "A simple Shoshone woman is of such great importance?" she shot back.

"Yes," Thunder Horn replied, rising. "In less than a moon, about the same time your baby is due, you will understand. Until then it has been decided you will be left in peace." His fingers paused. "Afterward, you have been pledged to me, and I will take you no matter how hard you kick and punch or how loud you scream."

An ominous shadow settled upon Winona's soul as the Minneconjou departed and a shiver rippled down her spine. She felt the baby kick, hard, and grasped her stomach again.

What was she to do? Winona asked herself. Escaping in her state was impossible. Even if she succeeded in stealing a horse and sneaking out of the village, improbable in light of the many sentries and dogs, she would not be able to make good time and was certain to be chased down by Thunder Horn. Oh! she reflected. If only my Nate was here! Seldom had she missed him as much as she did right then and there.

The only note of good news was that she would be left alone for a month or so, until the baby was born. Winona rubbed her belly and sang softly to soothe the grasshopper inside of her. She was grateful for the respite. Perhaps she could use it to her advantage.

Who was she deluding? In another three weeks she would be so big and heavy she couldn't outrun a turtle, let alone flee across the prairie with Minneconjous nipping at the heels of her moccasins.

Since sitting up had aggravated her discomfort from the jostling she had received when captured, Winona reclined on her back and sighed at the relief she experienced. Short-lived relief, for no sooner did her physical discomfort end than her emotional torment resumed. For the hundredth time she worried about Nate and Zach and Shakespeare. Biting her lower lip to keep from crying out, she resisted the overpowering fear that flooded through her, fear she would never see them again. Her mind balked at the thought they might be dead.

But for the very first time, a tiny voice in the depths of her being whispered that they just might be.

"Lord! I think this old coon is still alive, Bob!"

"You're plumb crazy, Griffen. Look at all the dried blood. And those claw marks. Lord! My stomach is churning something awful."

"Churn in the other direction, you lunkhead. I done washed these buckskins a few weeks ago and I don't aim to have to wash them again until fall."

"Who are you calling a lunkhead, you coffee cooler? Why, I have half a mind to chuck you in the river just for the sheer hell of it."

"Try and we'll get in a racket for sure."

The words echoed hollowly in Shakespeare McNair's mind, as if he was at one end of a long, winding tunnel and they were at the other. Dimly, he became aware of being touched, of a weight on his chest. Then the pain hit him, a terrible, writhing mass of pain so acute it seemed to tear him apart at the seams.

"If this hos is dead," the one named Griffen said, "how come his heart is still beating?"

"The devil you say."

"Listen for your own self."

Through the shroud of agony enveloping Shakespeare he felt a new weight on his chest. He tried to open his eyes but his eyelids were weighted with lead. He tried to speak but his lips wouldn't move.

"I'll be dogged!" Bob exclaimed. "You're right for once. Come on. Help me."

A scream welled in Shakespeare's throat as the world tilted and rocked and a searing, burning spear ripped through him. He was conscious of moving, or rather of being moved, and his stomach did some churning of its own. The sickening sensation lasted a full minute, then he was still again, both outwardly and inwardly.

Shakespeare tried to collect his jumbled thoughts. Where was he? What had happened to him? A wispy fog floated in his brain, cutting him off from his memories. He longed desperately to remember anything but could not. All he knew was his name and the harrowing, chilling pain. Oh, the pain!

Someone was speaking but Shakespeare could no longer distinguish the words. He was falling, plummeting into the depths of the wispy fog. Vainly he tried to slow his descent by flailing his arms and legs but he wasn't a bird and there was no resisting gravity. The fog encased him in a clammy black sheath. His mind shrieked defiance, was immersed, and knew no more.

Until suddenly Shakespeare snapped wide awake and saw myriad stars sparkling in the celestial vault overhead. At first he thought he was dreaming or delirious but then he felt a cool breeze caress his feverish face and smelled the fragrant aroma of wood smoke. He attempted to sit up but a wave of dizziness turned him as weak as a kitten before he could raise his head more than an inch. "This is a slight unmeritable man," he quoted aloud, and was startled at hearing himself speak.

There was a crash close by his side, as if someone had knocked something over, then a string of curses followed by, "Bob! He's come around! He talked!"

"I heard him," a sleepy voice grumbled. "Tarnation. Did it excite you so much that you had to send the coffee pot flying?"

"I just didn't expect it," Griffen said. "He made me jump."

"Clown!" Bob complained, but there was a friendly inflection to his barb.

Shakespeare saw a pair of faces appear above him. One was like the full moon, expansive and bare of hair. The other was rugged and sported a full beard. "Costard and Don Armado, I presume?" he said.

They exchanged glances and the bearded one remarked, "The attack rattled his thinker. He figures we're some danged foreigners."

"Maybe the fit will pass," suggested the other. Smiling broadly, the man with the round face said, "Don't you fret none, Mountainee Man. Me and my partner here, Lane Griffen, will stick with you until you heal or go under. I'm Bob Knorr. Junior, that is." He began to offer his hand, then looked at McNair's chest and rapidly withdrew his arm.

"You have a name, old-timer?" Griffen inquired.

"I wasn't babbling," Shakespeare said.

"What?"

"I was quoting from old William S., the Bard of Avon."

"Where's Avon?" Bob interjected. "I've been from one end of the States to the other and never heard of it."

"England," Shakespeare answered. Instantly he was assailed by more weakness. In his current state saying so simple a word was akin to running five miles. Uphill.

"I knew a Britisher once," Griffen said. "Fine man. Clerked a dry goods store in Boston." He idly stroked his beard. "He hailed from London town, as I recollect. Never mentioned no Avon."

"No, no, no," Shakespeare said softly, lacking the strength to explain.

"I'll fetch you a cup of coffee and some jerky to chaw on," Bob offered, hurrying off.

"And I'll wash all the mud and gore off your face and out of your hair," Griffen said. "We would have done it sooner but we didn't want to wake you. You needed to rest." He gently touched McNair's shoulder. "We guessed you were lying there about two or three days before we found you. Another day and you would have been a goner for sure."

Shakespeare wanted to ask what had happened to him but Griffen disappeared. He tried to sit up but this time couldn't even lift himself off the ground. An odd itchy sensation on his face and neck distracted him, reminding him of the comment about mud. And gore.

Where had the gore come from? Shakespeare mused. Why couldn't he remember what had happened to him? He dimly recalled rain, a godawful lot of rain. There had been people with him, hadn't there? People he should know. People he was fond of. But who were they?

Lane Griffen returned bearing a small pan filled with water and a piece of buckskin. "This will have to do," he apologized. "We're all out of beaver oil and castoreum or I'd make a salve for your wounds."

"What wounds?" Shakespeare asked.

"You haven't seen yourself?" Griffen rejoined in mild surprise, and coughed. "No, I suppose you haven't yet. Well, all in due time." Dabbing the bunched buckskin in the pan, he commenced wiping off McNair's face and beard and throat. "Lord, mister. You are a pitiful mess. Never seen so much mud on any one person before."

Bob Knorr materialized. "I'll hold off giving him this coffee until you're done."

Griffen merely nodded. He was bent low, the better to see what he was doing in the pale glow of the campfire. Unexpectedly he straightened, blinking rapidly. "It can't be!" he exclaimed.

"What can't?" Bob said.

Bending again, Griffen worked faster, brushing at the mud with frenzied strokes, his eyes widening more and more with each passing moment. "I thought it was brown but your beard is white!" he said to the mountain man. "And your face! I know you now! You're Shakespeare McNair! It's great to see you again."

Shakespeare stared at the man's agitated features and tried to dredge up the memory of where they had met. It, like every other memory, eluded him.

Griffen seemed to sense his hesitation. "What's the matter? Don't you remember the rendezvous two summers ago? And that time we met at Fort William?"

"I wish I could," Shakespeare said, his failure galling him tremendously.

"How can you forget?" Griffen asked in disbelief. "We spent a whole night drinking and carousing with Bridger and some of the boys. You won the contest to see who could balance a pipe on his nose the longest."

Bob placed a hand on his partner's arm. "Let him be. That bear attack must have been a terrible shock to his system."

Bear attack! Shakespeare stiffened, nearly crying out. In his mind's eye he saw himself frantically searching the north bank of the swollen Yellowstone for his precious book on the Bard. He heard again a rumbling growl and saw the hulking figure of a grizzly fifteen feet away. There had been no time to think, no time to do anything except lift his Hawken and take a bead as the behemoth bore down on him like a runaway wagon. He recalled firing, recalled a jolting, smashing impact, and then he'd flown through the air for a score of feet. After that his mind was as blank as an empty chalk slate until the two men found him.

"I suppose you're right," Griffen was saying. "We'd best let him rest some more."

Shakespeare twisted to regard the younger man. "Lane? You were the lookout at the fort when I was there, weren't you?"

"Sure was," Griffen said, and laughed happily. "You do remember after all!" He paused. "Whatever happened to the pard of yours, Nate King?"

A lightning bolt ripped Shakespeare from head to toes and he snapped off the ground as if shot from a cannon without being aware he had done so. Everything came back to him in a stark rush of horror and in his dismay he cried out, "Nate!"

The two trappers were by his side in a twinkling, each taking an arm. "There, there," Griffen said. "I didn't mean to upset you. Better lie down a while."

"Please," Knorr stressed. "A man in your condition shouldn't overexert himself."

"My condition?" Shakespeare said dully, trying to come to grips with the magnitude of the calamity that had befallen him. Glancing down, he discovered a blanket that had slipped partway when he sat up. As he looked it fell onto his lap, revealing his chest and belly. "Dear God in heaven!" he breathed.

The bear had only slashed him once but that had been more than enough. Its four-inch claws had torn five jagged furrows from his sternum to his right thigh, shearing through him as easily as a hot knife parted butter and tearing out long strips of flesh.

In the flickering firelight Shakespeare could clearly see exposed bones and glimpsed several of his internal organs. Vertigo struck him like a physical blow and he went limp and would have fallen if not for his kindly benefactors who lowered him down and covered him again.

"We've cleaned it the best we could," Bob said softly. "In the morning we'll bandage you up and hope infection doesn't set in."

"You're a lucky man," Griffen remarked.

"Lucky?" Shakespeare said feebly.

"To even be alive. You must be one tough cuss."

"I don't feel so tough." Shakespeare closed his eyes, wanting to do something he hadn't done in ages: curl into a ball and bawl like a baby. In all his years on the frontier, years of fighting hostiles and wild beasts and contending with the elements themselves, this was the lowest moment of all, the moment when he stared defeat in the face and wrestled with his own soul for his salvation.

"Is there anything else we can do?" Griffen inquired solicitously.

"Pray," Shakespeare said.

Bob Knorr knelt and plucked at a stem of grass. "This might not be the best time to bring it up, old hos, but Lane and me were talking some while you were unconscious. We have an idea and we need your opinion." He broke the stem in half. "It's your life at stake, after all."

"What idea?" Shakespeare asked. He went to shift a leg to relieve a cramp, thought of his innards squishing about as he moved, and held himself still.

"Let me backtrack a bit," Knorr said. "About five weeks ago a bunch of us left St. Louis after stocking up on powder and balls and such. Lane, here, needed a new Hawken and gewgaws for his wife, who's staying with the Flatheads. Which is a long story in itself and——"

Griffen gave a snort of impatience. "I never met anyone who can beat around the bush like you do. Get to the point before he passes out again."

"Let me tell it my way," Bob said, tossing the stem to the ground. Turning to Shakespeare, he continued. "Anyway, there were eleven of us left St. Louis together, seven hivernans and four greeners. We figured we were better off sticking together for protection, until we got to the Mandan villages, that is. There we learned the Blackfeet have been on a rampage all along the southern boundary of their territory. Old Mato-tope, the grand chief of all the Mandans, had just heard the news himself."

Griffen had been fidgeting the whole time his partner talked. Now he took up the narrative, saying, "Mato-tope advised us to break up into little groups. He thought we'd have a better chance of sneaking past those damnable Blackfeet if we weren't in one big outfit."

Knorr spoke the instant Griffen took a breath. "So we divided up into three groups and left the Mandans about two days apart. Lane and me were the last ones to leave."

"The others will get to the spot we agreed to meet at before we do," Griffen said, "and they're supposed to wait for us. It's about forty to fifty miles from here."

Shakespeare was having difficulty staying awake; the drone of their words was gradually putting him to sleep. He shook his head to clear it and said, "Neither one of you has gotten to the point yet."

"It's this way," Bob responded. "One of our number is an old hand at patching up folks and critters. Why, once he sewed up a horse that had its guts torn out by a panther and the horse lived! Saw the operation with my own two eyes. They were the biggest stitches you'd ever want to see."

"And we figure he can do the same for you," Griffen concluded. "We'll have to push to get you there lickety-split, and we'll have to keep our eyes skinned the whole time for Blackfeet, but we're willing to try if you say the word."

They didn't fool McNair. Both were acting casual about their proposal but Shakespeare realized it was fraught with danger for the two of them. Pushing meant going without sleep, traveling day and night to reach their friends swiftly. And going without proper rest in Blackfeet country was an invitation for trouble.

Their senses would be dulled by fatigue, making them more vulnerable.

"What do you say?" Lane goaded.

Shakespeare looked at each of them. Here they were, one a complete stranger and the other a passing acquaintance, and they were willing to put their lives in peril for him. He admired their sacrifice, but he had to say, "It would be best for all concerned if you went on and left me."

"Why best?" Griffen asked.

"I doubt I'll last a day in my shape," Shakespeare replied. "You'd be wasting your time."

"You've lasted this long, haven't you?" Knorr retorted.

"And we'll decide what is a waste of our time and what's not," Griffen declared.

Bob nodded and beamed. "So it's settled! We leave at dawn. We'll use our blankets to tote you to the canoes. The rest should be easy."

Shakespeare argued, or tried to, but they would have none of it. He might have debated until dawn had sleep not claimed him. Vaguely, he was aware of having his wounds dressed, of having strips of cloth bound around his chest and abdomen.

The gay chirp of sparrows brought Shakespeare back to the land of the living when a trace of pink lined the eastern horizon. He heard a commotion and twisted his head to see the Yellowstone only ten feet away and the two trappers loading their belongings into a pair of canoes. In the second canoe space had been left for him. Spare blankets had been spread out to make him comfortable.

Shakespeare delved deep within himself and discovered his despair of the night before gone. Living things are inherently tenacious, and he now wanted to live so badly that the notion of dying brought a lump of regret to his throat. There were those who might say he'd lived a ripe, full life. But to his way of thinking he still had another ten or twenty years to go and he wanted to enjoy every minute of them. Footsteps intruded on his reflection, drawing his attention to his benefactors, who were approaching. "Morning," he greeted them.

"We're all loaded," Bob Knorr said. "First a cup of coffee all around and then we'll shove off."

Lane Griffen bent down. "Are you up to eating anything, you think?"

Shakespeare was going to say he was hungry enough to eat a horse whole when a twig snapped loudly to his rear and the two trappers stiffened, their eyes widening in alarm. Gritting his teeth, Shakespeare was able to turn far enough to see the creature responsible for breaking the twig, and on doing so he felt his blood run cold.

It was the grizzly. And it abruptly reared on two legs and vented a fierce roar.

Chapter Nine

The instant young Zachary King realized he was trapped by five young Blackfeet, he whirled toward the right side of the gully and tried to claw his way to the top. He got a handhold, managed to dig a toe into the hard earth, and then was grabbed from behind and yanked.

Tumbling hard onto his shoulders, Zach tried to regain his footing. He saw the Blackfeet converging and lashed out with a foot, upending one. The rest were on him before he could do anything else, pinning him under their combined weight.

Had the Blackfeet been whites, they would have rained down a hailstorm of punches, perhaps breaking Zach's nose or pulping his lips. Instead they had tossed their weapons aside and were striving their utmost to take him alive. Hands seized his wrists, his ankles.

Zach fought with all the fury of a terror-stricken youngster, breaking free and bucking and punching and flailing his legs. He connected twice, much to his satisfaction. But the outcome was preordained, especially when one of the older Blackfeet boys produced a length of rope and quickly slipped a loop over Zach's left arm. He heaved and tugged, his face flushed from his effort to tear loose. This time he was thwarted. And with one arm useless, the other was soon snared.

Zach tried to ram a heel into the stomach of a boy in front of him. Another batted his leg aside. Then both legs were held fast, he was flipped onto his side, and both wrists were bound behind his back. He fought back tears of frustration at being captured when another hour would have seen him safely away and on the trail to rejoining his folks.

The five Blackfeet stepped away from him. All breathed heavily. Several were bruised and one had a dirt smudge on his right cheek. They stared at Zach in amazement, apparently unable to believe they had caught him, it had all happened so fast.

Zach still had his legs free. He tucked them under him and rose to his knees, intending to turn and flee. The tallest of the boys, divining his plan, suddenly lunged, grasping his arm. Another Blackfoot took the other side.

"You danged whippersnappers!" Zach roared, as might his Uncle Shakespeare at a passel of pesky kids. "Let me go, you hear! I'll rip your lungs out if you don't!"

A skinny boy blinked, then laughed and said something that set all five to laughing. He reached out, pinched Zach's shoulder.

"I'm real enough!" Zach declared in Shoshone. "I'm the son of Grizzly Killer, and if you know what's good for you, you'll cut these ropes off right this minute!"

The mirth subsided. The Blackfeet regarded Zach with keen interest. Zach wondered if they had understood him and said, "Yes, I speak Shoshone. I should. They are my tribe."

None of the Blackfeet responded although the skinny one's eyes narrowed.

"Do you know the tongue?" Zach asked. "Talk to me if you do!"

A heavyset boy addressed the skinny one, who pondered a moment and said a single word. Then he and the other two not holding Zach retrieved the discarded weapons.

"What are you fixing to do?" Zach demanded. "Rub me out on the spot? Or take me to your village to butcher me with everyone looking on?" He clearly remembered the signed words of Cream Bear, "We do not kill children." But after all he had heard about the atrocities Blackfeet committed, he was unwilling to believe anything one of them claimed.

The Blackfeet headed up the gully, hauling Zach with them. He resisted at first, digging in his heels until one of the boys commenced kicking him in the shins every time he gave them any trouble. After several kicks he decided to go along and die with dignity.

It developed that the gully wound for hundreds of yards, to within a stone's throw of the village. Zach gulped as he was pushed up over a gravel–strewn slope and into the open. He barely registered the stately painted lodges or the peaceful scene of dogs lounging, children playing, and women engaged in scraping hides. All he saw were the warriors, many seated and talking, others mending shields or making arrows or sharpening knives.

The skinny boy hoisted a lance and yipped like a proud coyote returning to its den with a fresh kill. He shouted excitedly, gesturing at Zach as the small group advanced.

From all directions Blackfeet came to see what the commotion was about. Zach lost count of the knives, war clubs, and tomahawks in evidence, and while inwardly he quaked at his impending doom, outwardly he composed his features so that he showed a calm face to those who would shortly gloat over his lifeless corpse.

A young girl, a twin of the skinny boy, was the first to reach them. She listened, incredulous, to whatever the boy told her, then stepped brazenly up to Zach and raked him from head to toe with the sort of look Zach was certain she would give an animal soon to be slaughtered.

"Go ahead, gloat!" Zach said, and grinned when she recoiled backward as if stung. "But you won't see Stalking Coyote on his knees begging for his life. No sir. Do your worst. I'm ready for you !"

Adults arrived, men and women, some so old their hair was entirely gray. They ringed the boys, scrutinizing Zach while the skinny one went on at some length.

A burly warrior stepped forward and snapped at Zach in the Blackfoot tongue. Zach merely glared. The warrior tried a different tongue which Zach thought might be Flathead but wasn't sure. Exasperated, the Blackfoot grabbed the front of Zach's shirt and gave him such a shaking his teeth rattled.

Just when Zach was certain the warrior was on the verge of whipping out a knife and lifting his scalp, a low, resonant voice rang out and the warrior released him and stepped back. Through the throng stepped an older man who had to walk with the aid of a staff because his left leg had once suffered a terrible accident, leaving his foot bent at a right angle to his body. He walked to the front line of onlookers, the Blackfeet parting before him as if he were a personage of some importance.

Zach suspected this might be a chief or a medicine man. He held his chin higher, recalling the talk he'd had with his pa about the likelihood of being captured by hostiles. "Never show fear, no matter what," Nate had advised. "Indians respect a brave man, not a coward. Show them that you have courage and they will not be as hard on you as they would be if you cringe and cry."

The important newcomer studied Zach a few moments, then merely nodded at the two boys holding Zach's arms and they immediately let go. The man smiled, a genuinely warm smile.

Even though Zach felt it necessary to put on a stern face, he melted under the kindly eyes of the oldster and grinned sheepishly. "I wish you spoke my lingo," he said wistfully in English.

"I do."

The heavily accented words were uttered haltingly, as if the old warrior had not used English in so long he was afraid he might not pronounce them correctly. But Zach understood, and his heart soared at finally being able to communicate. Until a glint of sunlight off the tip of a lance reminded him who he was communicating with.

"Speak little English," the kindly man said, saying the last word so that it sounded like, "Ennnn-gleese."

"How?" Zach blurted. "Who—-"

"I White Grass," the Blackfoot said, touching his chest. "Learn English far winters ago. From white man." He pointed. "You who?"

"Zachary King, sir, at your service," Zach said, being polite as his folks had taught he should always be.

White Grass cocked his head, peering at Zach's arms. Stepping forward, the old man saw the rope and scowled. He barked orders at the boys and the skinny one hastily unfastened the bindings.

As the rope fell free, Zach smiled at the stately warrior, saying, "Thank you, sir."

A puzzled look came over the Blackfoot. Tapping his chest again, he repeated, "White Grass. White Grass."

"I know, sir," Zach assured him.

The puzzled look deepened. Then White Grass made a gesture with his hands that oddly enough reminded Zach of a shrug more than it did any sign language he had ever seen.

"Sir," the old man said, once more touching his chest. "Sir be it. Sir me."

Abruptly, Zach understood. He had used the word so many times that White Grass mistook it for a name. "No—," he began, and changed his mind. Trying to explain might only further confuse the matter and annoy his savior and he dearly wanted to stay on the old man's good side.

"No?" White Grass said.

"Sir is fine," Zach said.

"Sir." The Blackfoot beamed, displaying fine white teeth that would have been the envy of any white man half his age. "Yes. Know. Come now." Wagging his staff, White Grass shooed the Blackfeet in his path away and headed deeper into the village.

Zach briefly hesitated. Every nerve screamed for him to bolt before the tribe butchered him as they had dozens of other whites. Only the realization he wouldn't get ten feet prompted him into scooting in the old man's wake. He was keenly aware of the many intense stares directed at him by the Blackfeet he passed. He couldn't tell if they were merely curious or eyeing him as the first Pilgrim must have eyed that first Thanksgiving turkey.

White Grass did not go more than twenty yards when he halted and raised a hand to his brow to screen his eyes from the harsh sunlight.

Zach looked and felt his breath catch in his throat. Five warriors were riding toward the village, two riding double. Even at that distance he recognized Bird Rattler and Cream

Bear. His feet spun of their own accord but there was nowhere to go. The entire population of the village had followed, forming a wall of enemies between him and the prairie. He gulped, pivoted, and jumped when a gentle hand fell on his shoulder.

The old man shook a gnarled finger at him. "Still be, Hackeryking."

"Zachery King," Zach corrected him. "Son of Grizzly Killer."

"Hackeryking," White Grass said. "Big chief come. Listen him say about you."

Big Chief? Zach wondered. Dread ripped at his innards as he remembered the encounter by the river. He knew without a shadow of doubt who the big chief would be and he bit his lower lip to keep from screeching at the bizarre twist of fate that had brought him to this lowest of low points in his life. Once the Blackfeet knew, he'd be hacked into so many bits and fed to their dogs.

The riders galloped up in a flurry of dust. Cream Bear drew rein and Bird Rattler slid off and approached, never once taking his gaze off of Zach. "So, horse thief," he signed when he stopped. "We meet again."

Zach heard whispering among the assembled Blackfeet and wished he could remember a suitable prayer to offer his Maker. This was it, he was certain. They would fly into a rage and swarm on him like wolves on a fawn.

White Grass leaned his staff against his side to sign, "You know this white boy, Bird Rattler?"

The chief launched into a long account in

his own tongue. Zach knew, just without a doubt knew, that every Blackfoot was hearing the story of how he took the brown stallion. Soon, very soon, they would close on him and it would all be over. He tried to shrink into himself and steeled his will against the inevitable. Belatedly, he heard a peculiar sound coming from behind him. He glanced around and was stunned to see a goodly portion of the Blackfeet laughing wholeheartedly, the men especially. And that skinny boy and girl were gaping at him in outright awe. Now what?

"Hackeryking," White Grass said.

Zach swiveled. "Yes, sir?"

"Very bad you," the old man said, and it appeared as if the corners of his mouth couldn't stop twitching. "Take big chief's horse."

"I didn't meant to," Zach said lamely. "It was sort of an accident."

"Axe-see-dent?"

"I didn't think I hit him that hard. And then the darn horse wouldn't stop no matter what I did and the next thing I knew it was bringing me right to your village and then I sort of stumbled onto those boys and—" Zach stopped the rush of words and took a breath to calm himself. Show courage! his pa had said. Not blather like an idiot.

White Grass was saying something. To Zach's amazement the Blackfeet roared with mirth, even Bird Rattler and Cream Bear. The thought struck him that maybe the reason the Blackfeet were so bloodthirsty had something to do with every blamed one of them being stark raving mad.

Unexpectedly the skinny boy and girl walked over to Bird Rattler. He listened to what the boy had to say, glancing now and again at Zach. Then Bird Rattler and White Grass consulted at length.

Zach wished the Blackfeet would do something other than stand there staring at him. He still expected the other shoe to drop soon, as his pa might say. Raising his chin high, he happened to gaze at the skinny girl, who smiled sweetly at him and then averted her face. He was so startled by this development that he didn't hear when White Grass spoke his name. Not the first time, anyway.

"Hackeryking? Your ears open?"

"Yes, sir," Zach replied dutifully. "I hear right fine. It's just that so much has happened I don't rightly know whether I'm coming or going."

"You coming," White Grass said. "Come with Sir in bit."

"Where to, sir?"

"You see."

Bird Rattler swung to the crowd and addressed them for the longest while in solemn tones. At the conclusion they began to disperse, except for an attractive woman in an elaborately beaded dress who stepped to the side of the tall warrior and received the sort of look Zach knew all too well from having seen his father give his mother the same sort of look countless times over the years. The woman put her arms on the shoulders of the skinny boy and skinny girl and together they walked off beside Bird Rattler.

Zach put two and two together and deduced the pretty woman was Bird Rattler's wife, the skinny ones their kids. White Grass nudged him, indicating they should follow. Zach couldn't imagine where they were going or why he wasn't bristling with arrows. But he wasn't one to look the proverbial gift horse in the mouth. In an attempt to win over the older man, he asked, "Are you a chief like Bird Rattler, sir?"

White Grass straightened with pride. "I watch Beaver Bundle."

Although Zach did not have the slightest idea what that meant, he nodded and said, "It sounds like a great honor, sir."

"Greatest, Stalking Coyote."

Zach gawked. "How do you know my name?"

"Bird Rattler tell." White Grass snickered. "Name wrong."

"Wrong?"

"Should be Big Little Horse Thief."

That made no sense to Zach either but he kept quiet and checked to see how many warriors were trailing them to prevent him from escaping. To his consternation there were only a dozen or so little children, some so young they waddled like ducks. On seeing him turn, they stopped, some of the very smallest cowering in fear. Shocked, Zach smiled to show them he meant no harm and a few made bold to smile in return.

Bird Rattler halted in front of a lodge so large there was no denying his status as a man of great prominence. He paused to survey the encampment and his family scooted inside ahead of him. Then he slowly entered.

White Grass beckoned Zach to do likewise but Zach balked. The girl had been friendly enough, but he had no idea what her father had in store for him. Given his theft of the horse, he wouldn't put it past Bird Rattler to bind him and hold him prisoner until the Blackfeet dragged him out to scalp him.

"Hackeryking?" White Grass said, jerking a thumb at the entrance. "Go."

"The horse." Zach said absently, not knowing how to explain and saying that which was uppermost on his mind.

"Horse?" The old warrior's brow knit, then he grinned and shifted to point.

Zach looked. Beyond the lodge grazed several fine mounts, among them the very brown stallion he had stolen. It must have come straight home, he realized, and wished that he owned such a superbly loyal animal.

"Go," White Grass repeated.

Swallowing his anxiety, Zach stooped and opened the flap. Through his mind ran the rules of proper lodge etiquette as taught to him by his mother: always go to the right and wait for the host to seat you, never walk between the fire and anyone else, and never talk unless asked to do so by someone older.

Zach straightened and felt oddly surprised at what he saw. The interior was spotless and neatly arranged, as fine a lodge as their own when they spent time with his mother's people. On the insulating lining hung a bow and quiver, a war shield, a medicine bag, and other things. Along the curved sides were stacked blankets, parfleches, rolled up buffalo-hide bedding, a sewing bag, a cooking bag, and other household gear.

Bird Rattler had taken the seat of the host toward the rear, behind the small fire that filled the lodge with the fragrance of burning wood. His wife and daughter were to his left, preparing a meal. The skinny boy sat on his father's right, giving Zach an oddly puzzled look.

"Come," Bird Rattler signed. "You are welcome in my lodge."

Zach shuffled forward, suspecting a trick of some kind. These people were being so kind, so downright friendly, they couldn't possibly be Blackfeet. He sat where indicated and White Grass sank down beside him.

"Chief want talk you. I help."

"What does he want to palaver about?"

"You."

Zach looked at the chief and would have quaked at the stern visage fixed on him had he not detected the warm glow of genuine kindness in the Blackfoot's lively dark eyes. He smiled—he seemed to be doing a lot of that this day—and received a sympathetic smile in return. "What about me?"

White Grass and Bird Rattler talked for some time, the chief doing most of it and the older man grunting agreement. Finally White Grass tapped Zach's knee.

"Hackeryking, chief say you much good rider."

"I wasn't doing much actual riding," Zach confessed. "Most of the time I was hanging on for dear life."

As White Grass would do throughout the subsequent conversation, he translated for the benefit of Bird Rattler, then said, "Chief say you good fighter at Elk At Dawn."

For a moment Zach was confused, thinking Elk At Dawn must have been one of the warriors in the chief's party by the river. "I remember poking my spear at Cream Bear," he said, "but I don't know any of the others."

White Grass stared at him, then extended an arm toward the skinny boy. "Elk At Dawn."

Zach faced the chief's son, who still wore his puzzled expression. "I am pleased to meet you," Zach signed. "I hope I did not hurt anyone when you caught me."

Elk At Dawn replied fluidly, "You fought like a mountain lion but no one was hurt." He paused. "We were hunting rabbits. Catching you was much more exciting. We will be the envy of all the boys."

Zach wanted to say more but the old warrior touched his elbow to get his attention.

"Chief want know where family? Want no double tongue."

"I don't rightly know where they are," Zach said, a lump forming in his throat. "There was an awful storm and we were separated. I kept expecting them to come after me but they never did." He bowed his head to hide the moisture seeping into his eyes. "That's not like them at all. My pa would move mountains to find me. He's the best pa anyone ever had."

"Other brothers, sisters you have?"

"No. Not yet. I might soon, though. Ma is in the family way."

"Where you live, Hackeryking?"

"The Rockies," Zach said. It occurred to him the warrior might not be familiar with the name, so he elaborated by pointing westward and saying, "In the big mountains where the sun sets. Do you know the ones I mean?"

"Yes. Many, many sleeps away," White Grass said thoughtfully, adding, "Too far. Too far."

"Too far for what?"

The old man ignored the question. "You good son? Listen father, listen mother?"

"Of course. I love them," Zach said. He glanced at Bird Rattler, who was studying him. "Say, why all this interest in my family? Why does the chief want to know what kind of son I am?"

White Grass laid a wizened hand on the boy's shoulder. "You be happy, Hackeryking. Never see mountains again. Never see mother, see father. But Bird Rattler like you, like you very much." He gestured at the inside of the lodge. "This be new home. Bird Rattler want make you his own son."

Chapter Ten

Nate King slept fitfully his first night in the Pawnee village. He tossed and turned on the bedding lent him by White Calf, deeply troubled about his family and yearning to go to them. By morning he had another problem. He began itching terribly, leading him to suspect the bedding was ridden with lice.

White Calf slept soundly, snoring loud enough to rouse the dead. He had shown up at the lodge about ten o'clock and profusely apologized for taking so long. There had been an important council in the chief's lodge, he'd signed, and he'd been obligated to attend. The medicine man had offered to cook a late meal but Nate had declined, the stench of the animal carcasses having totally ruined his appetite.

Nate had demanded to know why a pair of warriors kept guard over the lodge. "Am I a friend or a prisoner?" he had signed. White Calf had assured him that his friendship was highly valued, and explained the two warriors were there to prevent anyone from badgering him.

Shortly thereafter they had retired, but not before Nate insisted the disgusting remains be removed. His expression must have betrayed his sentiments because White Calf had apologized even more ardently than before and revealed the dead animals—-or at least parts of them—-had been used by White Calf in certain ceremonies. "But if they displease you, Sky Walker," the medicine man signed, "I will take them out and feed them to the village dogs."

It had done little good. Nate sat up and accidentally took a deep breath. The odor churned his stomach. It amazed him that the medicine man abided the smell on a daily basis without complaint. Throwing off the smelly buffalo robe he had used to cover himself, he stood, staring up through the ventilation hole at the faint tinge of pink in the sky. Dawn was not far off. Once the sun was up, he would ask to see the chief. By noon, if all went well, he would be on his way to find his loved ones.

Taking the flintlock, Nate slipped out through the doorway while the medicine man snored on. He expected to find guards but there were none. Nor, in fact, did he see anyone moving about yet in the village, not even dogs.

This was his chance! Nate hastened around to the back of the lodge. Undergrowth and a few trees were all that separated him from the river. He crept through the brush until he could see the gently gurgling water. It would be child's play, he reasoned, to enter the river and follow it westward for a few miles, then head out across the prairie. The Pawnees would be unable to trail him, and if they did scour the river banks it would take hours for them to find his tracks, if they did at all. His only regret was that there were no horses nearby so he could steal one. He considered going back into the village after a mount but decided not to tempt fate.

Nate dashed to the water's edge and was set to plunge his foot in when a low cry to his left drew his attention to a tableau that froze him in place.

A young, lovely Pawnee, an early riser, had ventured to the river to wash a cooking pot and utensils. She was on her knees, the pot in one hand, a tin ladle she had no doubt received in trade with white men in the other. Her features were ghostly pale from fright. As well they should be.

At that point the river narrowed. Standing on a gravel bar opposite the young woman was a large black bear bearing a white blaze on its chest. Ordinarily black bears avoided humans and were considered nowhere near as dangerous as their grizzled cousins. Occasionally, however, there were exceptions, and this proved to be one.

As Nate set eyes on the bear, it left the gravel bar and started across the river toward the petrified woman. All she had to do was turn and race into the village. Her shouts would bring warriors on the run and they would make short work of the interloper with their lances and arrows if it had the audacity to pursue her. But she was too scared. She gaped, like one mesmerized.

The bear rumbled deep in its chest.

Heedless of the consequences to himself, Nate called out in Shoshone, "Run, girl! Run!" He could not stand there and allow her to be slain, which was exactly the fate she would suffer unless she regained her senses and got out of there. The Pawnee, though, didn't seem to hear him. She squatted there, easy prey for the hungry bear.

Nate looked back at the village, hoping against hope others were awake and someone else had noticed the woman's plight. The spaces between the lodges were vacant, and not a single wisp of smoke curled over a solitary dwelling. "Damn lazy tribe," he muttered, drawing the flintlock.

By now the bear was halfway across the river. Emboldened by its quarry's lack of movement, it surged faster, plowing through the water like a great hairy boat.

"Run!" Nate bellowed, but the young woman might have been deaf for all the effect his yell had. She only had eyes for the bear, which would be the last sight she saw unless something was done.

Veering toward her, Nate aimed the flintlock. He would rather have had the Hawken, or any rifle for that matter. Pistols were fine for small game and men at short range but woefully inadequate for larger animals. Still, the .55-caliber smoothbore packed a hefty wallop. He sighted on the bear's head behind the ear,

148

and when the huge black brute came within a dozen feet of the woman, he fired.

The blast galvanized the woman where nothing else had. She started, jumped erect, and fled into the village, screaming at the top of her lungs.

At the shot the bear crumpled, but only momentarily. Rising, it shook itself, roared, and glanced around for the source of its terrible pain.

"Oh, hell," Nate said. He went to flee, then realized he couldn't possibly hope to outrun the bear and if it pulled him down from behind he was finished. Nor was there time to reload.

The black bear roared again, and charged.

Tossing the flintlock onto the bank, Nate drew both his tomahawk and his butcher knife. He had no choice but to fight. And as he'd learned from hard experience, the surest way to win a fight was to take it to the enemy and not wait for the enemy to come to him. So, voicing the war whoop of a Shoshone warrior, he raised his weapons and sprang to meet the bear.

The beast was almost to the shore. It drew up short at this unexpected development; rarely did prey turn on it. Surprised, and not thinking clearly due to its head wound, it reared on its hind legs to intimidate its prey with its bulk and size.

Nate came to the edge of the water and launched himself into the air. Tingling from head to toe with primal blood lust, he arced the tomahawk downward with all his strength while simultaneously thrusting the butcher knife outward. Both scored, but so did the

149

bear, swinging a huge paw that clipped him on the shoulder and sent him flying head over heels into the river.

Cold, murky water closed over Nate. His mouth had been open when he went under, allowing water to gush down his throat. Sputtering and gasping, flailing wildly, he managed to break the surface and suck in needed air.

Except the bear was there, rearing like a monster of old, mouth agape in a hideous snarl, blood pouring from its split skull. It swiped at him with startling speed.

Nate ducked under the first blow, was nicked by the second, its long claws ripping his buckskin shirt wide open and slicing into the skin. His moccasins found purchase, enabling him to stand. The water level rose as high as his waist, just high enough to impede his movements as he darted to the right to evade another slashing strike. Claws whisked by his ear so close his hair was fanned by the air.

The black bear roared once more, then dropped on all fours. Lips pulled back to expose its glistening teeth, it closed in, but warily. It had learned its lesson well. The agony searing its head and chest had taught it that the two-legged creature, although puny in size, was capable of inflicting great pain.

Nate hefted both weapons while back-pedaling. He needed an opening so he could deliver a lethal blow but the bear had its head low, chin brushing the surface. Thinking he could anger the brute into exposing its neck, he feinted, flicking the butcher knife. The black bear jerked its head aside the first time but was slower the next, and by the merest fluke the tip of the knife seared into an eyeball.

A tremendous roar that seemed to shake the trees at the water's edge issued from the bear's throat as it dabbed a paw at its now ravaged eye.

Shouts had broken out in the village but Nate dared not take his gaze from the bear to see if the Pawnees were rushing to his aid. Not that he expected them to. He was an outsider, a strange white man. And from the looks they had given him the day before, a lot of them would be all too happy to see him rubbed out.

The bear suddenly fixed its sole good eye on the source of its torment. If it was possible for a bear's face to reflect raw, savage hatred, this bear's did as it moved in for the kill.

Nate twisted aside as razor teeth crunched together in the very space he had occupied. He brought the tomahawk flashing down, catching the bear above the ruined eye, the keen edge biting deep—-and holding fast. Nate tried to wrench the tomahawk loose but it refused to budge. The bear, snarling horribly, rammed into him, its shoulder slamming full into his torso.

Bowled over, losing his grip on the tomahawk, Nate found himself being pushed under the water by the bear's enormous weight. In desperation he reached up, looping his arm around the animal's thick neck, and clung on for dear life. The black bear gave a violent shake to dislodge him but Nate gripped its hair firmly, resolving to hold on no matter what it took.

Nate was in the river up to his shoulders. His legs bumped the bear's as the beast swung back and forth, seeking to hurl him loose. Belatedly he realized he still clasped the butcher knife, and with the thought came action. He plunged the long blade into the underside of the bear's neck, burying it to the hilt. The bear went into a frenzy, bawling and pawing at him but unable to hook its claws in his body.

Water poured over Nate's shoulders and splashed on his face as the bear whipped this way and that and snapped its head upward and sideways. All the while Nate kept stabbing, over and over and over again. Blood spattered his cheeks, his throat, his shoulders. Soon the water itself turned crimson.

The bear reared back, trying to stand. Nate's body served as an anchor, dragging its head back down. It kept trying to rip him open but its claws could not find their mark.

Nate must have stabbed the bear twenty times. His arm was growing heavy, his shoulder aching. Given the alternative if he stopped, he continued to stab, stab, stab, making a scarlet sieve of the brute's throat. Suddenly the black bear whirled and barreled through the water at a swift, lumbering pace, as if it had a destination in mind. Nate's feet scraped the bottom of the river, then his legs, his thighs. Seconds later he was being dragged over dry ground and he realized the bear was on terra firma.

And here the bear could get at him. It drove the back of a shaggy paw into Nate's stomach, knocking him loose and sending him sprawling. Dazed, Nate sat up. He saw the bear rear, saw its paws lift to cave in his fragile human head. Scrambling backwards, he attempted to escape but his slick hands slipped and he fell as the bear swung.

No, the bear wasn't swinging; it was falling. Shoving up, Nate dived to the left but was a fraction of an instant too slow. The black bear crashed down, its body hitting his lower legs, smacking him flat and pinning him to the ground.

Nate shifted, fearing the bear would turn and rake him. He was elevating the butcher knife when the blank look in the bear's good eye registered. Pausing, Nate took a few breaths to calm himself, then tentatively pushed at the bear a few times. There was no reaction. Nor would there ever be one.

The black bear was dead.

Nate sagged onto his shoulder, suddenly exhausted. He closed his eyes and rested his forehead on his forearm, letting his racing blood slow. Another few moments and the bear would have had him. He would never have seen his beloved family again.

Intuition more than anything Nate heard gave him the feeling he was being watched. Raising his head, he discovered he was right. It appeared as if every last inhabitant of the Pawnee village was gathered a dozen yards off staring at him with mixed emotions. The majority gawked, apparently unable to credit the testimony of their own eyes. The aged chief was there, as was the tall warrior who had treated Nate with such hostility. And at the forefront stood the young woman who had been spared by Nate's timely intervention. There was, however, no sign of White Calf.

Nate did not like lying there virtually helpless. He tried extricating his legs but the bear was too heavy. Bending, he placed his hands on the beast's neck and shoved as hard as he could. The carcass hardly moved.

Soft footsteps made Nate snap around, ready for the worst. It was only the young woman, advancing fearfully. Nate assumed she was scared of the bear and slid his knife into its sheath so he could sign, "The animal is dead. You need not be afraid."

The woman hesitated, her features reminding Nate of a terrified doe about to bolt. "I am a friend," he signed. "I would never hurt you."

She smiled, or at least her mouth creased in a lopsided imitation of a smile, and her slender hands moved. "Question. Are you hurt, Sky Walker?"

"I kill grizzlies all the time. A little bear like this cannot harm me," Nate joked to put her at ease. To his dismay, though, her apprehension mounted and she backed up a step. "What is wrong?" he asked, "I promise you the bear can hurt no one."

At that juncture a commotion broke out among the Pawnees, and shortly the familiar figure of White Calf barged through their midst. The medicine man halted on seeing the bear and blinked in astonishment. He glanced at Nate, at the bear again, and then did something peculiar. White Calf tilted his head back and howled in wolfish glee while spinning in a small circle.

Nate had to laugh. The man was a loon, plain and simple. He saw White Calf hop a few times like a demented jackrabbit. Then the medicine man dashed over, hands working energetically.

"Congratulations, Sky Walker! You have slain the father of all black bears with your bare hands!"

"A dose of steel did the job," Nate responded. "And do not make more out of this than there is. I do not want your people to get the wrong idea."

White Calf cackled and spun to address the tribe, accenting his speech with grand flourishes.

More than ever Nate longed to be able to speak their tongue. The Pawnees listened in rapt absorption, glancing often at him and the dead bear. Neither the venerable chief nor the tall warrior seemed overly pleased.

Nate became impatient to be freed. Should the Pawnees take it into their heads to kill him, he would be powerless to resist. "Dunderhead!" he interrupted to get the medicine man's attention, then resorted to sign. "Am I supposed to lift this bear off me all by myself or do you think some of your people would be kind enough to help?"

"I understand," White Calf signed slyly. "You are testing us to see if we are worthy." He barked words at the Pawnees and gestured at Nate but no one moved to help. Impatiently he tried again, more stridently, and when his outburst failed to produce a result, he turned livid and shrieked at them while motioning at the heavens as if calling down the wrath of all their gods.

Nate did not know what to make of the Pawnee behavior. He'd nearly lost his life helping one of their own. Surely that should count for something. When it became apparent he could not rely on their aid, he faced the bear and resumed pushing to shift the body off his legs. He made no headway and was about to give up when shapely arms reached past him and someone else's strength was added to his.

Nate glanced up and was surprised to find the young woman he had saved. He smiled to show his appreciation. She smiled in return, an anxious sort of smile, giving the impression she dreaded having her head bitten off if the whim struck him.

Evidently the woman's act served to reassure the rest. Fully three-quarters of the Pawnees crowded forward, so many that White Calf had to motion many back. It was the work of a minute to roll the bear clear.

Nate stood, plucking bear hair from his leggings. The Pawnees stepped back to give him room. Straightening, he signed sincerely, "I thank you all." To the young woman he said, "Such a pretty one should be more careful. I would hate to think you would end up in the belly of a grizzly."

The woman gasped, a hand pressed to her mouth.

Now what had he done? Nate wondered. The Pawnees, he concluded, had to be the most eccentric tribe he had ever run across. The sooner he was shy of them, the better. He stepped to the bear, gripped the haft of the tomahawk with both hands, then yanked to free the head. After wiping it clean on the bear's hide and tucking the tomahawk under his belt, he moved along the river bank seeking his pistol. The Pawnees in front of him parted, almost stumbling over one another in their haste to get out of his way.

Nate was sure he knew exactly where he had tossed the flintlock, yet when he came to the spot the pistol wasn't there. He scoured the grass inch by inch and saw where some stems had been bent as if by a heavy object lying on them. Turning to the river, he checked the muddy bank and the shallows.

The pistol had vanished into thin air. Since that was impossible, Nate deduced that someone had taken it. There was no dearth of suspects; he had an entire village to pick from. He scanned their faces, hoping the guilty party might somehow give himself away.

White Calf approached. "May I ask what you are doing, Sky Walker?"

"My gun is gone," Nate signed.

"Perhaps it fell in the river and is buried at the bottom," the medicine man suggested.

"No, someone took it," Nate said.

"Do not worry yourself. I will find the one who has done this and return it to you," White Calf pledged.

Nate doubted he would ever see the flintlock again. Guns were valuable on the frontier, especially to Indians who so rarely obtained firearms. When they did, the weapons were inferior fusees. A warrior must have noticed the prized flintlock and picked it up while no one was looking. Nate suspected the culprit would hide the gun until he quit the village. He had no choice but to accept the loss.

The Pawnees were beginning to disperse, but not the venerable chief and the tall warrior. They approached side by side, the chief as calm as could be, the warrior's right hand dangerously close to the hilt of his big knife.

Nate was set to greet them properly in sign language when White Calf stepped in front of him and spoke rather harshly. The chief halted, his demeanor suggesting he was more puzzled than offended. Not so the warrior, who retorted angrily and motioned for the medicine man to get out of the way.

Nate had tolerated about all of the medicine man's nonsense he was going to tolerate. Shouldering White Calf aside, he said, "I am glad to see both of you again. And I would be highly honored if we could smoke a pipe together. There is much we must talk about."

The tall warrior unaccountably scowled. "I do not care to talk with you, Sky Walker. All I want is for you to leave my people and never come back."

The chief put a hand on the other's arm but the tall warrior shrugged it off and continued in the same vein. "We did not ask you to come. We do not want you here. Even if White Calf is right, which I very much doubt, mixing the two is not wise. You have your own kind and you should stay among them."

Nate plastered a smile on his face to demonstrate he wasn't offended and responded, "Many of my kind live among Indians. Some have taken Indian women as wives. Mixing the two can often be beneficial to both."

"We are flesh and blood, not clouds."

The significance of the remark eluded Nate. Since he was getting nowhere with the fiery warrior, he turned to the older man he believed to be a high chief. "Question. How are you known?"

"Mole On The Nose," the elder Pawnee answered without hesitation.

Until that moment Nate hadn't noticed the very prominent mark on the tip of the man's nostrils. "Are you a chief?"

Pivoting, Mole On The Nose encompassed the lodges with a sweep of an arm. "My people," he signed, in effect saying, "This is my village. I am chief over all."

"And you?" Nate signed, nodded at the firebrand.

"I am Red Rock, head of the Bear Society," the tall warrior boasted proudly. "And I say again, Sky Walker, go home."

Nate learned two things. First, Red Rock fixed on an issue like a dog on a bone and would not let go. Second, Red Rock was a formidable warrior, perhaps the equivalent of a war chief. He knew this because Indian societies were elite memberships restricted to individuals of note, and Bear Societies especially were invariably made up of warriors possessing exceptional courage and fighting prowess. Just as this thought crossed his mind, he had an opportunity to test the merits of his reasoning firsthand. For Red Rock suddenly pulled his knife and waved it angrily.

"Go! Now! Or die! "

Chapter Eleven

It was several hours after sunset when someone slapped the entrance flap of the teepee several times. Winona sat up and arranged the hem of her buckskin dress over her bent knees. "Come in," she said in English, counting on whoever was out there to understand the tone if not the words. The flap parted and her stomach bunched with dread that it would be Thunder Horn. Instead the seamed features of the old woman appeared.

"I am sorry to intrude," Butterfly signed. "But I have been sent by the council. They want to talk to you."

"Now?" Winona responded.

"Now."

"It is so late."

Butterfly walked slowly over, stooped as always. Long ago her back had been bent by an internal malady that warped her spine. "For this also I am sorry. They are meeting late because of you. They want to ask you questions so they may go to their lodges and their beds."

The implication filled Winona with unrest. Evidently Thunder Horn had spoken the truth when he claimed the entire tribe had a stake in her welfare, but for the life of her she couldn't comprehend how this could be. She rose, then smoothed her dress, stalling so he could gather her wits about her. "Of what importance am I to the council of the Minneconjou?"

"You must ask the council. I am a messenger, no more."

"Why do they send you and not a warrior to escort me?" Butterfly's aged visage cracked in a grin. "They think you would be less likely to scratch my eyes out than the eyes of a man. And, too, Thunder Horn is my grandson."

"What good would it do me to attack anyone?" Winona said forlornly, patting the small mountain her condition had made of her belly. "I could not run very far in my state."

"No," Butterfly agreed, her wizened hand reaching out to stroke Winona's abdomen. "Your time is not far off."

"At least a moon," Winona said without confidence.

"Much sooner, my pretty Shoshone," Butterfly signed. "I should know. I have helped more women give birth than any living Minneconjou. In ten sleeps, twenty at most, you will deliver your baby." She smiled encouragement, revealing the gap where three of her upper front teeth had been. "But do not worry. I will be at your side." Butterfly pointed at the flap. "Now we really must go. Compose yourself. No one will do you any harm."

The night air was refreshingly cool on Winona's face after having been confined in the teepee for so long. Winona arched her back and walked stiffly across to the biggest lodge of all, the old woman at her elbow. She paused before entering to flag her courage and absently gazed to one side. Thirty feet away stood a warrior. Another warrior was an equal distance from her on the other side. Had she been up to making a run for it they would have caught her in seconds.

Butterfly snickered. "You must have very long nails, pretty Shoshone." She bent, lifted the flap. "In you go. And it might help you to remember they are only men."

Despite herself, Winona grinned. She was still grinning as she straightened inside, and her grin widened when she beheld the curious stares of many of those assembled.

Here were gathered the top Minneconjous, the leaders of that most numerous division of the Sioux. Foremost among them was a gray-haired warrior who held the seat of honor. On either side, forming two curved prongs, were ten men, all dressed in their finest buckskins, many adorned with headdresses and beads.

Winona squared her shoulders and moved down the center of the aisle formed by the two rows of men, keeping her eyes on the gray-haired warrior. She did note that Thunder Horn sat three positions from the high chief, on the right. This told her Thunder Horn was a warrior of some distinction, more than she had thought, more than was good for her welfare.

When a few feet from the gray-haired man, she knelt and gave a slight bow. No one had addressed her yet. She could practically feel their eyes boring into her, assessing her character by her appearance and her bearing. The lodge smelled of pipe smoke and cedar.

The gray-haired man cleared his throat. When Winona raised her head, he signed, "I am Runs Against. I will ask you questions and you will answer with a straight tongue. If you lie to us, we will find out, and when your baby has come you will be punished by your new husband, Thunder Horn, who has—"

Winona surprised herself and shocked the assembled chiefs by interrupting with sharp gestures. "I am most sorry, Runs Against, but as I have made plain to Thunder Horn again and again, I already have a husband and will accept no other."

Stunned quiet ensued. For a woman to speak out of place was a serious breach of conduct. For anyone to interrupt an older warrior was even worse. And for someone to break in on a chief was virtually unthinkable.

Thunder Horn leaned forward to get attention and signed, "You all see what I have had to deal with. She is beautiful, yes. But she does not know her proper place. Shoshones must not rear their children to respect their betters."

"Show me a better," Winona rejoined, "and I will give him the respect he is due." She glanced quickly at Runs Against, whose indignation had flushed his cheeks red. "I apologize, great one, for offending you. I wanted you to know the truth. On this, as in all matters, I will speak to you with the straight tongue you requested."

The square-jawed warrior to the left of Runs Against cracked a grin. "She is clever, this one," he signed. "She holds out bitter roots in one hand and honey in the other."

Winona guessed they had previously agreed to rely solely on sign language for her benefit, and was glad they had. Otherwise she would have been left in the dark in more ways than one.

"Only you would see humor in this, Penis," Runs Against responded testily. "You always see things to laugh about that others do not."

"With a name like mine can you blame me?" Penis signed, provoking hearty laughter that seemed to break the air of tension hanging heavy in the council lodge.

Runs Against chuckled, then became severe. "I will overlook your conduct this once, woman. Not twice. Do you understand?"

"Yes," Winona answered.

"Good. Let us begin." Runs Against made a teepee of his fingers and pondered a short while. "We already know your name and the tribe you belong to. Tell us more of your people, of where they live."

"In the mountains far to the west."

"We know this information already," Runs Against signed. "Tell us exactly where they are to be found, not just at this time but during each moon that follows."

A flicker of fear sprang to life within Winona, She could think of only one reason the Minneconjous would desire such information: so they could send war parties to attack the Shoshones. "My people never travel the same route twice," she signed. "And since I have not lived among them for many moons, I would not know where to find them at this time."

"I warned you about lying," Runs Against said. "You would have us believe you do not live with your own kind?"

"My husband, Grizzly Killer, has a wooden lodge high in the mountains near the one my people call Eagle Peak. It is there I live."

"Who ever heard of making a lodge from wood?" Runs Against signed. "Can it be moved when all the game has been killed off? Can it be rolled up and loaded on a travois and taken to a better camping place?" He surveyed his audience. "Truly only a white man would build such a thing."

More laughter further relaxed the chiefs. Winona felt the baby kick but didn't touch her stomach.

"I believe you because we have seen these strange wooden lodges with our own eyes," Runs Against told her. "But how can you stand to live in such a place?"

"It is warm in winter, cool in summer. It is spacious and dry and never needs mending," Winona replied. "What woman would not prefer such a home?"

Runs Against had a ready answer. "No Minneconjou woman would. But we must remember you are Shoshone. Tell us, Winona. Thunder

Horn has said you speak the tongue of the whites. How well do you know their language?"

"My husband has often told me I speak it better than he does himself."

"Ha! Not likely." Runs Against wagged a finger at her. "Straight tongue, remember?"

"If he were here he would confirm it."

"Speak, then. Say something in the white tongue," Runs Against commanded. "Anything at all."

Unbidden to Winona's mind came snatches of conversations overhead at the annual rendezvous. While Nate seldom used such language himself and she never did, she had no reservations about doing so on this occasion as she was certain no one would be able to translate. "As you wish, you arrogant old fart. Your mother was a whore, your father a jackass," she said in a level voice while smiling sweetly. "You are a stupid son of a bitch who thinks he can outfox me but I will outfox you and the rest of these dung eaters and when I am done your own women will point at you and laugh and say there goes the old fool who was tricked by a mere Shoshone." She had their complete attention so she went on, still smiling. "I have never been one to hate others simply because they are from a different tribe, but I tell you here and now that if I could, I would fill the breechcloths of all of you with red ants after staking you to the ground. And then I would tie a stallion over you and give it water to drink until it could not hold the water in any more. This way you would earn a new name. Instead of Runs Against, everyone would call you Pissed On."

None of the chiefs moved or signed when she finished. A few shared glances. Then Runs Against raised his arms. "What do you think, my brothers?"

"She could be trying to trick us," signed a man whose headdress was attached to the horns of a buffalo joined by a thick leather band. "She said gibberish thinking we will believe it is the white tongue."

"There is one way to be sure," Runs Against signed, turning to a warrior with a large comma of hair hanging against the side of his face. "You claim to know a little of the white's bird talk, Long Forelock. Is Buffalo Hump right? Does she know it or not?"

This was unforeseen. Winona fought to hide her anxiety at being found out. She glanced at the warrior with the forelock, wondering where in the world he had learned her husband's language. Once he told them the truth, they would take her out and let the Minneconjou women stone her to death, or perhaps leave her stranded on the prairie with no food, no weapons, and maybe no clothes.

Long Forelock pursed his lips, deep in thought. He looked straight at Winona and she swore she detected a hint of fear in his eyes. Why that should be, she had no idea. She convinced herself it must be her imagination.

"What do you say?" Runs Against prompted shortly. "If you know some of the white tongue, you must have some idea of what she told us."

"I do," Long Forelock signed.

Winona bit her lower lip. Had she not been pregnant, she would had made a dash for the entrance.

"She plays us for fools," Long Forelock signed, and there was muttering among the chiefs. "She teases us. She would have us think she does not think highly of the Minneconjous when she does. She said that she has heard many tales of Minneconjou bravery in battle, and now that she has met us she knows they must be true. She thinks we are pleasing to the eye. And she admitted to liking Thunder Horn more than she has let on."

No one was more shocked by the warrior's statements than Winona. Her expression of utter amazement seemed to lend credence to his words, and many of the men gazed on her in a new light. Foremost among them was Thunder Horn, who beamed as would the owner of a fine new mare.

"So the truth is known," Runs Against signed, chortling. "Did you really think you could keep it secret, woman?"

Winona had no choice but to play along. If she disputed Long Forelock they would chalk it up to womanly pride. "He did indeed understand most of my words."

"Most of them?"

"All except those concerning Thunder Horn. I did not admit to liking him more than has been apparent. I admitted to disliking him more than I dared show."

The relaxed atmosphere evaporated like morning dew under a hot sun. Frowns and scowls replaced the smiles and grins. Everyone studiously avoided looking at Thunder Horn, who had gone as rigid as granite.

Winona had overstepped the bounds again,

and this time she had openly insulted a noted warrior. But the way she saw it, she'd had no choice. Had Thunder Horn left the council thinking she was attracted to him, he would have become insufferable, hounding her daily to become his woman, refusing to take no for an answer.

Now, ringed by hostile glares, Winona had second thoughts. Somehow she must salvage the moment and get back in Thunder Horn's good graces. Just not too far back in. "I wish Long Forelock had understood all my words," she signed. "I do not dislike Thunder Horn personally. Anyone can see he is a Minneconjou of importance, and any Minneconjou woman would be delighted to be his mate. No, I dislike him just as any woman dislikes a man who has gotten the better of her, as he did when he captured me. As you would dislike anyone who bested you in a fight."

Winona held her breath, gauging the impact. She had appealed to their warrior vanity because vanity was the prime weakness of most men. Although women were branded as more vain due to the greater amount of time they spent making themselves attractive, every woman knew the contrary was true and how to use that knowledge to their advantage. Whites or Indians, it made no difference. Men were men, and there wasn't one alive who liked coming out second best at anything.

Some of the resentment faded from the faces of the Minneconjous. Thunder Horn actually grinned, which Winona took as a bad omen.

"I am sorry," Long Forelock signed to Thunder Horn. "My knowledge of the white tongue is limited. Sometimes I mix words."

Runs Against tapped the ground so everyone would look at him. "I am the one who should apologize," he signed. "I thought Long Forelock was telling another of his tales when he claimed to know the bird talk. I will never doubt him again." He stared hard at Winona. "Now back to the matter at hand. You have proven you were not lying. You must know the ways of the whites very well indeed."

Before Winona could stop herself, she answered, and she realized she had made a grave mistake the second she lowered her hands. "My husband says I am as at home among his people as I am among mine. I even know the written tongue of the whites and can read the small signs they put on paper."

A murmur of excitement broke out. Half the chiefs began conversing with a neighbor. Runs Against and Penis huddled together, with Penis doing most of the talking. They were obviously thrilled by the revelation.

Why? Winona asked herself. The Lakotas weren't on the friendliest of terms with the white trappers and traders, so of what possible significance was her ability to them?

Runs Against signed for silence. "Tell me, Shoshone," he then said, "is it not true that the whites place great value on the squiggly signs they so love to write?"

"Yes," Winona confirmed, thinking of the trade contracts between the trappers and the fur companies. "They use them to bind each other to promises they make."

"Their word is not enough?"

"In their personal dealings, yes," Winona explained. "But when they engage in trade and hold council with one another they always want their agreements put down in great detail so there will be no misunderstandings in the future."

"And they never break these agreements?"

"It is rare for them to do so once they have put the squiggly signs down."

"It is as we hoped." Runs Against looked very pleased. "Tell me more, woman. Let us say you were out on the prairie and you saw a party of whites in the distance. Let us say you want to go to them but you do not want to get shot before they realize you are friendly. Is there a way you could do this?"

"A white flag," Winona signed, "such as the flags our own societies sometimes make for themselves."

"Only the one color?"

"Yes. To the whites it means, 'I come in peace.' They will never shoot someone holding one."

"A white flag for whites," Penis signed. "How very appropriate."

For a while Runs Against sat in contemplation and Winona began to think they were done with her when he cocked his head and signed, "Do your people have many guns, Shoshone?"

"Some," Winona answered.

"How many?" Runs Against pressed.

Winona had no intention of disclosing that thanks to her husband the Shoshones owned more rifles than any surrounding tribe, enough to insure they could hold their own in any tribal clash. "Ten," she lied, the true total being many times that number.

"That is all?" Runs Against rubbed his chin. "What about steel knives and tomahawks and fire makers?"

"Too many to count," Winona signed honestly. "For fourteen or fifteen winters now we have been trading beaver hides to the whites for items we wanted. Looking glasses, blankets, pots and pans, material for dresses, and much more."

"So the Shoshones are a rich tribe," Runs Against remarked.

"In small things," Winona responded. "But we are not rich in horses, like the Comanches and the Nez Perce, or rich in numbers, like the Minneconjous."

"Still," Runs Against signed, "it is good to be rich in the small things. Everyone is happier when their hands have much to keep them busy." He paused. "No one likes to be poor."

"I know I would be happy if my wife had one of those looking glasses," Penis interjected. "Maybe then she would spend all her time admiring herself instead of nagging me."

The laughter was contagious. Winona grinned, forgetting for a moment she was among enemies, letting down her emotional guard only to have it immediately pierced by the next words Runs Against signed.

"As for you, woman, you will forget about this white man you took as your husband and change your mind about Thunder Horn. Like it or not, in a moon or so you will become his wife. I have given my word on this."

"Never," Winona countered.

Runs Against sighed and signed more slowly, as might a patient father to an erring daughter. "Why can you not get it through your head that you have no choice in the matter? From the day you were captured you belonged to the Minneconjou to do with as we please. And it pleases us to have so lovely and healthy a woman bear many strong boys so the Minneconjous may continue to thrive and prosper."

"I would rather die than be the wife of Thunder Horn."

"Why? As you pointed out earlier, every eligible woman in the village would be delighted to move into his lodge."

"Then let him pick one of them. There is only one lodge for me, the wood lodge high in the mountains, the one I call my home."

"You will never see it again."

"Whether I do or whether I do not, there is only one man for me and his name is Grizzly Killer."

"Wagh!" Runs Against declared aloud, which was as strong an oath as an Indian used. His hands moved in angry, jerking gestures. "You are enough to give a man fits! Why are you being so unreasonable? Did this Grizzly Killer put a spell on your heart?"

"Yes," Winona signed.

"You admit it?" Runs Against asked in surprise. "How did he bind you to him? Did a spirit help him? Did a medicine man sell him a magic flute? Did he use a special potion?"

"He used something very special," Winona signed, and when she had their complete attention, she added, "He used love."

None of the chiefs so much as moved for a full minute. Penis broke the uncomfortable hush by signing at Thunder Horn, "You would do well to put this Shoshone from your mind, friend. Her heart is bound in iron." A sly twinkle lit his features. "But if you are still interested in a wife, I will gladly trade you mine for a good horse."

Everyone except Thunder Horn was smiling. "No," he signed absently, his gaze fixed on Winona.

"Very well," Penis said. "It does not need to be a good horse. Any one will do." He sighed heavily. "It does not even have to have four legs."

The lodge rocked with mirth but this time Winona didn't let her guard down. She waited with stony reserve for the interrogation to resume but received a flick of dismissal instead.

"We are done with you, woman. You may go," Runs Against directed. "You will remain in your lodge except for short walks each day. Butterfly will tend to your every need. You have but to ask her and it will be done. Take care of yourself so that you will be ready when the time comes."

Winona obediently rose and turned. Butterfly awaited her, and together, flanked by the two warriors, they departed. Winona drank in the sweet air, grateful the session was over, the chief's parting words ringing in her brain: "Take care of yourself so that you will be ready when the times comes."

Ready for what?

Chapter Twelve

Shakespeare McNair, Lane Griffen, and Bob Knorr were riveted in place by the paralyzing sight of the massive grizzly rearing on its hind legs and opening its gaping maw to roar. A relatively recent wound on the side of its head, a deep furrow dug by a lead ball, was all the evidence Shakespeare needed that here was the same bear responsible for cutting him open and nearly rubbing him out. Automatically his hands sought the pistols he would ordinarily have at his waist, but there were none. Nor did he have his rifle. He was unarmed, weak, defenseless, totally at the mercy of a creature that had no mercy.

Shakespeare's only hope lay in the two free trappers. He glanced at them just as they did the last thing he expected; they broke and ran.

The grizzly came down on all fours and advanced, its great head swinging ponderously from side to side. It stared straight at Shakespeare, and McNair felt the icy hand of death stroke the nape of his neck as the bear's warm breath fanned his face. He went rigid, not so much as a muscle twitching, his eyes locked wide. Sometimes——but not always—bears wouldn't touch someone if the person played possum.

Growling suspiciously, its raspy breaths like the puffing of a steam engine, the grizzly stopped and sniffed loudly, its warm nose brushing Shakespeare's chest. Shakespeare resisted an urge to cringe away. Steeling his nerves, he neither moved nor made an outcry, not even when the bear nipped lightly at his shoulder, its teeth shearing the buckskin but hardly breaking the skin.

Abruptly, the bear twisted its head and opened its mouth. Saliva dripped onto Shakespeare's cheek. This was the end, he told himself. It was going to finish the job, eat him right there on the spot. He saw its glistening teeth, saw its tongue as the head bent toward him. Its bulk blotted out the sun and most of the sky. I'm dead he reflected, and offered a heartfelt prayer to his Maker that his end would be swift and painless.

Then the bear froze. Loud shouts had erupted. Snarling in annoyance it turned to ascertain the source.

Shakespeare McNair looked and nearly shouted for joy. Lane and Bob had run off, all right, but only as far as the canoes to retrieve their rifles. Both men were twenty yards away, jumping up and down and hooting to draw the grizzly off.

"Come on, you bastard!" Knorr cried. "Let's put some lead in your diet!"

"Here, bear! Try me!" Griffen chimed in. "Why don't you try eating someone who can fight back, you cowardly monstrosity!"

The grizzly did not like the taunts. Roaring its challenge, it moved toward the pair of trappers with astounding speed for such a gigantic animal.

Shakespeare's heart leaped into his mouth. Should anything happen to the two trappers, he was doomed. He wanted to shout "Look out!" to them but it was too late and unnecessary. Besides, they were ready.

In unison the strapping frontiersmen tucked their rifles to their shoulders and cocked the hammers. Lane Griffen held a Hawken, Bob Knorr a Kentucky rifle. They sighted on the grizzly's head and when the bear had only fifteen feet to cover, they squeezed triggers.

At the twin blasts the bear stumbled and slid several yards, almost to the feet of the trappers. Lane and Bob whirled and ran, each in a different direction. Reloading on the fly, they cast glances over their shoulders to see which one of them the bear would pick.

It was Griffen. Snarling viciously, the grizzly pushed up off the grass and took out after him, paws pounding the ground like hammers. The instant Knorr saw this, he halted and quickly finished reloading, his fingers flying. Lane Griffen had begun to curve back toward him, which in turn induced the bear to angle sharply to intercept Lane. And that gave Bob Knorr a clear broadside shot.

At the report the bear staggered, slowing and shaking its head as if it were being assailed by bees. Looking around, the beast spotted Knorr, then charged.

Immediately Lane Griffen stopped, aimed carefully, and fired. The ball caught the bear low on the side and brought it to a lurching halt. Roaring louder than ever, it whirled toward Lane and again headed for him.

Meanwhile, Knorr was reloading. He poured black powder directly into the muzzle instead of taking precious time measuring the grains in his palm. Next he frantically wrapped a ball in a patch, crammed both into the end of the barrel with his thumb and used his ramrod to shove them all the way down.

The grizzly had gained on Lane Griffen. Realizing he couldn't outrun the hairy behemoth, the bearded man whirled, letting go of his Hawken in order to grab the pistols at his waist. He cleared his belt, leveled both simultaneously, and fired at the exact second Knorr fired the rifle.

Three balls tore into the bear. This time, though, it did not stumble, did not slacken its speed. Growling hideously, the grizzly barreled toward Lane Griffen, who at the very last moment threw himself from its path. The bear kept on running, but not very far. It slowed, blood flecking its mouth, then stopped and pawed at its side. Legs buckling, it collapsed and lay there, feebly attempting to stand.

Lane reloaded his rifle ahead of Knorr. He

walked up behind the bear, placed the barrel so close to the top of its head that hairs brushed the metal, and squeezed off the final shot.

Thrashing wildly, the grizzly shuddered and snarled, both movement and sound growing weaker and weaker until it sagged lifeless on the bloody grass.

"Tough son of a bitch," Bob Knorr commented.

"These devils are too damned hard to kill for my tastes," Lane said.

Shakespeare nodded his agreement. Grizzlies always had been notoriously tenacious of life. It was not uncommon for one to absorb eight, nine, even ten balls in the lungs and other vital organs and still not keel over. One of the first white men to encounter them, none other than Meriwether Lewis of Lewis and Clark fame, had often said that he'd rather tangle with two Indians out after scalps than a single grizzly. And Indians themselves regarded the bears as so fearsome that some tribes accorded the same coup status to slaying one as they did to slaying an enemy warrior. Which explained why the Shoshones were in such awe of Nate King. He'd killed more than any man, white or red, ever.

Griffen and Knorr jogged over.

"Are you all right?" the former inquired.

"We saw it take a bite out of you and feared you were a goner," his partner added.

McNair touched his torn shirt. "Almost, but not quite." He gazed into the distance and quoted, "To die, to sleep. To sleep, perchance to dream. Ay, there's the rub, for in that

180

sleep of death what dreams may come, when we have shuffled off this mortal coil, must give us pause. There's the respect that makes calamity of so long life. For who would bear the whips and scorns of time, the oppressor's wrong, the proud man's contumely, the pangs of despised love, the law's delay, the insolence of office, and the spurns that patient merit of the unworthy takes, when he himself might his quietus make with a bare bodkin?"

"What?" Bob Knorr said.

"You must be feeling a mite better if you're quoting that old book of yours," Griffen remarked.

"That old book," Shakespeare repeated with a tinge of melancholy. "Would that I still had it. My most prized possession, the immortal works of the Bard, gone forever, destroyed by one of Nature's tantrums. I suppose there's poetic irony in that, boys, but for the life of me I can't appreciate it."

"Is that why you're so sad?" Lane Griffen said. "Didn't we tell you?"

"Tell me what?" Shakespeare responded, hardly daring to believe the deduction Lane's question inspired.

"I'll show you." Lane spun on a heel and sprinted to the canoes.

Bob Knorr hunkered down to examine McNair's wounds. "The sooner we get you bandaged up, the less I'll be worried about your innards oozing out if you make any sudden moves." He glanced at the bear. "If we had the time, I'd take a couple days to skin that cuss and treat the hide so we could wrap you in it for the journey."

"Blankets will do fine," Shakespeare said, craning his neck in an effort to gaze past Knorr. He could hear Griffen running back but couldn't see whatever the man was bringing.

"We found your guns," Knorr mentioned offhandedly. "Your pistols were stuck under your belt. The Hawken was lying half in, half out of the river. I cleaned and oiled it myself. Wasn't busted or anything."

"I'm grateful," Shakespeare said. Lane Griffen appeared, holding a waterlogged bundle, and Shakespeare felt the sort of constriction in his chest a man feels when setting eyes on a long lost lover after a lengthy absence. "William S.!" he said softly.

Griffen handed the bundle over. "Actually, if it's poetic stuff you like, I'd say it's pretty darned fitting for a man to be saved by his own book."

"How's that?" Shakespeare asked, not paying much attention as he swiftly unwrapped the heavy blanket stained by water marks.

"We wouldn't have found you except for that bundle," Lane explained. "We were paddling along when I saw it snagged on the limb of a partially submerged tree. Got me curious so we went over to investigate and as Bob was untangling the blanket we spotted you." He paused. "It done saved your bacon, old coon."

The blanket parted, and there it was, the leather cover slightly marred by new water marks. "William S.," Shakespeare said again, and forgetting himself and his condition, he gave the book a gentle hug.

"Lordy," Knorr said. "If you get this excited

over books, you must be a regular hellion with the ladies."

"It's not just *any* book," Shakespeare said, gingerly turning the pages. Only a third of them had been touched by the water, and although some lines had smeared, none were illegible. "It's the sum and substance of what we are."

"I have to differ," Lane Griffen said. "Only the Good Book is all that, and more."

"True as far as that goes," Shakespeare said, tenderly running a finger along the edge of a page. "The Good Book tells us who we are and why we're here and what we have to do if we want to go on living once we cast off this moral coil. Old William S., on the other hand, gives us a peek at what makes us tick. Read *Hamlet* sometime. Or *Romeo and Juliet*. You'll understand then."

"I've heard of that Hamlet feller," Bob Knorr said. "Isn't he the one who boiled a batch of witches in their own cauldron?"

"You're thinking of *Macbeth*," Shakespeare said dryly.

Griffen had turned to gaze inland. "Maybe this isn't the best time to sit around chawing about books," he reminded them. "There's no telling who might have heard those shots. We are at the border of Blackfoot country, if you'll recall."

"I should have thought of that my own self," Knorr said, rising. "Let's forget the coffee and light a shuck before we have uninvited company."

It took all of fifteen minutes. Shakespeare lay propped in the second canoe, swaddled in blankets, his precious book on his lap, while

183

Lane Griffen paddled strongly to take them out into deeper water. In the first canoe Bob Knorr glanced over a shoulder and waved cheerily.

"Don't you fret none, McNair," Griffen said. "Once we hook up with our friends, Jacob will have you patched together good as new in no time. Might take a couple of hundred stitches, but he's a real patient man."

"I can hardly wait," Shakespeare said. And, in truth, he couldn't. The excitement and exertion had taken their toll, leaving him weak and flushed and feeling feverish. He tried not to dwell on the furrows in his flesh because every time he did he shuddered uncontrollably.

The gentle motion of the canoe lulled Shakespeare into drifting to sleep. He suffered disturbing dreams, all involving rampaging grizzlies tearing into his unprotected body, only snatches of which he remembered on awakening. Pushing up on an elbow, he scanned the tranquil stretch of river ahead.

Lane Griffen heard and looked back. "Figured you'd be out most of the day. It's the middle of the morning now. How are you holding up?"

"I've felt better," Shakespeare said. His fever had worsened while he slept and he felt as if he could fry eggs on his forehead. "Wish I could do my share of paddling."

"Leave that to us," Lane said. "We know you'd do the same on our behalf if things were reversed." He dipped the paddle smoothly in a steady rhythm. "Folks need to look out for one another, just like the Good Book says. My pa made that clear to me before I was knee high to a grasshopper." Lane grinned at the fond recollection. "Pa was a preacher man."

"Surprised you didn't follow in his footsteps," Shakespeare mentioned.

"I was fixing to," Lane responded. "Then I met me the finest woman this side of Creation. Abigail was her name, and she loved me as much as I loved her. So I decided having a family was more important than spreading the Word."

"Where is your lady love now?"

The trapper broke his rhythm. "I wish to God I knew, McNair. Two years ago next month she disappeared."

"Indians?"

"Piegans. I made the mistake of taking her into the mountains with me to trap. Everyone warned me not to do it but I was too pigheaded to listen. Thought I could handle anything that came along." His voice wavered, acquiring a haunted aspect. "Why is it we think we're invincible when we're young?"

"For the same reason we think we know all there is to know and that no one can possibly teach us a thing about life," Shakespeare said, making himself comfortable. "The way I see it, we're always about twice as stupid as we think we are and four times as ignorant."

"Ain't it the truth." Griffen stuck the paddle in the water and held it there, steering the canoe around a floating log. As he resumed trailing Knorr, he continued his account. "Things went really well for about a month. We made us a lean-to high in the pines where no one could find it and I'd go off most mornings to check

my traps while she worked on the hides of
the beaver raised the day before." He looked
skyward. "I tell you, McNair, it was heaven on
earth."

"True love always is."

"Yep. Anyway, one afternoon I came back
to the lean-to as usual and she was gone, the
lean-to smashed to bits. There were plenty of
moccasin tracks, Piegan prints by the cut of the
soles. They'd taken her north so I went after
them hell bent to wipe the varmints out."

"Did you ever catch up with them?" Shakespeare asked when the trapper's voice trailed
off.

"No." The word was little more than a whisper. "I tried. Lord, how I tried. Hunted for
months, until the first snow came. It was
hopeless." Griffen's shoulders sagged. "Later
I heard tell from a couple of voyageurs of
a rumor about a white woman living with a
band of Piegans up toward Canada. They had
no notion of where the tribe could be found or
I would have headed right out."

"And now?"

"Now I'm about plumb out of hope," Griffen confessed. "God knows what she's gone
through. Even if I find her, she might be too
ashamed to want to come back. Sometimes that
happens, I hear."

Shakespeare was having a hard time keeping
his eyes open. Sleepiness pervaded his body
and his brow was hotter than ever. "If she loves
you she'll never give up hope," he said, putting
a forearm over his eyes. "You should do the
same."

"Easier said than done, McNair," Griffen said. "Hope is a lot like faith. Both are precious commodities, and when we run out it's not simple to stock up again."

"Sure you haven't been reading old William S.?"

"I don't read anything any more. Not even the Good Book."

"You should—" Shakespeare began, and had no idea whether he finished the statement because the next thing he knew he was sitting up and the sun sat balanced on the western horizon like a red plate standing on edge and about to slip off the end of a table. "Sorry," he mumbled. "Drifted off again."

"In your shape I'd do the same," Griffen said. "You'd be wise not to do much moving around until we get there."

"When will you pull over for the night?" Shakespeare asked, relishing the idea of that cup of coffee the grizzly's attack had denied him and a good night's sleep beside a warm fire.

"We're not. Bob and I stopped earlier while you were sleeping. We agreed to push on through the night."

"Too dangerous," Shakespeare advised. "By morning you'll both be too tired to keep your eyes skinned for hostiles. And I certainly won't be of much use."

"It's for your benefit that we're doing it," Griffen said. "We can reach Jacob that much sooner."

"No. I won't have you jeopardizing yourselves needlessly on my account."

"You don't have a say in the matter," Griffen

declared bluntly. "We already have our minds set, so that's that."

"Darned idiots," Shakespeare groused, knowing full well he would be unable to dissuade them and admiring their grit despite his misgivings. Placing a hand behind his head, he surveyed the countryside.

The Yellowstone River ran straight for as far as the eye could see, a scenic blue ribbon in the midst of the vast green grassland. Cottonwoods and willows lined both banks, the branches of the willows hanging so low they seemed to touch their reflections on the surface. To the south grazed a small herd of buffalo. In the undergrowth on the south bank several deer stood watching the canoes glide past. Overhead a red hawk vented the unique screech of its kind. On the north bank sparrows and a jay frolicked. On the plain to the north nothing moved, not so much as a solitary antelope.

And to the north lay the heart of Blackfoot country. Shakespeare had no idea how many villages were spread out over the countless square miles encompassing their domain. A fair guess would be dozens. Like the Sioux farther south and the Comanches way down near Mexico, the Blackfeet were a powerful tribe whose power in part derived from their well-nigh limitless numbers. That, and their confederacy.

Some years ago the chiefs of three tribes—the Bloods, the Piegans, and the Blackfeet—had smoked the pipe and formed a loosely knit alliance that became known as the Blackfoot Confederacy since the Blackfeet were the guiding lights and the real power behind the league.

Now the Confederacy controlled an empire a third the size of the eastern United States. They terrorized trappers, drove out traders, and generally made life miserable for anyone who had the gall to set foot in their territory. No amount of palaver could change them. No amount of trade goods would sway their attitude. They were implacable.

Shakespeare knew them well. Perhaps too well. And he would not like to see the two young trappers fall into their clutches because of him. So he resolved to stay awake as long as he could to help them keep watch.

"Is it true what they say?" Lane Griffen asked conversationally. "That you were one of the first out here?"

"I was," Shakespeare admitted.

"When was it? Shortly after Lewis and Clark went through?"

"Before them."

Griffen nearly upended the canoe, he turned so swiftly. "You're tickling my ribs, McNair. No whites had gone west of the Mississippi before '05. Everyone knows that for a fact."

"Just like everyone once thought the world was flat, for a fact, and just like most folks in the States, even today, call the country west of the Mississippi the Great American Desert because they just know, for a fact, that nothing will grow here and it's as dry and lifeless as the Sahara."

"Point taken," Griffen conceded. "So what was it like way back then?"

"Not much different than what you see around you," Shakespeare reminisced. "There was more game. And there weren't quite as many Indians, but all the tribes, even the Blackfeet, were friendly in those days——"

"They were?" Griffen asked in astonishment.

"None friendlier," Shakespeare said. "About a half-dozen whites were living with different Blackfoot bands when Lewis got into his famous racket with a small bunch of Blackfeet trying to steal the guns of his party. Once the word spread that whites had killed Blackfeet, those whites living among them were told to pack up and ride out or be roasted over an open fire." He ran a hand along his eyebrows, noting how hot his skin was to the touch. "Most of those men had Blackfoot wives. A few had small children. They didn't like giving up their loved ones, but they liked the notion of dying even less. So they went."

"The wives and children must have gone through sheer hell."

Shakespeare swallowed, then licked his lips. "I would imagine so," he said hoarsely.

Griffen suddenly stopped paddling and asked, half to himself, "Now what the dickens has him so excited?"

Bob Knorr had also ceased paddling and was jabbing a finger at the north side of the Yellowstone. Shakespeare twisted to see why and spotted riders out on the prairie, hastening toward the river. Toward them. And although the distance was a quarter of a mile or more, much too far for him to note details, he knew they were Blackfeet.

Chapter Thirteen

The Blackfeet Indians were human beings just like everyone else! In all the brief years of Zachary King's existence, this was the most shocking insight to date. He would sit outside Bird Rattler's lodge of an evening and gaze in bewilderment at the peaceful variety of activities taking place, activities just like those the Shoshones engaged in, and he would shake his head in amazement.

This third night of his stay in the village was typical. Not far off, at the edge of the prairie, a young warrior sang a love song, and although Zach didn't know the Blackfoot tongue, he could guess at what the warrior was singing: a plea for a sweetheart to meet him outside the camp. Shoshone men did the same thing.

Already the night-singers were making their rounds, moving around the great circle of lodges, jingling bells and venting whoops as the mood struck them.

The lodges themselves were brightened by fires within, so that each lodge seemed to glow with a radiant inner light. Zach thought of them as oversized upright fireflies. The setting was serene, and it so reminded him of a typical Shoshone village that he became heartsick to see his own people again.

From certain lodges arose drumming and chanting. Special ceremonies and dances were taking place within, and they would carry on until late.

Outside a nearby lodge several warriors were doing a begging dance. As Bird Rattler had explained the dance to Zach the night before, custom called for the owner of the lodge to come out and give food to those doing it. The dance was not done because the warriors were so poor they had no food. Rather, they danced to test the generosity of the lodge owner.

Zach sighed sadly and gazed at a bright star all by itself on the northern horizon. He felt a lot like that star, all alone in the world with no one to confide in, no one to share his turmoil.

The flap of Bird Rattler's teepee rustled and out came Elk At Dawn and his sister, Bluebird.

"Ho!" Elk At Dawn said aloud before reverting to sign language. "Why do you sit by yourself so much, Stalking Coyote, my brother to be? It is not good to be alone all the time."

"Perhaps he misses his family," Bluebird signed. Ever since Zach's arrival she had taken a special interest in him. At mealtimes she took it on herself to fill his bowl and be sure he had seconds the instant he finished the first helping. She unrolled his bedding at night, rolled it in the morning. Her parents had been so amused by her antics they had nicknamed her, "Stalking Coyote's Shadow."

Zach didn't know what to make of her attention. Deep down he had a suspicion but he refused to admit it to himself. Now, gazing on her smooth, lovely features and seeing the genuine warmth in her adoring eyes, he was tempted to take her aside and reveal the sorrow eating at his heart.

"How would you like to see a dance?" Elk At Dawn broke Zach's train of thought.

"What kind?" Zach responded, not really caring.

"The Society of Brave Dogs is having one," Elk At Dawn said. "They are the ones who keep order in the village and punish those who do not listen. They are some of the bravest warriors in all the Blackfoot nation." He plucked at Zach's sleeve. "Would you like to go see them? We were not invited but I know how we can sneak in."

The prospect of adventure was more than Zach could resist. Plus it would take his mind off his woes. "If you want, I will go."

Earlier Zach had witnessed the Brave Dogs parading through the encampment in time to music. Each man had carried a folded blanket over his left arm and a rattle in his right hand. They marched in pairs, from the most prominent members to the least, announcing their dance as they went along.

The Shoshones also had societies, also held dances. But Zach had never seen any people so fond of singing and dancing as were the Blackfeet. Somehow he had got the notion into his head that they would always be grim and mean to one another. So bloodthirsty a people had to be. But the Blackfeet loved to laugh, to have a grand time. They were in love with life and showed it in all they did. Which only added to the mystery surrounding them.

Elk At Dawn led the way across the camp to where the dance lodges of the Brave Dogs were located. Silhouettes of figures flitted about inside one, accompanied by laughing and shouting and music. Elk At Dawn walked up behind the lodge, checking both ways to insure no one was watching, and, bending quickly, lifted the lower edge of the hide and squeezed underneath.

Bluebird went next, graceful as her namesake.

Zach came last, freezing momentarily when he saw the many spectators ringing the interior. But no one paid any attention to them so he crawled the rest of the way and stood beside the skinny duo.

The dance was already in full stride. Wearing only breechcloths and moccasins, the warriors in the society spun and leaped and shrieked in exuberant glee. A few had bone whistles on which they blew shrilly. Some sang. A quartet of dancers had been painted over with pale clay and held sticks adorned with eagle feathers. Two other dancers wore elaborate headdresses adorned with the ears of bears and numerous bear claws. Black streaks had been painted from eye to eye; the rest of their faces were painted red.

Elk At Dawn leaned close to Zach and signed, "Do you see the four smeared with clay? They play the part of wolves and are herding the other dancers toward the center of the lodge as a wolf pack herds buffalo."

Indeed, the other dancers were pretending to be packed closer and closer together. At one point, when all the 'buffalo' were crammed tight, the two warriors dressed as bears came to their rescue, scattering the wolves. The spectators cheered the bears on while deriding the 'wolf pack'.

"What does it mean?" Zach signed. Long ago his father had revealed there were always underlying meanings to everything Indians did, including their dances.

"Without the buffalo, my people would die," Elk At Dawn signed. "So we ask for the buffalo to be protected that there may always be plenty for everyone."

The Shoshones often did the same, only differently. Zach watched the dance be repeated several times, at a loss to comprehend how the two peoples could be so alike and yet one had the reputation of being the most fiercesome tribe on the frontier while the other was known to be the friendliest.

After the fourth dance Elk At Dawn motioned and slipped out of the lodge the same way he had entered.

Zach held the hide up so Bluebird could pass under, and she gave him such a strange look that he feared he had done something grievously wrong. Outside, stars filled the firmament, and a cool breeze from the northwest fanned his long hair.

The three youngsters strolled toward Bird Rattler's lodge, so alike in dress and appearance that a casual onlooker would have assumed they were three young Blackfeet.

"You have not answered my father yet, Stalking Coyote," Elk At Dawn unexpectedly signed.

Zach was slow to reply. "I have not made up my mind. It is all too soon. I have only been here a few sleeps."

"My father does you a high honor," Elk At Dawn signed. "I do not see why you are slow to accept. And my friends all agree with me."

Bluebird gave her brother a light shove. "Let him alone!" she chided. "If you were lost, among strangers, your heart would be as sorrowful as his."

Elk At Dawn grinned and signed mockingly, "Stalking Coyote's Shadow! Stalking Coyote's Shadow! Stalking Coyote's Shadow!"

Squealing, Bluebird delivered a slap that would have made her sibling's head ring but Elk At Dawn skipped nimbly aside and ran off, calling her new nickname aloud over and over. She muttered in her own tongue, then glanced at Zach and signed, "All brothers are idiots! I do not know one girl who does not agree with me."

"I might have a sister of my own soon," Zach signed, then stopped, the uncertainty eating at his insides like a handful of tiny ravenous shrews.

"I would love to be your sister," Bluebird signed brightly. "But I know that I am not the one you are thinking about."

They neared Bird Rattler's lodge with its promise of light and warmth and caring and Zach abruptly wanted nothing to do with it. Veering off, he made for the plain, planning to spend time alone to sort his thoughts. An elbow brushed his and he found Bluebird keeping pace. "You should go back," he signed. "The air is chill."

"Am I a baby that I can not stand a little wind?" she shot back.

"I would not be good company."

"You can not possibly be worse company than my own brother," Bluebird responded, "and if I can endure his, I can tolerate yours."

Halting, Zach placed a hand on her arm and nearly jumped when a tingling jolt coursed through him clear down to his toes. She seemed to feel the same sensation because she voiced a little, "Ahhh!" and took a step back as if she'd been bitten by a black widow spider.

"I am sorry," Zach signed. "I do not know what caused that."

"It is as my father says," Bluebird replied. "You have powerful good medicine."

"Your father said that about me?"

"And much more. He thinks you will grow up to become a mighty warrior of great benefit to your tribe. I heard him say, 'The Shoshones's loss is our gain.' He has seldom been so impressed by a boy."

"Incredible," Zach said in English, and resumed walking until he stood outside the border of pale light cast by the lodges. He welcomed the darkness. It closed around him like a sable garment, seeming to shut his cares and woes out like a robe that kept the cold from him on a bitter winter's day.

Twisting, Zach admired the celestial spectacle, a habit he had picked up from his father who was enamored of lying out late on any given summer's night and gazing long and thoughtfully at the stars. Zach had once asked why his pa did such a thing, and Nate had answered, "To try and figure it all out, son. To try and figure it all out." Zach still had no clear idea of what his pa had been talking about.

Bluebird primly folded her hands at her waist and stared at his profile. "I do not want to upset you any more than you are already, but if you would care to talk about the things that have been bothering you I would be very glad to listen."

The blissful moment of inner peace was gone. "I would not know where to begin," Zach lied.

"With your family would be the logical place."

Zach looked at her. Women, his father had once told him, had a keen insight into the innermost nature of things and people. They often pretended to be silly and shallow when in truth they were more perceptive sometimes than men. Now here was this snip of a girl seeing into the secret depths of his soul, proving his father right once again. "I miss them," he signed frankly.

"I do not blame you."

"My heart is torn in half," Zach continued,

the emotional wall he had erected beginning to crumble. "It would be different if I knew for sure they had been rubbed out. But I do not." He gazed forlornly southward. "For all I know, they might be scouring the area around the Yellowstone for me. Or one or both of them might be laid up somewhere, hurt and dying, needing me. Yet I am stuck here."

"They are not anywhere near the river," Bluebird signed, and swiftly lowered her hands as if she had blundered in revealing the information.

"How can you be certain?" Zach demanded.

Bluebird hesitated. "I should not be telling you this," she signed. "My father wanted to do it when the time was right." She bit her lip, then continued. "He sent men to hunt for your parents the first day you came to our village and they have been searching ever since. Each evening they send someone to report. I am sorry to say that so far they have not found a single sign."

Her use of the word 'hunt' rekindled Zach's dormant fears about the Blackfeet. "Why is he doing this?" he asked, worried Bird Rattler was going to capture his folks, torture them, and rub them out.

"It was to be his secret," Bluebird signed with reluctance. "He hoped to be able to take you back to them."

Zach was flabbergasted. Fortunately he was using his hands to communicate. "He would do that for me? Why?"

"He feels very sorry for you. When he was about your age he lost his father."

Once again Zach was jarred by the gulf

between his ingrained notions of the Blackfeet and how they really were. "I will not let on you told me," he assured the girl. "And I am very grateful to your father."

"He is the most wonderful of men."

"I feel the same way about my father."

Minutes elapsed and neither moved or signed. Zach fidgeted, uncomfortable. He had the feeling something was expected of him but no idea what it might be.

"I must be honest with you," Bluebird signed at length. "I would be very happy to have you live in our lodge. I like you very much."

"And I like you."

"My mother says I care for you too much."

This was new territory and Zach floundered, unsure of the proper response or action. "I did not think it possible to care for anyone too much," he signed.

"Come," Bluebird signed, turning. "Let us walk together a while."

Zach would rather have stayed where they were but she was already strolling along the perimeter of the light, delicate hands clasped under her chin. He caught up and leaned close so she could see his fingers when he signed, "We must not be gone too long. Your father and mother will worry."

"Not very much. I am a long way from becoming a woman."

Puzzled by the statement, Zach did what all men do when flustered by women: he changed the subject. "How long have your people camped at this spot?"

"Two moons," Bluebird disclosed. "In anoth-

er moon we will strike camp and head northwest to the mountains for a council with the
Piegans and the Bloods."

A ripple of despair flowed through Zach. Once
the Blackfeet left, any chance he had of seeing
his folks again was gone for good. He owed it
to his parents to escape before then.

Bluebird did not notice his agitation. "The
council will be a long one," she had gone on.
"There is much the three tribes must talk over.
And there is a grievance my father must lay at
the feet of the Piegans." She laughed. "I wish I
could listen in on that meeting!"

"Why?" Zach asked, not really caring.

"It concerns Cream Bear. I believe you have
met him?"

"Yes. I tried to poke his eyes out with a
spear."

"It is just as well you did not. He has enough
problems with his new wife. Six moons ago he
traded nine fine horses and a rifle to a Piegan
for her, and she has made his life miserable
every moment since." Bluebird laughed gaily.
"Adults! They can be so silly."

"So what does Cream Bear intend to do?"
Zach inquired to keep the conversation going
while racking his brains for a way of slipping
from the village unnoticed.

"He wants to give her back to the Piegan who
sold her and have his horses and rifle returned.
He claims the Piegan deceived him by saying
she would be an obedient wife and that she
knew how to cook and sew and tend horses
well. The truth is that she hisses at Cream Bear
like an angry snake all the time, burns his food

at every meal, and when she sews his clothes, they soon fall apart."

"Can she tend horses at least?"

"She is as capable there as she is at everything else. So far she has lost three of them."

"I am glad she is not my wife," Zach joked, and wondered why Bluebird laughed longer and louder than was called for.

"Cream Bear has had enough of her. If he had not given so much, he would have cast her out of his lodge long ago. She would surely starve to death because no one else would take her in. Not even my father, and he is the kindest of men."

"Why does she act the way she does?"

Bluebird stopped and faced him to respond. Abruptly, she pointed upward and cried out in the Blackfoot tongue.

Tilting his head back, Zach spied a shooting star blazing across the heavens. He longed to be like it, to be able to fly wherever he wanted to go. Had he the power, he would streak straight into the arms of his folks.

"Do you see that?" Bluebird signed. "It goes to the northwest, the same direction we must go when we break camp. The medicine men will take it as a good omen."

For a strange and fascinating moment, as Zach gazed on her awestruck features, he was struck by her beauty and felt an almost irresistible urge to kiss her. He'd never experienced anything like it before. The urge startled him, and he drew back, afraid of doing a deed guaranteed to see him parted from his hair.

Bluebird had eyes only for the shooting star

and gazed longingly at the sky long after it had disappeared. "Our lives are a lot like that," she signed.

Zach failed to see any comparison but refrained from saying so in order not to offend her. He scanned the village, saw some of the camp dogs frolicking and yipping at one another. Bird Rattler's lodge was much farther away than he had figured. "We should start back," he signed. "I do not want your parents mad at me."

"I suppose you are right," Bluebird signed, patently disappointed.

Their shoulders touched now and again as they walked, and Zach was sure she did it on purpose because when he moved slightly to the right she did the same. "Thank you for listening to me," he told her.

"I wish I could do more," Bluebird replied.

Suddenly Zach thought he heard the rustle of grass off in the night. Automatically he stepped between the girl and the prairie to protect her in case a wild animal or worse prowled nearby. "Did you hear that?"

"A rabbit, perhaps. Or a coyote."

"Or a bear. Or an enemy warrior."

Bluebird giggled. "Do you always expect the worst?"

"My father taught me to always expect the best but be prepared for the worst," Zach clarified. "Only a fool lets down his guard in the wilderness."

"Grizzly Killer must be a very wise man."

The reminder added fuel to Zach's sadness and he walked on, into the dim glow of the outermost lodge. He deliberately kept his face to the plain so she couldn't see his face. Blue-bird, though, tugged on his sleeve. He had to plaster a smile on his lips and swung around to see her hands move.

"I am so sorry for you," she signed.

"Do not be. I will see my father again. My mother also."

"If the situation were reversed, I do not know if I would have your confidence." Bluebird glanced in all directions, then reached out to clasp his hand and give it a gentle squeeze.

Zach was taken unawares. She had no sooner touched him than her hand was gone, giving him no time to react.

Just then, from the ring of darkness, came a womanly titter. Zach and Bluebird stopped. From out of the grass strolled a young warrior and his sweetheart, hand in hand. They walked past, the warrior giving Zach a knowing wink and his sweetheart patting Bluebird on the head. In moments they were gone among the lodges, the woman's titter wafting on the wind.

"I would like to be her," Bluebird signed.

"Let us hurry," Zach said, doing just that.

A pair of night-singers riding double on horse-back appeared, their melodious voices matched in perfect harmony. The man handling the reins stopped and leaned down, regarding Bluebird critically. He addressed her in their tongue.

"Use sign for the benefit of our guest," Blue-bird responded, her hands moving stiffly as if she was annoyed. "And to answer your question, Raven Wing, yes, my father knows I am out this late and does not object."

The rider studied Zach. "You must be trustworthy, boy. But I would never let my daughter out without a chaperon at Bluebird's age." Clucking to his horse, he rode off and the two men took up their song where they had left off.

Bluebird sniffed, then walked faster.

Zach wondered if he would be in trouble for going off alone with her. Engrossed in his thoughts, he didn't notice the lodge in their path until he nearly blundered into it. On its side had been painted the likeness of a large white bear. From within issued the shrill voice of a woman in a language Zach understood, and it was the very last language he expected to hear in a Blackfoot village.

"Don't like the way I cook your venison! So what? You can choke on it for all I care, you miserable red devil! You and all your kind should be wiped off the face of the earth, just like President Andrew Jackson wanted to do!"

Stunned, Zach gaped at Bluebird, who apparently guessed why and signed, "Oh. I forgot to tell you. That woman Cream Bear bought from the Piegans is white."

Chapter Fourteen

Nate King could have drawn his butcher knife or tomahawk and sprung to meet the threat of the enraged Pawnee warrior named Red Rock there on the bank of the river by the Pawnee village, but he didn't. He stood calmly, arms folded, as the brave stepped up to him and waved a knife in his face. And he could be so composed because he knew that members of a Bear Society were renowned not only for their skill in combat but also for their integrity and character. A man of Red Rock's standing could no more murder someone who would not fight back than he could slay a tribal member in cold blood. The brave was bluffing, trying to scare Nate into leaving. Or so Nate hoped as he looked the Pawnee in the eyes and refused to be cowed.

Mole On The Nose settled the matter by

sliding between them and gently pushing the warrior backward while speaking in a soothing tone. Red Rock lowered his knife and glowered at Nate, then gestured in disgust, wheeled, and stormed into the village.

White Calf seemed well pleased. He nodded once, clapped Nate on the back, and motioned. "Let us go. I will prepare your breakfast, Sky Walker," he signed.

Nate pointed at Mole On The Nose. "I want to talk to him," he signed.

"Why?" White Calf replied suspiciously.

"It is proper for visitors to pay their respects to the chief," Nate signed, which was the truth. Usually a newcomer was treated to a fine meal at a formal supper and introduced to lesser chiefs, medicine men, and others of influence.

"There is no need to trouble yourself," White Calf signed. "I will talk to him for you. Think of me as your spokesman for all your dealings with my people."

The oily smile the medicine man used to accent his remark galled Nate. "I do not need a spokesman," he signed testily. "I am perfectly capable of speaking for myself." So saying, he stepped up to the chief and made the sign for 'friend'.

Mole On The Nose had witnessed the exchange in silent contemplation. Now he glanced at the medicine man and said something that caused White Calf to turn scarlet and clench his fists. Then Mole On The Nose appraised Nate a few moments. "I am pleased to make your acquaintance, Sky Walker," he signed.

"And I, yours," Nate replied. "I was hoping

to smoke a pipe with you last night but did not have the opportunity."

"That can be remedied this night. I invite you to my lodge for supper. And I will also invite the leading men of my people, that they might see for themselves whether White Calf speaks the truth about you."

Now Nate was the suspicious one. "What has he been saying about me?"

"That you are our friend, that you are here to help us, that the Sioux will pay for their savagery with much blood and many scalps."

Nate didn't understand the significance of the reference to the Sioux but he filed it at the back of his mind for future consideration and cut to the quick. "Then White Calf has spoken with a straight tongue. I am a friend of the Pawnees, as I proved just now by saving one of your women from the bear."

The chief gazed at the slain beast. "I have heard of men killing bears with only a knife or tomahawk, but until I saw it with my own eyes I did not really believe anyone could do so." He swung toward Nate. "There is a rumor you have done the same thing to grizzlies."

"I have," Nate verified. "It is not something I would like to make a habit of. They are very hard to kill." He thought the chief would laugh at his jest, or at the very least crack a grin. Yet Mole On The Nose only appeared more somber.

"I must keep reminding myself you are not like us, not like normal men at all."

"There you are wrong," Nate begged to differ. "Deep down we are not all that different."

"Do you have a heart like we do?"

"Of course," Nate signed, surprised by the silly question.

"A brain?"

"Yes."

"Do you bleed when wounded, thirst when long without water, go hungry when without food?"

"All those things I do," Nate signed.

The chief digested this. "Even so, you come from somewhere else, a land we can never visit in this life. You are as different from us as night is from day. And while it pains me to say so, I must agree with Red Rock. You had no business coming here. You should have stayed among your own kind."

Nate would not have taken the chief for a bigot. In his travels he'd met many Indians who despised him simply on the basis of the color of his skin. Even among the Shoshones there were some who resented his adoption into the tribe and disliked his union with Winona. "I am sorry to hear you say so," he signed. "I hoped I could count on you as a friend."

Mole On The Nose did not sign anything for a while. "I will try to be your friend, Sky Walker," he mentioned finally, "but I am first and foremost devoted to the welfare of my people. If your coming will cause them hardship I can never look on you as other than you are."

"I have no intention of causing the Pawnees any grief."

"Good. Until tonight." Mole On The Nose started to leave, then indicated the medicine man. "You may bring this one with you. He knows how to find my lodge."

No sooner did the chief get out of earshot than White Calf was at Nate's side. "Why did you do that, Sky Walker? Why have yourself invited to the lodge of your enemy?"

"He does not trust me. That is all."

"You are wrong," White Calf insisted. "He dislikes you as much as Red Rock but he is more dangerous because he is the most influential. Tonight he will fill your belly and pretend to be your friend when all the while he will be looking for a way to turn the people against you."

Nate couldn't conceive of the elderly chief committing such an act and signed as much.

"Only because you do not know him as well as I do," White Calf said. "He rules our people with an iron fist, and anyone who disagrees with him is made to suffer. For many years he and I have been at each other's throats because he resents anyone having as much power as he does. Many times he has tried to bring me down but so far I have held my own. My medicine is more powerful than his."

Could it be? Nate mused. He had difficulty imagining Mole On The Nose as a tyrant but he had known it to happen. Some chiefs became so full of themselves they lorded it over their people like medieval feudal lords.

"You must keep a rein on your tongue and your eyes sharp tonight," White Calf warned. "Do not say anything he can use against you. Trust no one other than those I say you can trust."

Nate made no response. In his book trust

had to be earned. He would be on his guard against treachery, sure enough, but that included treachery from the medicine man.

Several warriors had gathered close at hand, men Nate remembered as being in White Calf's band when they found him. White Calf gave them instructions and they went over to the black bear and began removing the hide, their knives flashing in the sunlight. "I will have a fine robe made for you," the medicine man signed.

The last thing Nate needed was a robe and he was going to say as much when an idea occurred to him. "That would be nice of you," he said. The bear had been in its prime, its coat lustrous and thick. Given its huge size, the robe was bound to be extraordinary, and quite valuable.

"Would you care to eat now?" White Calf asked.

"Lead the way."

Village life was returning to normal. Smoke from cooking fires wafted from every lodge. Children were outside playing. Some of the warriors were going through simple rituals to greet the new day.

Nate shrugged off the many stares thrown his way, foremost among them the ill-disguised disdain of Red Rock and a small group of warriors standing with him. Fellow members of the Bear Society, Nate figured. He smiled at them but he might as well have been smiling at figures carved from stone for all the effect it had.

On nearing the medicine man's lodge, Nate

slowed. He wasn't about to eat anything in there, not while the rank odor lingered. Since White Calf had been waiting on him hand and foot, he decided to test how far he could push by signing, "I will take my breakfast out here in the sun. The same with all my meals from now on."

"As you wish."

Nate sat cross-legged as the medicine man turned to the entrance. He saw a pile of fresh bones near the lodge and recalled the snapping and growling the dogs had made when devouring the animal remains. He also recalled something else he had been meaning to ask about and clapped to get White Calf's attention.

"Yes, Sky Walker?"

"I saw a human skull in your lodge last night. What was it doing there?"

"I keep them all."

The implication brought Nate right back to his feet. "There is more than one?"

White Calf grinned and beckoned. Smirking like someone about to reveal the greatest treasure of all time, he walked to a nearby lodge much smaller than all the rest and paused outside the entrance. "There are some who criticize me for my collection. But I feel I honor those who have gone on to the spirit realm by preserving reminders of their sacrifice." Crouching, he motioned at the dark hole of an opening. "You may go in first."

Nate did not care to turn his back to the man for even a moment, but he did so now, his curiosity compelling him to squat and enter. As he straightened he saw a shaft of sunlight streaming in the smoke hole at the top, but nothing else. His eyes required half a minute to adjust to the murk, and when they did, he stepped back a pace and gasped, wishing they hadn't.

There were skulls everywhere. They had been arranged in a circle around the base and hung suspended from the ceiling by leather cords. Four had been placed on high stakes imbedded in the earth. At the very center of the lodge three skulls formed a short row, their empty sockets fixed on the doorway as if mocking those who entered with the answer to the eternal riddle.

"It is impressive, is it not?" White Calf signed, having slipped in beside Nate.

Nate fought back his revulsion and responded. "Where did they all come from?"

"Again you test me," White Calf grinned. "Perhaps one of them is the reason you came."

"Tell me!" Nate signed, and there must have been a reflection of his feelings in either his gesture or his demeanor because White Calf blinked a few times and began signing rapidly.

"Surely those who are on high know all about the offerings made to them? So you must know of our ceremonies, and of those who give their lives that our crops will grow and our people will live long and prosper. For many generations we Pawnees have been offering choice sacrifices to Tirawa, the God of gods, so that he will bless us with good fortune."

The man was talking about human sacrifice! Nate realized, and barely suppressed a shudder. There had been rumors about the Pawnees, but he'd always chalked the tall tales up to overactive imaginations. He scrutinized the pale assortment of horrid skulls, trying to assess if they were old or new. Most were the same modest size, leading him to sign, "Your people sacrifice children?"

White Calf laughed hysterically. "What do you take us for?" he rejoined. "We Pawnees are not savages! No, we do not offer children. We offer only the choicest of morsels to Tirawa." He smacked his lips as if at the prospect of a hearty meal. "Young women."

"My God!" Nate said aloud in English.

"Why do you appear upset?" White Calf inquired. "Our sacrifices must meet with approval or Tirawa would have sent us omens to let us know we should stop." Stepping to a skull impaled on a stake, he rubbed the smooth pate as a man might stroke the head of a lover. "At the last one I delivered the song," he signed proudly. "Would you care to hear?"

Nate was too confounded to answer, but that didn't stop the medicine man, who went on as if he had.

"It was the Morning Star ceremony, the most special of all. What a grand sight it must be from the clouds! At daybreak the woman is brought, naked, to the posts set up for the occasion. Wood is piled under her and lit. Then a warrior chosen for the occasion shoots her once, under the arms, with a sacred arrow. It is crucial for this warrior to have perfect aim, otherwise the whole ceremony is spoiled."

White Calf held the skull up to the sunlight, his eyes adoring it, and set it down reverently slowly. "Then we must work quickly, before the fire consumes her. All the males of age run over and put an arrow into her so that when they are done you can hardly find bare skin from her knees to her neck. Males not of age have someone shoot for them. Afterward the arrows are pulled out, except the first one."

A vivid, gruesome image of the victim, slumped over, blood pouring from scores of holes, made Nate want to retch. He looked at the medicine man, aghast, but White Calf was lost in the bliss of his recollection.

"The sacrifice is cut open by myself or another medicine man. We reach into her chest and can feel her warm blood gush over our hands. Swiftly we smear our face with it and step back so the women can strike her with sticks and spears to earn coup. When they are done, the song is sung, and our people pray to Tirawa to have compassion on us in the moons ahead and give us all we will need to multiply and grow strong."

White Calf raised his voice in a singsong chant while signing these words: "Life ends that life may go on. One dies for many that many flourish. From life, blood. From blood, life." Chest swelling with pride, he signed, "I created the poem myself. What do you think?"

"It is very fitting," Nate answered.

"A great moment in my life," White Calf said with evident regret that it had passed. "At the next Morning Star ceremony, Raven Beak will have the honor." Giving the skull on the stake a farewell pat, he turned. "Are you ready to leave?"

"I have seen all I need to."

Once out of the grotesque shrine, Nate asked, "How do you pick the woman to be offered to Tirawa? Do all those in the village draw lots?"

The medicine man chuckled. "Are we fools that we offer up our own women when we can capture a maiden from another tribe who is every bit as pleasing in Tirawa's sight?" He ticked off previous victims on his fingers. "Osage, Mandan, Arikaras, Kansas, Otos, Sioux, Cheyenne, Blackfeet, we have offered them all to our god at one time or another. Personally, I prefer maidens from the last three tribes. They fight like wild women until the last, defying us tooth and nail. Once a Blackfoot girl bit off the thumb of the medicine man binding her."

"How often do you sacrifice?" Nate had to know.

"The Morning Star ceremony is held once very twelve moons. There are lesser ceremonies at which we offer maidens if we have them on hand. Unfortunately, there usually is a shortage. Sometimes three, sometimes five times in twelve moons. It all depends."

"Do the other tribes know?"

"Some suspect but have no proof. If they did, they would all rise up against us at once and rub us out."

"I know of no other tribe that does this," Nate commented in sign. "Why do the Pawnees?"

"We always have," White Calf signed simply. "From the times of our ancestors we have made sacrifice to Tirawa and we have never been defeated in battle, never had our villages burned to the ground, never known famine or thirst." Close to his own lodge, he halted. "There is a tradition among us that once, back in the dawn times of all things, our people lived far, far to the south in a country that never grew cold, where there were snakes as long as ten men and a river as wide as the prairie, where there were no buffalo and the whole land was covered with trees. The tradition goes that we began to sacrifice in those times and have done so ever since." He looked at Nate. "But, of course, you already know all this."

The rumors Nate had heard had in no wise hinted at the full horror of the Pawnee practice, and Nate settled there and then on finding a way of bringing it to a halt. He didn't know how he could achieve it, but come hell or high water he would.

White Wolf hunkered to go into his own lodge. "So. You must be famished by now. How much deer meat would you like?"

"I am no longer hungry," Nate signed.

"Really? Well I am." The medicine man glanced at the skull lodge. "I am the same way after a ceremony. And just talking about a sacrifice makes me starved enough to eat the offering!" Laughing at his quip, he slipped within.

With new eyes Nate King gazed out over the Pawnee village. He saw the children scampering about, saw women cleaning utensils and shaking out bedding, saw warriors in idle conversation or mending weapons or tending horses, and thought of them sinking arrow after arrow into the quivering form of a helpless young maiden. It was all he could do not to rail at them, to open his mouth wide and scream sense into their blood–soaked brains.

Nate was no stranger to atrocities. He'd seen whites butchered by Indians, Indians butchered by whites. He'd seen the handiwork of the Blackfeet and their allies, seen a woman mutilated, seen a man mangled by buffalo. Yet those were acts committed in the fiery crucible of warfare or the normal consequences of living in the raw, brutal wilderness.

The Pawnee sacrifice of innocents was drastically different. It was the willful extinction of guiltless lives according to custom, a barbaric, outdated practice participated in by an entire people.

Nate couldn't understand why someone didn't speak out against it. Was there no one in the Pawnee nation with a conscience? No one who saw the great wrong they were doing for the vile abomination it really was? He gazed on the peaceful setting, at the scores of Pawnees busy with daily tasks, and instead of a tranquil village saw instead a pack of human wolves in idle repose, waiting for the next chance to bury their fangs in a new victim.

The rest of the day passed slowly. Nate spent most of the time pondering, as his mentor Shakespeare would put it, the 'human condition.' He strolled about the village under the watchful eyes of a pair of warriors no doubt sent by the medicine man to keep track of him. Twice he walked to the river to search fruitlessly for his pistol.

When the sun slipped into the western vault of the sky, Nate returned to the lodge. He no longer looked forward to the impending supper, and had no interest in getting to know Mole On The Nose better. He wanted nothing more than to be shy of the Pawnees. To that end, he plotted his next escape attempt.

White Calf stepped out dressed in his finest splendor. A red cap crowned his head. A wolf skin had been draped over his shoulders. His buckskins were new, his moccasins too, and both had been beaded lavishly. The first words from his hands were, "Are you hungry yet?"

Nate allowed as how he might be able to swallow a few bites.

"How you get by on so little food is a mystery to me," the medicine man signed. "Your appetites are not those of a human being, Sky Walker." He snickered slyly. "But why should they be?"

"Did I wear the guards out?" Nate asked.

A blank look came over White Calf. "What guards?"

"Do you take me for a simpleton?" Nate retorted. "All day I was followed by warriors, everywhere I went. And I resent it."

"I am sorry, but they protected you for your own good," White Calf signed. "You have seen for yourself that there are those who want to kill you. I do not intend to let that happen." He adjusted his cap. "Are you ready to go?"

"As ready as I will ever be."

The pounding of drums issued from a lodge they passed. Outside another a man and woman argued, a rare public display having to do with the woman's tardiness in fetching water. In front of yet another an older warrior carved up a freshly killed buck. "Sky Walker!" he signed on spying Nate. "I will give extra thanks to Tirawa tonight for your saving my granddaughter."

"That was a masterly stroke," White Calf signed when they had left the warrior behind. "More of my people have come around to our side. And when I am done, they will all look up to us with the respect we deserve."

Nate was about to explain that the encounter with the bear had been an accident when he noticed Red Rock and other men entering a lodge.

"The Bear Society," White Calf signed, his contempt transparent. "They are the ones you must watch out for. Should they be able to convince the people you are less than I say, your days will be numbered."

"Red Rock would like nothing better than to gut me," Nate agreed with the medicine man for once.

"It would be much worse, believe me."

"What can possibly be worse than dying?"

"How you die." White Calf stopped. "If Mole On The Nose and the Bear Society prevail, your skull will join the rest."

"What?"

"Why must you always pretend you do not know things? You are as aware as I am that our sacrifices do not always involve maidens." White Calf brushed at a bit of dust on one sleeve. "Sometimes we sacrifice men."

Chapter Fifteen

"Damnation! It's Blackfeet!" Bob Knorr bellowed in alarm as seven dusky riders sped toward the north shore of the Yellowstone. "Paddle like hell, Lane, or we're gone beaver!"

Shakespeare McNair could do nothing except lie there and watch the young trappers bend their shoulders, stroking powerfully, sending the canoes flying toward the south bank. His Hawken had been reloaded for him but he was too weak to pick it up and too woozy from his fever to hit anything beyond ten feet even if he could.

The Blackfeet bore down on the Yellowstone at a gallop. Oddly for them, they rode silently, airing none of the customary war whoops warriors incited themselves with.

Once the canoes passed the center of the river, Shakespeare slumped onto the blankets.

They were safe so long as they stayed out of rifle and bow range. And he couldn't see the Blackfeet plunging into the Yellowstone after them, not when the braves would be sitting ducks.

"This should be far enough," Lane cried to his companion as he steered the canoe up river. Resting the paddle on his thighs, he allowed the speed they had built up to drift them along as he picked up his rifle.

The Blackfeet reached the water's edge and trotted parallel to the Yellowstone. Two held rifles, the rest bows, arrows nocked to their sinew strings. They made no overt hostile gestures, another oddity.

"Why ain't they trying to pick us off?" Bob Knorr mused. "It's spooky the way they're just staring at us like that."

"They may be heathens but they're not dunderheads," Griffen said. "They know they can't get at us so they're putting the evil eye on us."

"Who are you trying to fool? Injuns can't hex worth a hoot."

A lean Blackfoot suddenly pumped his rifle in the air and yelled the same two words again and again.

"What's he doing that for?" Knorr asked. "Does his armpit itch, you reckon?"

"He want's something, but it beats me what," Griffen said.

Shakespeare leaned over, the better to hear. Wind whistled inside his head and thunder rumbled in his stomach. His mouth tasted bitter. He was sicker than he'd been in a coon's age and as helpless as a baby. Still, he could translate. "He wants you to go over to their side."

"Not in this life," Griffen said. "He must think we have rocks between our ears."

"Or else he figures we're greenhorns and we'll mistake them for friendlies," Knorr suggested.

The Blackfoot uttered a string of sentences, waving inland the whole time.

"Now what?" Griffen said.

"Maybe he's extending an invite for you to go meet his sister," Knorr said.

"No," Shakespeare interjected. "He wants us to go visit his village. He says it's important."

Lane and Bob both laughed, which had the effect of confusing the Blackfeet. "Sure!" Griffen declared. "Once we're there, the whole blamed tribe jumps us and has us hairless and skinless in three shakes of a dog's tail. No thank you."

Shakespeare saw the Blackfeet jabbering like chipmunks. He was as mystified as the younger men. Knowing how devious the Blackfeet could be, he chalked their bizarre antics up to a trick on their part, just as Lane believed.

Once again the lean Blackfoot shouted across the water, the same word a dozen times or more.

It was hard for Shakespeare to hear. The whistling in his head was now more in the nature of a howl. To compound matters, his vision swam periodically, rendering the shorelines as murky as the water under the canoe. "What's he saying now?" he asked.

"Wish I knew," Griffen said. "Doesn't sound like no red lingo I ever heard." He paused.

"Acker-eee-ing, I think it is."

"Something like that," Knorr concurred. "Makes no sense."

Shakespeare slumped, the last vestige of strength deserting him. It made no sense to him, either. Or did it? A vague feeling that he should know the phrase nipped at his consciousness, a persistent pricking that faded as his sentience did.

Abruptly, night replaced day. Shakespeare sluggishly opened his eyes to behold stars where the azure sky had been. In front of him came a series of light splashes, the dipping of a paddle into the Yellowstone. "Lane?" he said, his mouth crammed with cotton.

"Right here, McNair. It's close to midnight."

"The Blackfeet?"

"Must have got their hands on some whiskey. They never did attack, never fired off a single shot. For the better part of an hour they kept us company, taking turns saying those three words, like they were chanting or something. Ever hear of them doing anything so harebrained?"

"Never."

"How are you feeling?"

"Pain pays the income of each precious thing."

"Huh?"

"William S.," Shakespeare said.

"How can you think about him, the shape you're in?"

"I've been worse off."

"When?"

"Before I was born."

224

Griffen shifted, his skin a pale contrast to the darkness. "The fever must be tearing you up. You're making less sense than those Blackfeet. Rest easy, old-timer. We're making good time."

"Time," Shakespeare mumbled, the stars fading in and out. "I remember the first time Caesar put it on. T'was on a summer's evening, in his tent."

"You're raving, man. Go to sleep."

Shakespeare tried to organize the jumbled bits of scattered thoughts in his head into a coherent whole and could not. "Sleep," he repeated, tottering on the verge. "To sleep, perchance to dream."

"We've already heard that one. Please, McNair. You need the rest. We'll stop at first light and dress your wounds again. It's all we can do for the time being."

"Time again?" Shakespeare said. An elusive quote dangled in front of him and he snatched at it as would a starving man at a morsel of food. "My pulse, as yours, doth temperately keep time, and makes as healthful music. It is not madness that I have uttered." He sank deeper into the canoe. "Or at least it did once."

"Hush, will you?" Griffen urged.

Shakespeare tried to lift his head, was unable. "What if I do not?" he quoted. "As, indeed, I do not. Yet, for I know thou art religious, and hast a thing within thee called conscience, with twenty——." His voice trailed off as he slipped into the nether realm of disjointed dreams. He thought someone pulled the blanket tighter around him.

And then it was morning. Shakespeare

blinked, licked his dry lips. With a herculean effort he rose on one arm. The scenery was much the same, the river flowing a shade faster. Griffen and Knorr had to paddle harder to overcome the current. "We should stop so you can rest," he commented.

"Soon," Lane said. "Around the next bend, if memory serves, is a clear strip of sandy shore where we can see for miles around. No one can sneak up on us there."

Griffen's memory proved accurate but they were unable to land. As they sailed around the curve the shore hove into sight, and so did a large female grizzly and her two cubs lying at ease, sunning themselves. The mother shot up off the ground, growling fiercely. She came to the edge of the water, glaring at the two canoes as they drew abreast of her. Then, mouth wide, she plunged into the river in pursuit.

The two trappers paddled for all they were worth and for a few tense moments it seemed they would lose the race. They had already veered shoreward in anticipation of beaching the canoes. Consequently they were a mere twenty feet from the she-bear when she jumped in.

Shakespeare was nearest the beast. He fingered his Hawken, doubtful he could lift it. The grizzly narrowed the gap with astounding rapidity, plowing through the water as if it were nonexistent. Just when Shakespeare braced for the impact of her heavy body against the canoe, salvation came from an unlikely source.

The two cubs had bolted to the top of the adjacent bank and stood watching their mother's heroics. One of them chose the very instant she was about to reach her quarry to bawl in distress and the second heartily took up the refrain.

On hearing the cries, the mother bear stopped to look around. She saw her cubs were in no danger and turned back to destroy the interlopers, but the delay had cost her.

The canoes flew up the river out of reach, Griffen and Knorr laughing nervously at their narrow escape. Thereafter they stayed in the middle of the river until certain it was safe to venture onto shore.

The excitement had taken a severe toll on Shakespeare. He sank onto his side, one eye level with the top of the canoe, too enfeebled to so much as lift a hand. In this position he dozed, and when next he awakened, it was afternoon. Someone had propped him on his back so that he could see over the side and covered him with a blanket. Both canoes were making good headway even though Shakespeare could tell the trappers were fatigued.

Over the next several hours Shakespeare fluctuated between wakefulness and dreamland. Every time he opened his eyes it was to a new sight.

Once he saw a panther of considerable size. It had killed a deer on the south bank, devoured a portion, and was in the act of hiding the rest in the brush. On hearing them it looked up, let go of its prize, and darted into the vegetation.

Later there were two antelope swimming from south to north. They passed close to the canoes, nostrils flared, eyes wide in fear.

Griffen was of a mind to shoot one for supper but Knorr pointed out the pair were lean and sickly looking so they permitted both to swim on untouched.

A third time, toward evening, Shakespeare saw several beaver at work on the north bank. The country on either hand was more broken than previously, with intermittent low hills. The bottoms had narrowed. Now there was more high grass and reeds bordering the river, and less timber.

The next time McNair awakened, the stars were out. He knew the trappers had hardly rested in over twenty-four hours, all on his account. His lips and mouth were moist, as if someone had recently trickled water down his throat. "Griffen?" he croaked.

"Back among the living, are you?" Lane responded. "How are you holding up?"

"My innards are on fire," Shakespeare confessed.

"I know. Which is why I've been giving you some water every so often and moistening your forehead. It's the best I can do until we rejoin our companions."

"How soon, you reckon?"

"It depends on if we can hold to this pace. Maybe tomorrow evening provided all goes well."

"When will Knorr and you sleep?"

"We won't. We've decided to go straight through."

"I'm that bad off, am I?"

"Hell, man. Anyone else would have been worm food long ago. What keeps you going I'll never know."

Shakespeare was inclined to do more talking but his body had the final say and he slept again. Feverish phantasms inhabited his dreams, creatures and figures unlike any ever witnessed by mortal man. Bears with two heads, beaver with claws and fangs, and more. Then she appeared, and he stirred, tossing fitfully. Long ago he'd shut his mind to anything having to do with her to spare himself the anguish. Now, seeing her beautiful face hovering over his, as young and vital as she had been the day they were forced to part, he felt the old gnawing pangs and reached out to touch her. "Little Doe!" he said in his dream. "Little Doe! What happened to you? How did your life turn out?"

Little Doe's cherry lips moved but Shakespeare couldn't hear her voice. A tear trickled from her right eye and rolled slowly down her face. He tried caressing her cheek but her features shimmered like the reflection on a lake and began to break apart. "No!" he cried. "Not again! Come back!"

The image wavered, fading in and out. "You were the first!" Shakespeare shouted in his dream. "You were always special! Always so dear!" He snatched at the ethereal face and it suddenly blinked out, leaving a black, gaping hole which in turn resolved into the nighttime sky. A hand was on his arm.

"McNair? McNair? Snap out of it, old coon! You're having a bad dream!"

Perspiration drenched Shakespeare. A shadowy form was bent over him. "Lane? Sorry."

"No need to be. Had me worried for a while the way you were thrashing around. I was

229

afeared you'd upend the canoe." Griffen placed a palm on McNair's forehead. "What language was that you were using?"

"Language?"

"You were calling out in your sleep. Injun tongue, I'd say. But none of those I know, like Flathead or Crow. Damned if it didn't sound more like Blackfoot. Do you know their tongue?"

"A little," Shakespeare said.

"Is it okay to go on?"

"Be my guest. I'll be fine now. Thanks." Shakespeare folded his hands over old William S. and sadly gazed at the darkened landscape. Seeing those Blackfeet had dredged up recollections better left alone. Or maybe it was just the end was near and his mind was coming to terms with all the unanswered questions in his life. She was one of them. Their separation had plagued him for years afterward, and he had often wondered if she had found another man to love. In morbid moments he liked to flatter himself that she had been so heartbroken she had mourned herself to death. But Little Doe had been too fond of living and too full of life to pass so meekly into the next world.

Sleep shortly claimed him. When his leaden eyelids cracked open, the sun grinned down at him. And a putrid stench clung to the air like the reeking clothes of a scab covered beggar. For a few harrowing seconds he thought the smell came from him. Then he looked up and saw the buffalo, or what was left of them.

On the north side rose a cliff one hundred and fifty feet high, the rock wall sheer and unbroken. At its base were scattered the fragments of hundreds of buffalo carcasses. Large bones jutted from the surface at scores of points, mainly rib cages and legs, forming a sort of buffalo graveyard with the ribs resembling outlandish tombstones. The shaggy brutes had been stampeded over the rim by Indians and finished off while they writhed and kicked in the shallow water. Some had probably drowned.

Along the shore lolled scores of wolves, all fat and lazy. Not a one bolted at the approach of the canoes. Tongues drooping, they stared in listless curiosity at the white men.

"It's a good thing there aren't more cliffs in this country," Griffen remarked, "or the silly savages would wipe out all the buffalo there are."

"Just like we're doing with the beaver," Shakespeare wanted to say, but did not make the attempt. For the longest while he lay there listening to the swash of paddles, the rippling of water. The hot sunlight added to his distress, leaving him as weak as a kitten.

A flurry of yelling brought him around for the umpteenth time. Shakespeare heard snorting and grunting and more splashing than a thousand paddles could make. He looked, and it seemed as if the river had sprouted an endless sea of horns and humps and tails. Buffaloes, hundreds upon hundreds of the dumb animals, were swarming across the river forty yards away. Both canoes had stopped and floated next to one another.

"Damn contrary cusses," Bob Knorr grumbled. "They would pick now to decide the grass is greener on the south side."

"It'll be half an hour before they're done," Griffen predicted wearily, then yawned. "Maybe we should go ashore and rest until then."

"Nothing doing," Knorr said. "We're both plumb tuckered out. We lie down and we won't be waking up for two days."

Shakespeare swallowed to relieve his parched throat, then dipped a hand into the water and cupped a handful to his mouth. It was tepid and tasted faintly of mud. The buffalo must have stirred up the sediment for quite a ways.

"What are you doing, old coon?" Griffen said. "Don't be drinking that stuff. Here." He passed back a half-filled water skin. "Spring water from the last one we stopped at. Need me to lift it for you?"

"Let's find out." Shakespeare tried, really tried, but he had the energy of a dead man. It was Knorr who moved his canoe alongside and solicitously held the skin so Shakespeare could drink until his thrist was slaked. As Knorr handed it to Griffen, Shakespeare reached for the top of the blanket covering his chest.

"No," Knorr said, grabbing his hand. "You don't want to see."

"It's that bad?"

"Worse. We're dressing it every chance we get but I'm afraid it's infected."

"Wish we were in Flathead country," Griffen said. "They have herbal cures for every ailment under the sun."

"Most tribes do," Shakespeare said, thinking of the many times he'd been made well by the varied natural remedies Indians had perfected out of sheer necessity. Most were remarkably effective, and he'd often thought it a shame that white men looked with such disdain on Indian cures when so much benefit could be derived from them.

The buffalo continued to pour across the Yellowstone. Bulls, cows, and calves held to a straight course, following in the wake of the animals in front. It was the same when Indians drove the great brutes over cliffs. The warriors would surround the herd on three sides and then make a tremendous racket, forcing the animals to flee toward the precipice. Once the lead bulls plunged over the brink, the rest followed, unable to see where they were going.

Shakespeare slept once more. His sense of time became distorted. Once or twice he revived, briefly. Then he was lying flat on his back on the ground and there were many voices around him instead of only two and knowing fingers were probing the extent of his wounds. He gazed up into kindly eyes framing a beard nearly as white as his own. "You must be Jacob," he said, his voice like the grating of gravel over tin.

"That I be, friend," said the other. "It's good for these old eyes to see an old beaver like yourself. Us Mountainee Men have to stick together."

"Lane and Bob?"

"Sleepin' like babes, they are, and I can't blame them, not when they paddled three solid days and nights with little rest to get you here."

"Can you patch me up?"

"You cut right to the gristle," Jacob said. "And you deserve a straight answer. So brother to brother, I'm lettin' you know it's up to you whether you live or not. I can clean the wounds, which will hurt like nothin' has ever hurt you before, and then sew you up so that your chest will look like a lady practiced her sewin' on you while drunk, but whether you live or not is up to you."

"That's honest enough," Shakespeare said, trying to smile. A cool breeze fanned his chest and goose bumps broke out all over his skin.

"I don't have much to kill the pain," Jacob said. "A little whiskey for when we begin, and then you'll have to clamp your teeth down on a piece of wood and hope I don't have to carve out the splinters in the morning."

"When?"

"Neither of us are gettin' any younger." Jacob rose. "I'll fetch my tools and be right back."

The moon took the place of the mountain man's face. Shakespeare stared at the shining crescent, speculating on whether it would be the last one he ever saw. If so, he really had no cause to complain. His Maker had accorded him a long, eventful life. He'd seen the country from one end to the other, gone places no white man had ever visited. He'd been married more times than most, sired children and had a dozen grandchildren, all scattered from Canada to Mexico. In short, he'd lived life to the fullest, and when all was said and done what more could any man ask?

Shakespeare did have one regret. He disliked

giving up the ghost without learning the fate of the King family. They were closer to him than many of his own kin, and he shuddered to think they had all been rubbed out in one fell swoop.

The moon was blotted out by Jacob's head. "About ready," he announced. "These boys are going to help me."

A pair of sturdy trappers knelt on either side of Shakespeare, clamping his arms in grips of iron. Another pair took hold of his legs in similar fashion .

"I can't have you floppin' around while I'm pokin' and cuttin'," Jacob said. "Wouldn't want to nick your vitals by mistake."

"Let's just get it over with." Shakespeare said. His head was lifted, then whiskey seeped between his parted lips. Molten lava cascaded down his throat, breaking him into a coughing spasm that went on and on. A stout length of wood was placed between his teeth and he bit down as hard as he could.

The firelight glinted off the blade of a Green River knife. "I want to apologize in advance for all the misery this will cause you," Jacob said softly. "If you care to scream, feel free."

Shakespeare McNair shook his head. He'd always been able to tolerate more pain than most, and he wasn't about to turn into a whiner at his age. He would control the pain, just as he did that time the Arikaras put a ball into his gut and that time a panther tore open his thigh from groin to knee.

Unfortunately, Shakespeare turned out to be wrong. He handled the probing, he handled the cutting off of thin slices of infected flesh. But when Jacob commenced stitching him up, inserting a thick needle time and time again into his skin while pressing his wounds closed, it surpassed all pain he had ever known. Pain filled him from top to bottom. Pain oozed from every pore in his body. Pain became the sole focus of his existence. The terrible agony was more than he could bear, and in time he did hear someone screaming and was not at all surprised to recognize his own voice.

Chapter Sixteen

It was several more days before Zach King saw the white woman. He'd spent most of the time in the company of Elk At Dawn and Bluebird, particularly Bluebird. Whenever she was free of chores they went for longs strolls around the village or for short distances out on the prairie. The Blackfeet became so accustomed to the pair of them being together that after a while no one made any wiseacre comments.

Zach did some adjusting of his own. As time passed and he realized beyond a shadow of a doubt the Blackfeet had no intention of killing him, he found himself growing more and more at home. Life among the Blackfeet was little different than life among the Shoshones. Oh, they dressed differently and held different ceremonies, but essentially the two tribes were much alike.

Only two things marred Zach's happy inter-
lude with Bluebird. The first was her father.
Bird Rattler had not pressed him, but Zach
knew the chief expected an answer soon about
his adoption. While Zach was honored, he had
no intention of staying in the village much
longer.

Not once had Zach given up on the notion of
finding his folks again. By rights he knew he
should have snuck off already, but he couldn't
seem to bring himself to leave Bluebird, which
in itself upset him immensely. His parents
should come first, he repeatedly told himself.

Then there was the matter of Honey Hair, the
wife of Cream Bear. Upon learning about her,
Zach had plied Bluebird and her brother with
questions and learned that the white woman
had been stolen by the Piegans from somewhere
high in the Rockies. He'd kept an eye on Cream
Bear's lodge, hoping for a glimpse of her. And
on the third day, fortune smiled on him.

Zach had risen early, as was his custom.
Bluebird was already up, helping her mother
fix breakfast. Zach smiled at them and went
outside. As he stretched and faced the rising
sun, he saw a blonde woman in a buckskin
dress emerge from Cream Bear's teepee and
head to the stream for water.

Casting a glance around to be sure no one was
watching, Zach ran toward the stream from a
different angle. He'd been there many times,
knew the trail by heart. At a spot where it wound
through high brush he crouched and waited for
the woman to show. As she came toward him, he
examined her face. Her features were pretty—

although not quite as pretty as Bluebird's—but lined with sorrow. Her shoulders slumped far too low for someone her age, and her gait was that of someone twice her years. He waited until she was close, then said in English, "Hello, miss. We need to talk."

Honey Hair nearly tripped over her own feet, she stopped so quickly. Her hand flew to her mouth and she dropped her waterbag. "Who ?" she exclaimed.

Zach rose from cover, checking the trail to insure no one else was on it. He gestured for the woman to follow him, saying, "I'm Zachary King, ma'am. I've been captured same as you. Please come with me. Hurry, before we're seen together."

The woman just stood there, shocked witless. "You speak English," she said, as one dazed. "Yet you don't look white." The light of intelligence returned and she inspected him carefully. "No, you're only part Injun. I can see that now."

"Please!" Zach insisted. Women used the trail at all hours of the day, most frequently during early morning and late afternoon. At any second they might be discovered.

Honey Hair nodded, then scooped up the water-bag. "I'm sorry. It startled me hearing English again after so long."

Zach made bold to take her hand and led her into the brush. Hunkering down out of earshot of anyone who might pass by, he looked into her lake-blue eyes. "I've already introduced myself proper-like, as pa says to do," he whispered. "But I don't know your name."

"Abigail," the woman said. "Abigail Griffen." Unexpectedly, tears gushed into her eyes. Her chin fell to her chest and she cried silently, her whole body shaking.

Zach was speechless. He'd had no idea how she might react, but certainly not like this. Under ordinary circumstances he would have let her cry herself out before prying into why, but time was of the essence. If they delayed too long, someone would come looking for them. And they mustn't be seen together or they would arouse suspicion.

"Whatever is the matter, ma'am?" Zach asked, touching her shoulder. "Why are you blubbering like a kid?"

Abigail Griffen stopped as abruptly as she had started. Sniffling, she dabbed at her eyes with her sleeve. "Again, I'm sorry. It's been ages since I said my own name. And I've been holding so much in for so long," Abigail coughed sheepishly. "What did you say your name is again?"

"Zachary King. You can call me Zach."

The first trace of a smile touched her mouth. "Fair enough, Zach. And you can call me Abby." She bent down. "How did you come to be here? Where are you from? Where's your family?"

"I'd like to tell you everything but we don't have the time," Zach emphasized. "What I need to know is whether you want to escape from the Blackfeet as badly as I do?"

"Escape!" Somehow Abby made that one word reflect all the hope and longing a human heart can hold. "Oh, my."

"I mean to make a break for the Yellowstone the first chance I have. Do you want to come?"

"Oh, my."

"What's wrong?" Zach asked, perplexed by her amazement. "I thought you'd want to go. Not that I'm nosy or anything, but I happened to hear you yelling at your husband the other night and it was plain you're not very fond of Indian life." He waited for her answer, which came in a most bewildering form.

Abigail suddenly embraced him, hugging him tight to her bosom and swinging him from side to side. "Oh, you sweet, wonderful boy, you! You have no idea! No idea!"

"Is that a yes or a no?" Zach tried to say, but his face was pressed so tightly against her chest his question came out all muffled. He could barely breathe. Putting his hands on her shoulders, he pushed back and sucked in air. "Please, ma'am. This is no time to be acting silly. Escaping is a serious matter."

"So it is," Abby agreed, sparkling with new-found vigor. "And aren't you the mature one for your tender years." She started to giggle, then froze on hearing low voices from the vicinity of the trail. Reminded of their peril, she paled and took his hand. "Goodness, I'm acting the fool! Very well. Yes, I want to escape. I'd about given up hope of ever doing so." She glanced at the plain. "Before I came to live with the Blackfeet, I was with the Piegans."

"I know."

"You do? Well, they lived up north a far piece. Or was it northwest? Either way, it was too far for me to try to make it to civilization on my own. My sense of direction is pitiful. Doubt I'd last two days out there by myself."

"Don't you worry none. Thanks to my folks, I can get around right fine. All we have to do is work out the best time to leave. And that won't be easy."

"No, it won't," Abby whispered. "The brave I'm living with won't let me out of his sight for more than fifteen minutes unless he's off hunting or with a war party, and then he sends his mother over to stay with me."

"We'll find a way," Zach said confidently. He thought he heard a shout in the village. "This is taking too long. We need to meet again to talk some more."

"Where and when?"

"Do you come for water every afternoon?"

"Have to. Cream Bear throws a tantrum if he doesn't have fresh water with his supper."

"I'll try to be here then. If I'm not, look for me again tomorrow morning."

"I will," Abby pledged. Impulsively, she took his hand in hers and squeezed. "And thank you, young man. You're a godsend in disguise. My sanity was on the verge of slipping, but now, thanks to you, I have real hope for the first time in years."

Zach was flabbergasted when she kissed him on the forehead. Water-bag over her arm, she hurried toward the trail. He went the opposite way and circled around so that he approached the village from the south.

Bluebird was outside the lodge. On seeing him she ran over. "Where have you been? We are ready to eat but my father has held off so you can join us."

"I went for a walk," Zach signed, and let it go at that. Inside the lodge the rest of the family waited. He took his seat, two places to the right of Bird Rattler, then signed, "Please forgive me. My mind wandered."

"Do not let it happen again, Stalking Coyote," the chief instructed, and smiled. "I am in a foul mood all day when I do not have my morning meal on time."

Thankfully, Indian meals were quite unlike their counterparts among civilized society. Had Zach been with a white family, they might have pestered him about where he had been. Indians, however, always ate in silence and reserved conversation for the end of the meal. Although to say the meal passed in silence is not quite right. Indians ate most food with their hands, gulping portions greedily and noisily, sucking soft edibles through their teeth, and drinking with loud hissing, slurping noises.

Zach had divided loyalties in that regard. His mother taught him to eat as her people the Shoshones did, and when visiting their tribe he ate as noisily as everyone else, which his father did not care for. That was because his father wanted him to always eat as quietly as a mouse, with his mouth shut, and to never speak with food in his mouth. So when at their cabin he did as his father requested, which bothered his mother. Sometimes, he'd decided long ago, there was no pleasing anyone.

Now, on finishing off a tasty cake, Zach smacked his lips to show his approval and leaned back on his hands, done. The chief regarded him intently.

"We must talk, Stalking Coyote."

Since no reply was required, Zach merely straightened. The moment he had dreaded was upon him.

"Since we first found you by the river, I have looked after you," signed Bird Rattler. "You impressed me with your courage, with your daring. My heart grew warm towards you. And so I offered to adopt you into my family, to make you as one of us."

"For which I was grateful," Zach signed when the Blackfoot paused.

"But not grateful enough," Bird Rattler said. "Most boys would have agreed right away. You have had more than enough sleeps to reach a decision, yet my eyes have not seen your hands sign the words I hoped to see. Why is that?"

Zach cleared his throat out of habit when all he had to do was raise his arms. He signed slowly, hoping to put off committing himself yet again. "A son cannot give up one father and take another lightly. Since I do not know if my natural father lives or has been rubbed out, I can not be untrue to him and become your son. Once I know, then I can. And let me add that White Grass was right when he told me there can be no higher honor than to be accepted as the son of Bird Rattler. You are a man my own father would be happy to call friend."

Bird Rattler had a reply ready. "All you have said is true. Your attitude is commendable in one so young. So it is with much sorrow that I must tell you your father is either no longer in this country or he is dead. Unknown to you, I sent warriors to search all the way to the river. They rode far and wide and found no trace of any whites except three trappers in canoes."

Zach perked up. He wondered if maybe his parents had lost their horses and made canoes to transport them up the Yellowstone. "Did they get a good look at these trappers?"

"Yes. All were men. Two were young whites, one with a brown beard, the other with no hair on his face. The third was a much older man with a beard as white as snow. He appeared to be very sick."

Zach's hopes were dashed. His father had a black beard, not brown. Shakespeare did have a white beard but he would hardly go off with other trappers and leave his friends to fend for themselves.

"I wanted to find your father, Stalking Coyote. Alive or his body, it did not matter. Since there was no trace of him, we must conclude he is gone. You must resign yourself to the fact that you will not see him ever again."

Before Zach could stop himself, he signed emphatically, "Never! The son of Grizzly Killer does not give up so easily!"

"I would expect no less from my own son," Bird Rattler responded. "So this is what I will do. You have seven more sleeps in which to accept your loss and give me an answer. If you do not, then I will cast you from my lodge for someone else to adopt. I have spoken." Pushing upright, Bird Rattler left.

Zach stayed only another minute. The others were watching him so fixedly he was embarrassed by their scrutiny and sought the open spaces outdoors. He had not gone far when a warm hand brushed his wrist.

"Be honest with me," Bluebird signed. "Do you like us?"

"With all my heart," Zach answered, and meant it.

"My mother is very upset you will not accept," Bluebird signed in such a way that Zach suspected she actually meant herself and not her mother. "She admires your devotion to your family but thinks you go too far."

Stopping, Zach swung around so suddenly Bluebird nearly walked into him. They were nose to nose, tiny red dots forming on her cheeks. "I have made myself as clear as I can," Zach signed. "If I was free to choose another family, I would choose yours."

"Then we would be brother and sister."

Forever after Zach would be unable to explain the urge that prompted him to sign, "I would rather be husband and wife some day."

Bluebird recoiled, gasped, and bolted like a frightened Colt, fleeing toward the prairie. Those she flashed past gave her puzzled looks.

Zach hastened off before anyone noticed him and put two and two together. Bird Rattler would be most displeased to hear he had upset her. Once he had lost himself among the lodges, he killed time by strolling aimlessly, intending to keep to himself until it was time to meet with Abby Griffen. He avoided Elk At Dawn and other boys, and once had to scoot behind a lodge when Bird Rattler and Cream Bear went by.

Less than an hour remained when Zach walked around the teepee of a noted warrior admiring the realistic buffalo painted on the hides and blundered into White Grass.

"Hello, Hackeryking. How you be?"

The last person Zach wanted to meet was the keeper of the sacred Beaver Bundle. Since arriving he had learned the position was one of the most revered in the tribe, higher even than war chief or medicine man. Every Blackfoot had a stake in the bundle because the welfare of the tribe was believed to be linked to its proper upkeep. There were many rules that had to be followed by its owner and all who came in his presence. Anyone who violated them risked bringing calamity down on everyone.

Keepers of the bundle had to be wise, kind, and caring. White Grass fit the bill, but he had one character flaw Zach found irritating: he loved to talk endlessly. Several times he had cornered Zach and gone on for hours. Zach suspected the venerable warrior was delighted to be able to practice his English, and it was just Zach's misfortune to be the one person other than Abby who spoke it. She wouldn't give White Grass the time of day.

"I am fine," Zach answered politely, adding, "but very busy. There is somewhere I must be in a short while."

White Grass placed a weathered hand on Zach's shoulder. "When I age you, same I do. Always be go here, go there." He chuckled at the remembrance. "Boys all same. White, Indian, it same, same, yes?"

"Yes," Zach agreed. Although, now that he thought about it, he'd had very few experiences with white boys his age. Being raised in the remote Rockies had its drawbacks.

"You give great chief answer yet?"

Zach was so accustomed to White Grass mangling the language that it always surprised him when a sentence was phrased correctly. "Not yet," he said. "I have seven sleeps in which to make up my mind."

"You do right thing." White Grass patted him on the shoulder. "Bird Rattler take care good of you. You grow be mighty warrior."

"He would do a fine job," Zach said while trying to come up with a plausible reason to excuse himself. He gazed toward Cream Bear's lodge and was horrified to see Abby leaving for the stream early. She never looked his way and was soon lost among the lodges.

"Something wrong, Hackeryking?" White Grass inquired.

"No. I just have to go. I promised to help Bird Rattler make arrows this afternoon. Will you excuse me?" Zach hated to lie but felt he had no choice.

The keeper Of the Beaver Bundle tilted his head and stared so long and hard at Zach that Zach became uncomfortable. "All right, Hackeryking," he said at length. "Go do what have to."

Zach bounded off toward the stream, then caught his mistake and changed direction, making for Bird Rattler's lodge. A casual glance back showed White Grass watching him, so he smiled and waved. Once out of sight he changed course once more and by a circuitous route was presently in the thick brush bordering the trail.

Abigail Griffen awaited him, kneeling with the water-bag in her lap. Her expression was unaccountably downcast. There were red marks under her eyes, as if she had been crying. And her hands twined and untwined restlessly. She glanced up, smiled wanly. "I came early in the hope you would too so we'd have more time to talk."

"I'm glad you did," Zach said, squatting. "Lucky I saw you."

Abby focused on her hands. "This is going to be very hard for me to do."

"Escaping? Don't worry. I'll have it all worked out ahead of time. If we plan it right, we'll be long gone before the Blackfeet miss us."

"No, no. Not that." A long sigh welled up from deep within her. "I've changed my mind about going."

Zach blinked. "You've what, ma'am?"

"At first I was giddy at the notion of seeing my own kind again," Abby said. "I don't think I touched the ground once all the way back to the lodge." She stopped, her voice choking off, and it was several minutes before she found it. "But then I had time to do some thinking and I realized I can't go back with you, no matter how much I want to."

Many a time Zach had been boggled by adult logic, but this instance left him thoroughly confounded. "I don't understand," he confessed.

"All you need to know is that I appreciate your offer very much," Abby said, touching his cheek. "It brought me to my senses in one respect. There's no going back for me, Zach. Not now, not ever. I was stupid to hope otherwise." She put the hand over her own heart. "There's only one thing left for me to do, I'm afraid. I just pray I have the courage."

Zach didn't like the sound of that. "Maybe if you'd explain, I can help."

Abby sorrowfully shook her head. "You're so sweet, but there's nothing you can do. Trust me. This is a matter far beyond your tender years. You see" —she paused, choking again, moisture rimming her eyes— "I was in love once with the finest man ever trod this earth. Lane Griffen was his name, and there wasn't a prouder woman anywhere the day I said, 'I do!' to him."

"Don't you still love him?" Zach asked when she covered her eyes with a palm and her shoulders gently shook.

"Oh God, yes!" Abby's voice sounded as if it came from the depths of a deep well. "But let me finish. I insisted on going trapping with him so he took me into the mountains against his better judgment. That's when the Piegans found me."

"So? If he loves you as much as you love him, he won't hold it against you."

"Not that, no. But something else he will." Abby visibly wrestled with her emotions. She stiffened her spine while drying her eyes. "There are some things a person can never forget nor forgive. Once you're much older, you'll understand."

"It's true I'm green in years, ma'am. But I'm not dumb. I learn as I go along." Zach paused. "I've seen how my ma and pa act. I've seen how much they love one another. I know there isn't anything in the world my pa wouldn't do for ma. He'd die for her, if need be. And no matter what she did, he'd forgive her."

"What's your point?"

"I should think it'd be as plain as the nose on your face," Zach said. "When a man loves a woman that much, he'll stand by her through anything. Your Lane will welcome you back with open arms."

"Never," Abby said wistfully, and suddenly she clutched at her throat and began to stand. "I have to go now."

"Wait!" Zach said, gripping her wrist. "Just hear me out. Please!"

"What?" Abby responded, halfheartedly tugging to free herself. "There's nothing more to say."

"There you're wrong." Zach thought frantically, certain she was going to do something awful if he didn't persuade her to come with him. "Listen. In six days we have to leave. I won't bother explaining why now." He let go and she didn't run off. "I think you're making the biggest mistake of your life if you don't go. Bigger even than going to the mountains when Lane didn't want you to. And you owe it to him, I figure, to decide for himself whether he'll forgive you or not. Saying he won't is like saying he never really loved you in the first place."

Abby made no reply for quite some time. She had gone as taunt as wire, the shifting of her face the only hint of the intense war raging within her. At last she came to life and whirled. "I'll think over what you've said." She took several steps, then stopped. "And Zach?"

"Ma'am?"

"You're going to make some lucky girl a fine husband one day."

Zach watched her dash through the brush and reflected that, young or old, it didn't matter. Females were downright strange.

Chapter Seventeen

Nate King had once heard a learned scientist discourse on the wonders of science and the new frontiers science had opened thanks to the telescope and the microscope. It had been the scientist's opinion that the latter instrument would prove invaluable to mankind in the years ahead. To demonstrate, he had let each member of the school audience peer into a microscope at the minute world of tiny organisms contained in a simple smear of water.

Now Nate knew how those organisms must have felt if they had been aware of what was going on. For every eye in the grand lodge of Mole On The Nose was fixed exclusively on him, and he felt as if he was being as closely examined as those organisms had been.

It had been this way from the moment Nate entered. The warriors had been talking and laughing until he poked his head inside. Then they had clammed up, regarding him in cold, stony silence.

Now, with the meal completed, Nate sat back and waited for the host to speak, as was customary. He had been seated in the place of honor to the left of the chief. The medicine man was to his left. On the chief's right sat Red Rock and other members of the Bear Society, as grim a bunch as ever lived.

"We will smoke," Mole On The Nose signed. His woman brought a pipe which he filled with tobacco from a small pouch at his side. He took small puffs as he lit, and when he had the pipe going he passed it to Nate, who took a long puff and in turn passed it to White Calf. So it went down the line and around to the row of Bear Society warriors. Then the trouble began. None of them used the pipe. Slowly, solemnly, one by one they passed it along until Red Rock held the peace pipe in his hands. "We do not want you here. We will not smoke," he signed, and gave it to Mole On The Nose.

Rarely did Indians insult one another in public. Rarer still did they insult a guest. Everyone looked at Nate to see how he would take it. He hesitated, unwilling to provoke the Bear Society, remembering White Calf's warning about the sacrifice of males as well as females. And while he sat there mulling how best to reply, the Medicine man bristled in his defense.

"How dare you be so rude!" White Calf signed angrily. "Do you want Sky Walker to call down the wrath of the gods on all our heads?"

Red Rock answered in Pawnee and was cut

off by White Calf's flying hands. "Use sign language, fool!"

Several members of the Bear Society reached for their knives. Red Rock did, and was rising when Mole On The Nose motioned for him to sit. "There is too much bad blood here," he signed. "We must remember we are grown men and not children who fight at the drop of a feather." His stern manner caused the Bear Society to simmer down, although each and every one hurled lances at Nate and White Calf with their eyes.

"I invited Sky Walker here tonight to learn more of the reason he has stepped down from the clouds to mingle with men," Mole On The Nose went on. "The last time this happened was in the days of Walks With Fire, in the time before our people left the land to the south and made the long journey to this region."

Red Rock had listened with growing impatience. "Do you believe he is who White Calf claims, then?" he signed.

"I had much doubt at first," Mole On The Nose replied. "It made no sense for a sky walker to be white. But then I thought perhaps we are being tested in a way we cannot grasp." He faced Nate. "This man does not act as most whites do. He behaves more like a human being. And when he killed the bear without a gun or bow I knew he is much more than he appears and might well be who White Calf claims."

Nate could stay quiet no longer. All along he'd known that the medicine man was talking behind his back, spreading stories. He had to know the truth. "Would you be so kind as to tell me White Calf's words?"

Red Rock snorted. "You know all things. Why bother to ask?"

"I have never said I know everything," Nate challenged.

Mole On The Nose lifted his arms but had yet to make a sign when White Calf jumped to his feet.

"No one need give an account of my words. I can speak for myself." He defiantly sneered at the Bear Society warriors, then at the chief. "Since you have forced this on me in an attempt to embarrass me in front of Sky Walker, I will tell everything."

The anger was thick enough to be cut with a knife. Nate wisely made no comment. Somehow he had become like a pawn on a chess board. He was caught in the middle between two opposing tribal forces, and at last the reason would be made clear.

White Calf strode into the open space between the rows of warriors. "It is no secret that for many winters the chief and I have not seen eye to eye on many matters. Nor is it a secret that some of our people, including the Bear Society, support him, while many support me." The medicine man's chin jutted like an accusing finger at Red Rock. "I have ever failed to understand why the Bear Society should back a leader who shuns warfare and shun one who is in favor of it."

"There is more to the quarrel than that," Red Rock objected.

"What is more important than the welfare of our people?" White Calf retorted. "If it were up to Mole On The Nose, we would let the Sioux ride right over us. We might as well hand over our women and horses to them the next time they raid. And while we are at it, we should cut off our own hair and offer our scalps to them in a special bundle so they need not bloody their hands lifting our hair themselves."

The chief shifted. "As usual you twist everything. I have never advocated surrender," he signed.

"No, but you have pushed for peace at the cost of lives and our honor," White Calf responded. "Who was it that sent four of our finest young men to the Sioux to sue for peace? And what did the Sioux do? They killed our young men, hung them upside down from tree limbs, and shot them full of arrows."

"You bring up one incident out of many over which we have disputed," Mole On The Nose signed. "I believed in what I was doing. We have lost countless lives to the Sioux. They have lost countless lives to us. It is in the best interests of both our tribes to smoke the pipe of peace."

"And has it never occurred to you that perhaps the Sioux do not want peace?" White Calf signed bitterly.

"He made a mistake," Red Rock broke in. "All men do."

"Leaders who make mistakes that cost lives should not be allowed to lead much longer," White Calf said.

"You are only jealous because more listen to him than listen to you," Red Rock signed.

"At least I stand up for the best interests of my people."

Nate was a fascinated listener to the acrimonious exchange, gleaning facts as they went along. Apparently the chief and the medicine man had been engaged in a long-running feud, a power play to see who wielded the most influence. That the Bear Society had sided with the chief, who was more interested in peace than counting coup, was highly unusual and reflected badly on the medicine man's character.

Mole On The Nose was gesturing for both parties to calm themselves. "This is not a time for name calling. White Calf has been asked to explain about Sky Walker and he agreed to do so." He stared at the medicine man. "Will you or not?"

"I said I would." White Calf signed. He thrust his shoulders back and adopted a grand pose. "Everyone here knows how religious I am. I pray every morning, every midday, every night. Constantly I seek the guidance of Tirawa in all that I do."

"No one here would doubt your devotion to your calling," Mole On The Nose signed.

Flustered by the unforeseen compliment, White Calf lost his train of thought for a few seconds, then resumed as if this were a speech he had rehearsed just for the occasion. "And so it is with my plan to repay the Sioux for their last visit. They killed nine warriors, stole thirty-seven horses, and took three of our women." Mentioning the raid twisted his face into a rabid mask of hate. "They must be repaid in kind. We must have vengeance, which is why I, and I alone, offered to lead our young men deep into their territory to pay them back." Pausing, he puffed out his chest. "I want them to cringe before the name of the Pawnees."

"About Sky Walker," Mole On The Nose prompted.

"You all know I went off to fast and pray recently," White Calf detailed. "I went to a special place only I know, where the spirits are strong, the medicine good. And while I stood there calling on Tirawa, it began to rain, just a little at first, and then of a sudden there was a downpour that nearly knocked me off my feet and the wind picked up, howling so fiercely I thought I would be blown into the ravine below where I stood."

Nate wasn't the only one hanging on every signed word. He could see the others were equally enthralled, especially those seated on his side of the lodge. White Calf's backers, he assumed, and listened as the medicine man continued.

"I was wet and turned to seek shelter in the trees when my eyes caught sight of something high in the sky above me. At first I thought it was a bird caught by the wind, but then I saw it coming lower and lower and realized it was a human figure and not a bird." White Calf paused. Like a crafty politician milking a crowd, he had the warriors under his spell and knew it. "I was too shocked to move. I had never seen a man fly before, never heard of such a thing except in the tales of the old times. I wanted to run but my feet would not obey me."

"What did you do?" one of the listeners signed anxiously.

"I just stood there," White Calf answered.

"And as the figure came lower, I saw that it was indeed a man and he was not flying or falling but was walking on the very air, walking right down toward me so fast there was no time for me to flee. I watched his legs move when my own should have been moving." He tapped his head. "He hit me, and that was the last I remembered until I woke up with Sky Walker bending over me."

Nate was the object of attention again and pretended not to notice. He was more interested in the story. Now he knew how he'd survived the fall from the whirlwind; the medicine man had cushioned his descent.

"I admit I was afraid," White Calf signed. "I will admit I broke and ran, thinking he was an evil spirit come to destroy me. I fled to a stand of trees and there prayed to be spared. And it was while I called on Tirawa that I saw the truth." He stopped signing a moment. "The man who walked from the sky had not tried to harm me after I revived. He had acted concerned, and tried to calm me when I panicked. I realized he was a friend, not an enemy."

Red Rock muttered in the Pawnee tongue.

"Would you call me a liar?" White Calf signed.

"No," Red Rock answered in kind. "No matter what I might think of you, I know you always tell the truth. But there must be a rational explanation."

"I would be happy to hear it."

Nate had the answer and was mulling whether to reveal the facts when the medicine man took up the tale.

"The answer came to me like a lightning bolt from above. This man was a sky walker, sent by Tirawa to help us in our fight with the Sioux just as Tirawa sent others from above to guide us in the early times. And Sky Walker, as I named him, was sent to me and not to Mole On The Nose as a sign that I had Tirawa's ear and Mole On The Nose did not."

Nate had to stifle a laugh. That anyone could seriously mistake him for a spirit being was too ridiculous for words. Until he recollected that Indians were a highly superstitious lot, much more so than whites.

Many tribes believed in a host of spirit beings believed to inhabit everything from animals to common objects such as trees and rocks. In order to stay on the good side of these spirits, the Indians conducted various elaborate ceremonies. They always sought good omens, shunned bad medicine. And anything they couldn't explain was chalked up to the supernatural spirit world. So perhaps, he reflected, it wasn't so ridiculous after all that the medicine man had mistaken him for a creature from above the clouds.

"I brought Sky Walker to our village for all to see," White Calf elaborated. "Many of you scoffed. Many of you scorned him. But he proved his power by slaying the bear and saving the life of Black Buffalo Woman."

Whispers passed from warrior to warrior as each commented on the account.

White Calf, though, was not done. "Now all of you must ask yourselves whether you will side with me or with Mole On The Nose. Will you sit on your backsides here in the village with him while the rest of us are off raiding the Sioux? Or will you add your bow and lance to the ranks of those who are true Pawnees?"

Some members of the Bear Society began arguing in soft tones with their fellows.

Nate gazed at the ground. Everything made sense now, from the panicked awe of the people to the reference to the Sioux, from the chief's peculiar questions about his brain and heart to Red Rock's mistrust and hatred. He had to decide what to do about it. Admitting the truth might earn him instant death since some of the warriors would think he had deliberately misled them. Or they might keep him prisoner until the next sacrifice. The situation being as it was, he figured he might be smarter keeping his mouth shut.

"You have ten sleeps in which to decide," White Calf was telling his audience. "Then we leave for Sioux country with Sky Walker at our head, and when we return we will bring more scalps than any Pawnee has ever seen at one time."

Nate's head snapped up. Sioux country was due south of the Yellowstone, much closer to where he had last seen his family than Pawnee territory. It was in his own best interests to go along. Somehow he might contrive to sneak away during the raid so he could begin his long delayed search.

"I have said all that needs saying," White Calf signed. "Sky Walker and I will leave you to talk this over." He moved toward the entrance.

Taking that as his cue to leave, Nate nodded at the chief and rose. The medicine man had paused to wait for him. As he caught up, Red Rock called out to them. White Calf faced around to hear what the warrior had to say, and Nate, desiring fresh air, slipped outside.

The crisp air was a wonderful antidote to the smoke filled lodge. Nate inhaled as he strolled a few feet from the entrance. A spark of hope had been rekindled within him, and he felt deliciously elated. So elated that he paid no attention to the soft rustle of moccasins in the night to his right. So elated that he would have perished had he not belatedly registered the metallic click of a pistol being cocked.

Nate spun at the same split-second the flintlock spat flame and lead. Something tore at his ribs. And then a pair of husky figures burst from the darkness with knives upraised. Sidestepping a wild lunge, Nate seized the warrior's wrist and heaved. Almost in the same motion he whipped into the second brave, blocking a blow with his forearms while delivering a punch to the stomach that doubled the man in half.

A volcanic chorus erupted in the chief's lodge. Footsteps pounded.

Nate caught the second warrior on the tip of the jaw with a solid right that dropped the man to his knees, then grasped the brave's knife arm to keep the man from burying the blade in his groin. The scrape of a sole in the dirt forewarned him the first warrior was almost upon him. Throwing himself to the right, Nate evaded a wicked downward swing that would have cleaved him open like an overripe gourd.

The warrior on the ground was not so lucky. He pushed erect when Nate released him, rising straight into the arc of the swooping butcher knife. The blade struck him in the left cheek, splitting the cheek open, and sheared through his lips and chin, down into his neck. Screeching abominably, the Pawnee sprawled over and clutched at his gushing wounds.

Nate only had one foe left to worry about. He pivoted. The blade hissed past his face. Lashing out with a leg, Nate heard the man's kneecap crack. As the warrior buckled, Nate stepped in, gripped the Pawnee's wrist, and pumped the arm as he might a pump lever, snapping the knife up, then down and in.

The second brave yowled as the blade tore into his abdomen. Tottering, he let go of both the knife and the pistol in his other hand.

Quickly Nate snatched the flintlock up. In the dim light streaming from the entrance he identified his own gun and he jammed it under his belt.

Warriors streamed from the lodge, surrounding the three combatants. Confusion reigned as everyone shouted at once, trying to find out what had transpired.

White Calf materialized in front of Nate. "Are you hurt, Sky Walker?" he signed urgently.

"Just a scratch," Nate replied, touching a new tear in his shirt. The skin had been broken, nothing more. "They ambushed me but they were too slow."

Bear Society warriors gathered around the stricken men to minister to them. Red Rock stood over the pair wearing a look of disgust.

Meanwhile the medicine man's backers flanked him, fingering their own knives and gazing expectantly at White Calf for the signal that would send the two sides flying at each other's throats.

Into the narrow gap between the two factions walked Mole On The Nose. He frowned at the writhing warriors, then at Red Rock. Whatever he said induced an angry outburst from the tall warrior. White Calf joined in, and for ten minutes they argued heatedly until White Calf turned on a heel and walked off. By then women had arrived and were helping staunch the blood.

Protected by a phalanx of the medicine man's supporters, Nate was escorted to the medicine lodge. He balked at going in, which was just as well since White Calf was letting off steam by walking in a circle again and again. In due course the medicine man halted.

"You should have heard him, Sky Walker! Red Rock claimed he had no idea why those two warriors attacked you. Men who are close personal friends of his. Men who are members of the Bear Society."

"He spoke with two tongues."

"All along I have been saying you could not trust him. Now you have proof." White Calf paused in his pacing. "I know what he was trying to do. He thought to show the people you are not Tirawa's messenger by having you rubbed out. Ha! Like a snake that turns and bites the hand that feeds it, his plan has turned on him and will make him appear foolish in the eyes of the people. They are not stupid.

They will guess who put the warriors up to it." He winked craftily at Nate. "And if they do not guess, I will whisper words in the ears of those who will make it a point to spread the truth abroad."

"Do you think he will try again?" Nate asked, not relishing the prospect of having to keep one eye over his shoulder at all times until they left for Sioux country.

"No. If he failed twice he would be the laughingstock of the village."

"Will he be punished?"

"Who would dare? Without proof, no one can even formally accuse him. And there will be no proof because the two you fought would rather have their tongues cut out than talk."

"Red Rock plans well," Nate signed.

"In his blundering way, yes," White Calf responded. "But I am far smarter and much more clever. And you are from on high. Between us we will put him in his place."

From the vicinity of the chief's lodge a piercing wail split the darkness.

"One of them has died," White Calf signed. "Good. Now more people will come over to my side."

Nate turned away from the lodge, his dislike of the medicine man soaring to new heights. The loss of human life meant nothing to the Pawnee. All that mattered was power, more and more power. Those flowery words about the welfare of the tribe had been so much empty air.

The comparison to a chess game was more accurate than Nate had realized. And he wasn't the only chess piece. In White Calf's estimation, everyone was to be manipulated so that he might attain his eventual goal of being undisputed lord and master of the Pawnee nation.

Being allied with such a man was almost more than Nate could stomach. Almost, but not quite. He would do practically anything in order to see his family again. So he would rein in his conscience until they reached Sioux country, and then it would be every man for himself.

A hand touched Nate's arm.

"I will go in and spread out the bedding," White Calf signed. "Three men will keep watch over us until morning in case I am wrong about Red Rock."

Nate caught a whiff of the stale odor inside. "Bring me clean blankets so I may sleep outside tonight."

"It is too dangerous."

"You will do as I say," Nate insisted, "or on my return to the clouds I will inform Tiwara that you refused to do the bidding of his messenger."

Surprise, and not a little fear, etched the medicine man's features. "You have become very demanding," he complained. "But I will do as you wish to show the depth of my devotion."

You do that, you damn hypocrite, Nate thought, his hand straying to the pistol. And when the time comes, I'll give you your due.

Chapter Eighteen

The answer to Winona's question came much sooner than she expected. The Minneconjous had hinted she would know in a month, but it was only a few days after her interrogation by Runs Against that several scouts thundered into the village at a gallop and shortly thereafter a delegation consisting of the high chief, Thunder Horn, Penis, Long Forelock, and several other notables showed up outside her lodge.

Butterfly had taken to staying with Winona day and night. Winona was in great discomfort much of the time and was grateful for the old woman's help. She feared the baby would be born much sooner than she had counted on, her fear compounded because Thunder Horn had made it clear he intended to take her into his lodge after the child came.

Prairie Blood

On this day, a bright sunny morning with a light breeze blowing from the northwest, Winona had just laid down after taking a short stroll to relieve cramps in her legs when masculine voices alerted her to the visit. She sat up but needed Butterfly's assistance to stand. Holding her hands on her belly, she went out.

"Woman, we need you now," Runs Against signed without preliminaries. "You will come with us and do as we say or you will be punished severely."

"Excuse me, great chief," Butterfly surprised everyone by insinuating a comment. "She did not sleep well last night and has been in pain all morning long. Could you not use her another time?"

Runs Against raised a hand as if to cuff her and Winona moved between them. "How dare you meddle in our business, old woman," he signed gruffly. "Go back inside and do woman's work and leave men's work to men."

Butterfly sadly bowed her head, then obeyed.

Thunder Horn moved forward to grasp Winona's elbow and steered her across the village. He, like all the warriors, had an anxious air about him, as if an event of crucial significance was about to take place.

Winona resented their treatment of Butterfly but did not provoke them. She had enough problems. She felt queasy, and the baby was kicking hard every so often. It was all she could do to keep her spine straight.

Runs Against overtook them on the right, Penis on the left. "This is important," the former signed. "You are going to translate for us.

You must translate exactly. Nothing must go wrong. Nothing at all."

"I will do my best," Winona signed.

"We will tolerate no mistakes," Runs Against warned. "Should anything go wrong, anything at all, we will hold you to blame."

Winona was guided toward a flat, rocky point jutting into the sluggish river. Many warriors were already there, scattered for scores of yards both up and down the shore. She was startled to see none were armed with any weapons except sheathed knives. She was even more surprised to behold a large red blanket had been spread out near the water, its ends weighted down with rocks. A battered tin pot containing pemmican and venison rested in the middle beside a water-skin.

Thunder Horn brought Winona to the blanket and gestured for her to sit. "Keep this in mind too," he signed as she did. "Soon you will be my woman. Should you humiliate me today by failing to do as we want, Runs Against's punishment will be as nothing compared to mine. As your husband I will have the right to beat you to near death if I so want."

The bestial gleam in his eyes assured Winona more than words possibly could that he meant every word. "I will do my best," she repeated, "but it would help if I knew what I was to do before I did it."

"And give you time to think of a way to trick us?" Thunder Horn responded. "We do not trust you enough yet to let you talk as you please." He pointed at Long Forelock. "And if you should decide to betray us, just remember he will let us know the moment you say anything you are not supposed to say."

Winona glanced at Long Forelock, who had the look of a man who dearly desired to be anywhere other than where he was. He smiled at her, a sickly sort of smile no one else saw.

Suddenly a warrior far down the river yipped and all the Minneconjous tensed. Runs Against, Penis, and several others stepped right to the water's edge. They appeared nervous, fussing with their buckskins or their hair.

Completely bewildered, Winona stared at the bend in the river everyone else was staring at. She saw the warrior at the far end of the line smile and wave like he was welcoming a long lost friend. A minute later the reason appeared, leaving her stupefied.

Around the bend came a bull boat. A popular transport for whites, bull boats varied in size depending on the number of buffalo hides used in their construction. The hides were stretched over a circular frame of pliable willow limbs and then smoked over a small fire. To render the craft waterproof, bear fat was smeared over the outer surfaces.

This one held three trappers, judging by their buckskins, and their gear. They held rifles and were eyeing the warrior at the end of the line with suspicion. Not until they cleared the bend did they see the rest of the Minneconjous, and one of the whites immediately worked his paddle, bringing the boat to a stop.

All the Minneconjous smiled and waved to demonstrate their peaceful intent. Some gestured toward the rocky point, trying to persuade the trappers to go on.

Runs Against looked sternly at Winona. "Yell to them. Tell them we mean them no harm, that we are their friends. Ask them to pow-wow with us."

"And what happens when they step ashore?" Winona asked. Under no circumstances would she be party to wholesale butchery, no matter how severely she was punished. "Will you rub them out?"

"Had we wanted their hair, they would have been dead when our scouts first set eyes on them yesterday morning," Thunder Horn signed. He jabbed her in the side with his thumb. "Now do as we say and be quick about it or I will bloody your nose!"

Winona still had no idea what the Minneconjous were up to, but she was fairly sure they wouldn't have gone to so much effort to lure the whites into a trap, not when they could pick the trappers off at their leisure from the riverbank. And, too, the Minneconjous wouldn't greet the whites virtually unarmed as they were if they planned to attack.

Advancing, Winona raised a hand and called out, "Hello, the boat! I am the wife of Nate King, a trapper! I must spell my name for you: W-I-N-O-N-A. These are Minneconjous. Be on your guard!" She looked at Long Forelock and smiled sweetly.

Runs Against likewise looked at the warrior. "What did she say?" he demanded.

Long Forelock licked his lips. "She told them that we are their friends and they have nothing to fear."

The three trappers were huddled in the bull boat, talking. A man with a bushy red beard faced around and put a hand to his mouth. "Minneconjous, you say? They usually kill whites. What the devil is going on?"

"I do not know," Winona shouted, "but I would not try to flee if I were you. This river is too narrow, too slow. They would easily catch you on horseback and wipe you out."

"What do they want?"

"For you to parley with them," Winona explained.

"What about?"

"They haven't told me yet."

Again the three trappers consulted. "We don't like this one bit," the man with the red beard informed her, "but I don't see as where we have any choice." He paused. "Are you their captive?"

"I am."

"Hang on. We're coming in."

Runs Against was a nervous wreck. Shifting back and forth from one leg to the other like an indecisive grasshopper, he inquired in irritation, "Why are you saying so much? Our request was simple. You should only say the words I tell you to say."

"Do I keep silent when they ask questions?" Winona retorted. "If I do, they will suspect something is wrong."

"What questions?" Runs Against simmered.

"They wanted to know why you want to hold a pow-wow. I told them I did not know."

"Good. Good." Runs Against patted her arm as a man would pat a child or a pet that behaved correctly. "Keep doing as you are doing, but always make your answers short."

The bull boat glided toward the point. Two of the men held rifles to their shoulders and warily regarded the Minneconjous while the man with the red beard paddled. When the boat was close enough, he set down the paddle, lifted a Hawken, and vaulted smoothly over the side into the knee-deep water. Splashing onto dry land, he transferred the Hawken to the crook of his elbow and turned to Winona. Astonishment overcame him on discovering her condition. "I'll be damned!" he blurted.

"You'll be dead if you don't keep your wits about you," Winona said while smiling to give the impression she was greeting him warmly. "I am supposed to tell you only what they want me to, but I'll add as I see fit."

The man nodded in admiration. "You've got gumption, lady." He studied the Minneconjous while remarking, "I heard you say your name is Winona King. That right?"

"It is."

"We heard about your husband at Jake and Sam's shop in St. Louis, where I bought this rifle here."

Winona knew he referred to the Hawken brothers.

"They spoke right highly of him," the man went on. "Said he's one of the best, along with Bridger, Carson, and McNair." He calmly scanned the warriors lining the river. "I'm Reed, by the way. Adam Reed. Just say the word and we'll try to free you from their clutches."

"You dare not," Winona cautioned. She'd taken a strong liking to this brash stranger who so gallantly offered to aid her. "You are badly outnumbered. They would cut us down before we reached your boat."

"I don't see any with rifles or bows," Reed said.

"Not out in the open," Winona said. "But knowing them as well as I do, I wouldn't put it past them to have warriors in hiding nearby, watching us as we speak."

"Didn't think of that."

Runs Against had abided all the chatter he was going to. Sidling next to Winona, he signed while grinning idiotically, "You talk too much again, woman. What is he saying? What have you told him?"

"He wanted to know if you could be trusted. I told him you could," Winona cheerfully lied. "And again he asked to know the reason for the pow-wow."

"Say that all will be made clear after we have eaten and smoked a pipe," Runs Against directed. "Tell him to have his friends come on shore, too. Tell him they have no need of their rifles. They are our guests."

Winona faced Adam Reed and relayed the chief's words, throwing in, "It's wiser if your friends stay in the boat. They can cover you if trouble breaks out. And whatever you do, don't set your rifles aside."

"Don't worry. We won't. As for Tim and Matt, they stay right where they are until I know what's what."

Runs Against was unable to hide his annoyance at the answer but he smiled nonetheless and signed, "Very well. Have him sit with us."

The chief, Penis, Thunder Horn, and Long Forelock all took seats on one side of the blanket. Winona knelt near the tin pot. Adam Reed, Hawken across his legs, sat on the other side. An uncomfortable tension hung thickly around them

"Have him eat and drink his fill," Runs Against commanded. "Impress on him that we are his friends. He has come in peace, he will be allowed to go in peace. Assure him of this until he understands it is true."

Winona complied. "But I wouldn't believe a word this old bastard says," she concluded.

Reed chuckled, then took a big bite out of a piece of jerky. "Where's your husband?" he asked, mouth full of the salted meat.

"We were separated during a storm," Winona said. "The last I saw, he was searching for our son along the Yellowstone."

"We're heading west ourselves," Reed said. "Since you won't let us take you with us, tell me how to go about finding Nate and I'll try and get word to him."

Before Winona could offer advice, the chief nudged her.

"It is time to speak at length of the reason we invited these whites to visit with us," Runs Against signed. "I want you to ask if they are trappers."

Reed confirmed they were.

Runs Against rubbed his palms. "Ask them if they would like to have more beaver hides than they can carry in ten trips to the white man's land."

"What is he up to?" Reed wondered on hearing the query. "Of course we would. But it would take years to raise that many."

Again, and for the next several minutes, Winona translated without embellishment. She was as surprised as Adam Reed when the ulterior motive of the Minneconjous became clear.

"For three men, yes," Runs Against signed. "Not for a whole tribe. Our warriors could make you rich with beaver. The river to the west is thick with them because we seldom kill them and we have not let any other whites trap there."

"Why would you do this for us?" Reed asked.

"Because we would like something in return," Runs Against said. "We hear that whites like to trade, to barter. So do we. In exchange for the beaver, you would give us something."

"What?"

"Before we get to that, I would like to know if a story I heard last spring is true." Runs Against gazed fondly at the Hawken, scratched his chin, and seemed to change subjects without thinking. "You whites always have very fine guns."

Reed, his confusion showing, boasted, "Our guns are the best there are. They're superior to anything the Canadians or Mexicans have. And they're a far sight better than the fusees the Hudson's Bay people offer for plews."

"This I have noticed," Runs Against agreed. "With such weapons, it is no mystery how you whites have been able to penetrate so deep into the mountains after beaver, defying the Blackfeet and the Utes in their own territory."

"They know better than to court lead poisoning," Reed said smugly.

The chief played with the pemmican in his hand a moment. "I have lived a long life, white man. Over the years I have seen many changes. When I was a boy, no one had ever seen a white. When I reached manhood, we saw them only once in a while. Now, your kind shows up everywhere, with more and more coming all the time."

"And there will be more yet."

"So I have heard. And yet, if not for your guns, your people would have been driven back to their own land with their tails tucked between their legs long ago. Is this not true?"

"I wouldn't go that far. We fight for what we want."

"So do we," Runs Against signed. "We fight the Blackfeet to the north and the Pawnees to the south and the Cheyennes to the southwest, and we do it just to stay alive."

Here Winona could not resist mentioning, "He is not being completely honest. The Minneconjou, like most other tribes, fight because they *like* to fight. They go on the warpath to count coup, not because they are forced to do it."

Reed nodded and said, "I've been trapping four years now, so I know a little about Injun ways." He looked at the bull boat. "I knew better than to try this shortcut west. I'd heard about the Minneconjou camping in the area every so often, but I figured I could sneak through their country without being caught." Reed sighed. "Never buck fate. It'll get you in hot water every time."

The chief was bothered by their extended discussion. "What are you saying now?" he signed at Winona.

"The white man says he hopes there will come a day when all peoples might live in peace," she said, putting her own wish in the trapper's mouth.

"Then he is a fool," Runs Against signed, and swiftly went on, "but do not tell him that! Instead, say that there can be no peace for the Minneconjou until we can protect ourselves properly."

"Tell this old buzzard to quit beating around the bush," Reed chafed. "What the hell does he want from us?"

"Guns," Runs Against revealed. "We want to trade beaver pelts for rifles and pistols. All the hides you can carry for all the guns we can carry."

Here Reed hesitated. "Do you figure he'll fly off the handle if I tell him no to his face?"

"He might," Winona answered. "Better to humor him." She took the initiative, signing, "The white man says your offer interests him. But there are problems. For one thing, how would he bring so many guns all the way across the prairie? The load would be too heavy for canoes or bull boats."

"He could pack the guns on horses," Runs Against proposed.

"It would take too many for only three whites to handle. And they would be easy prey for other tribes."

"Then he could bring the guns in small lots," Runs Against was undaunted. "Just so we get them all."

Winona elaborated for the trapper's sake. "Play along with him," she said. "Agree to everything. When you're long gone you can laugh at his expense."

"All right. Tell the conniving bastard I accept his offer. Tell him I'll think of some way to bring in the guns."

The Minneconjous were elated by the reply. They chatted animatedly until the chief signed again.

"There is one more thing. We would like him to sign a paper such as the whites use when they trade with one another so he will be bound by his word."

"Where the devil did they ever hear about contracts?" Reed marveled, and laughed. "Sure, if that's what they want. There's no need to let them know that as far as the law is concerned, any deal we work out isn't binding." He glanced at Winona, his brow knitting. "And while you're at it, tell him I have a condition of my own. You come with us or the deal is off."

"I can't tell him that," Winona said.

"Why not?"

"He will not take it well."

"Let me worry about how he takes it. If he wants guns badly enough, he'll agree."

"It is too risky."

Runs Against slapped her arm. "What does he want? Why do you argue?"

"Tell him," Adam Reed insisted.

Caught in the middle, Winona rashly gave in even though her intuition blared a siren wail not to do so. "The white man says he agrees to all your terms provided you agree to one of his."

"Which is?" Runs Against asked.

"He wants to take me with him."

All four Minneconjou leaders became as still as ice. A deathly pallor crept up Runs Against's face. He glared at Reed, then at the two men in the bull boat. "And why would he ask such a thing?" he demanded.

"He likes me," Winona fibbed for Reed's benefit. "He thinks it would be of great benefit for him to have a woman who can speak the white tongue and use sign."

"Does he indeed?" Runs Against gave the pot of pemmican an angry poke with his toe and said some words in Sioux that brought scowls to the faces of the other warriors.

"I don't like this," Winona said to the trapper. "You must get in your boat and leave, now, before it's too late."

"He won't lay a finger on us," Reed declared. "Not and ruin his chance of getting his hands on some guns."

Runs Against looked at Winona. "I knew you would try to deceive us. Just as I knew Long Forelock does not speak the white tongue well enough to catch you."

"I have not tried," Winona said, but was rudely hushed by a barked.

"Do not lie to me, Shoshone!" Runs Against railed. "I read your faces. Either this one knows you, or he knows your white husband, or you have told him about yourself and he seeks to save you." Leaping to his feet, he turned his spite on the trapper. "You were a fool, white man! Other whites will come along, and eventually we will find one to do our bidding. But it will not be you!"

"Run!" Winona cried to Adam.

But it was too late. The chief made a chopping motion, and even as Reed pushed upright several arrows thudded into his chest. The men in the bull boat raised their rifles, took aim, and died under a shower of shafts pouring from the undergrowth. One of them screamed briefly as he fell. As swiftly as that, it was over.

Winona began to rise, to step to Reed, when fingers gouged into her arm and she was yanked off the ground and shaken until her teeth rattled.

"I warned you!" Thunder Horn signed. "I told you what would happen if you humiliated me." He shoved, sending her stumbling sideways.

It was useless to concoct an explanation. Winona saw their relentless fury and retreated, fearing for her baby. She bumped into a brave standing behind her, and before she could go around him, Thunder Horn was on her.

"You are not mine yet so I cannot give you the full punishment you deserve. But I can make you sorry for your treachery. Very, very sorry."

And with that Thunder Horn proceeded to drag Winona off by the roots of her hair into the village.

Chapter Nineteen

Zachary King had never been so nervous in all his young life. Crouched behind high weeds, he observed women coming and going from the favorite spot for filling water-bags. He'd often seen older boys hiding nearby to catch a glimpse of their sweethearts but had never, ever figured he'd be doing the same himself. Sort of.

Two women were leaving. The segment of trail visible from Zach's hiding place was empty save for them so he sank onto his elbows and knees and plucked at the grass. It had to be today, he told himself. Tomorrow he would be gone and he didn't want to leave without saying something.

Zach had a plan. That very afternoon, Bird Rattler, Cream Bear, and others were leaving to hunt buffalo. In their absence, he proposed to steal a horse, or two, and flee south.

A new figure appeared on the trail and Zach's heart skipped a beat. She had finally come, as she usually did at this time of the morning. He snuck closer to the stream, his moccasins soundless on the soft grass.

Her eyes were downcast, as they had been so often since that last day they talked. The bag was held loosely in her left hand by a strap, half dragging. She reached the pool, then knelt and dipped the bag in the water.

Tip-toeing up behind her, Zach gently ran a finger along her hair. She jumped as if set upon by a panther and cried out, whirling and dropping the water-skin.

"You! " she signed.

"I did not mean to spook you, Bluebird."

"Well, you did." Flustered, the girl picked up the bag and brushed off dirt. "I thought you were more mature than most boys your age, but you are like the small ones who delight in scaring anyone they can."

"I came here to talk," Zach persisted. "You have been avoiding me ever since the other day and I would like to know why."

"Go away and do not bother me. Unlike you, I have work to do." Bluebird jammed the whole water bag under the surface. Zach moved around so he could see her crimson face. "Please. We might never have this chance again."

"What are you talking about?" she signed indignantly.

Realizing he had slipped up, Zach quickly responded, "To be alone like this. Other women will show up soon."

"I hope they do so you will leave."

Feeling his heart tearing inch by inch with each caustic reply, Zach made bold to lightly touch her wrist. "Do you really mean that? Because if you do, I will leave now and never impose on your time again." She stuck her nose into the air, and Zach, crestfallen, turned to go.

Bluebird instantly snatched his sleeve. "I have changed my mind. I want you to stay, for a while At least. Long enough to tell me why you said those terrible things you did."

At a loss, Zach said, "I would never insult you, not in a hundred winters."

"You spoke of us being husband and wife!" Bluebird reminded him, her tone implying he had violated every rule of conduct known to mortals.

"What was wrong with that?"

Uttering a sound that closely resembled the angry nicker of a horse, Bluebird stood. "Was it such a small matter to you? I suppose you go around talking of marriage to every girl you meet."

"You are the first one I have ever thought of in that way," Zach admitted, shame-faced. "And I have no idea what got into me. Maybe it had something to do with you being the prettiest girl I have ever met. And the kindest, too."

By her posture, a stinging retort had been on the tip of Bluebird's tongue. On hearing his excuse, she relaxed, her temper subsiding. "Straight tongue?" she signed.

"I would never lie to you."

Bluebird could not meet his gaze. She glanced down, yelped, and frantically plunged both hands into the stream to rescue the water-bag, which was slowly sinking to the bottom of the pool. She missed.

In a twinkling Zach knelt next to her and bent low, sticking his face into the cool water. His outstretched fingers scraped the bag and he leaned farther. As his fingers closed on it, he lost his balance. He tried to get a purchase on the bank but his slick hand slipped. Lacking support, he started to pitch headfirst into the stream.

Quick thinking on Bluebird's part saved him from a dunking. She lunged, wrapping both arms around his chest, and heaved backward with all the strength her slender form could muster.

Together they rose, Zach dripping wet, the water-skin in his right hand. He turned, and without warning they were nose-to-nose, pounding heart to pounding heart, the smiles on their lips freezing. He had an overwhelming urge to kiss her, the very first such urge he had ever had, but as he bent his face to hers she broke out in raucous laughter and pushed him away.

"You should see yourself!" Bluebird signed despite her hysterics.

Zach stared at the surface of the pool. His face and head were dripping wet, but in his estimation he didn't look all that funny.

Bluebird calmed down and took the bag, which she closed and draped over her shoulder. "Care to walk me back?"

"I would be glad to."

Neither made a comment until they entered the village. Zach brushed water from his hair, all the words he had rehearsed the past few days gone. So he signed, "You still have not told me why you were so upset with me."

"I should not have to. But girls are always wiser than boys, from the cradleboard to the grave." Bluebird was smiling again, her old radiant self. "When you are older maybe you will understand."

"My father says men and women were not meant to understand one another. He says they are as different as the sun and moon."

"Your father is very smart. It is a pity you do not take more after him."

Zach laughed, enjoying her good-natured ribbing. Until that second he had not realized how much he'd missed her company. Or how much he would miss it when he left to find his folks.

"Are you ill?"

"No. Why?"

"Your face," Bluebird signed. "For a moment you had a sick look." She put a hand to his forehead. "You do not feel hot."

"I am fine," Zach stressed. He saw the lodge was not all that far off and slowed in order to have more time with her. Their elbows brushed and his arm tingled.

"What are you thinking?" she inquired.

"About my stay here. It has been a happy one so far, except for you being mad at me." Zach surveyed the serene encampment. "I sure have learned a lot in a short while."

"Such as?"

"Blackfeet are not the beasts everyone else claims."

"Who would say such vile things about us?"

"Trappers. Soldiers. Other tribes," Zach listed them. "Practically everybody I have ever met."

"Where do they get such crazy ideas? What do we do that they should think so poorly of us?"

"Your people refuse to live in peace with the whites, for one thing."

"Is that wrong?"

"Once I thought it was."

"My mother told me they would kill off all our beaver, take our land for their own."

"That they would," Zach signed. "And now that I see the problem from your point of view, I see things differently." He gazed upon the village, watching children frolic and women tanning a hide and several warriors gambling, and he realized he no longer despised the Blackfeet as he once had. Nor did he fear them as much as before. They weren't fiends incarnate. They were Indians. Nothing more, nothing less. "I will always look back on this time as special," he signed.

Bluebird kicked at a small rock, then scrutinized his features. "You make it seem as if you will not have more special times among my people in the future."

Zach had blundered. To alleviate any suspicions she might harbor, he signed, "Who can tell what the future holds for any of us? My father says we must take each day as it comes along and make the best of the time we are given in this life."

"I hope you do turn out like him," Bluebird signed. "I will make a record of all your sayings for our children." She took another step, then jerked her head as if stung on realizing what she had said.

"So you have had the same thoughts I have," Zach said.

"A few, perhaps." Bluebird's bashful streak was showing again. She gave him a sisterly smack on the arm and broke into a run. "We both talk too much at times. Come. I will race you."

Zach barely won, even though she carried the heavy water bag. Laughing gaily, she went in. He stood there catching his breath and caught sight of Abigail at work beside Cream Bear's lodge She was on her knees, pounding strips of dried buffalo meat into tiny pieces and mixing them with berries to make pemmican.

Bending to peer into Bird Rattler's lodge, Zach saw Bluebird helping her mother sort through a sewing bag. He slowly backed away, turned, and swiftly walked to Cream Bear's teepee. Zach stopped in its shadow and pretended to be checking his left moccasin for a stone.

Abby glanced at him. "What are you doing here?"

"We need to talk, ma'am."

"Make it quick. Cream Bear is gone but he'll return at any minute. He's preparing for a buffalo hunt later."

"I know. That's why I'm taking this chance." Zach removed his moccasin and felt around inside. "I'm leaving as soon as the sun sets. If you want to come, you're still welcome to."

"Why are you going so early? You should wait until the middle of the night when everyone is sound asleep."

"No, ma'am, I shouldn't. If anything goes wrong and the horses or some of the dogs start a ruckus, every warrior in the village will rush outside lickety-split. They'd all be after us in no time." Zach upended the moccasin and acted puzzled, as if he couldn't find the stone. "But right after sunset no one will pay much attention to a few yapping dogs or bother to check if a horse or two whinnies."

"I don't know—" Abby said.

"There's another thing to consider," Zach went on. "The Blackfeet can't track at night." He gave the moccasin a shake. "Well, they can, but they'd have to use torches and it would slow them down a lot. We'd have a big lead on them."

"You keep saying we."

"I'm sorely hoping you'll come, ma'am. This is no place for you. You'd spend the rest of your days as miserable as a wet hen."

Several warriors were passing close to the lodge. Abby resumed pounding the meat until they were gone, then mentioned, "I haven't made up my mind yet. One minute I'm torn one way, the next minute another."

"You have until sunset. About ten hours, I reckon." Zach pulled the moccasin back on and stood. "I don't want to leave you behind, but I have to go while the going is good. So with or without you, once the sun goes down I'm riding out."

"Wait!" Abby said. "If I do decide, where will we meet?"

"Behind Bird Rattler's lodge, where he tethers his horses," Zach signed.

"He won't like having his animals stolen."

Zach grinned as only a brash boy could. "I did it before. And my ma always says that things get easier the second time around." He strolled toward Bird Rattler's teepee. Halfway there someone hailed him.

"Hackeryking!"

"Oh no," Zach said to himself.

The keeper of the sacred Beaver Bundle had a blanket draped over his slim shoulders. Smiling paternally, White Grass set a hand on Zach's shoulder. "Walk with me. "

Zach yearned to rejoin Bluebird and spend as much time as possible in her company before evening came. To refuse, however, would be an insult to the revered warrior and remarkably bad manners. Since his folks had taught him to always respect his elders, he let himself be led off.

"I thinking we have words while still can," White Grass said.

"What do you mean by that?" Zach responded, his pulse racing out of fear the Blackfoot had been on the other side of Cream Bear's lodge and heard every word he'd told Abby.

"I old. Very old. Not many winters left."

"Oh," Zach said, relieved. "Don't worry. My pa has a friend who has to be ninety if all the tales he tells about his early days are true, and he's still got plenty of vigor and vim left in him."

"Vigor and vim?" White Grass repeated.

"Energy. Strength. Life."

"Life. Yes. Life precious."

They walked aimlessly on, Zach chafing at the delay. He knew enough not to rush the warrior. White Grass would get to the point in his own good time.

"What I say, Hackeryking, maybe you no remember till long time come. Maybe then understand. Savvy?"

"Sure I do," Zach said, when actually he didn't have the foggiest notion what the warrior was getting at. All he was concerned about was returning to Bluebird.

"We Blackfeet not bad as many like say. Not killers. Not butchers. No worse Sioux, Shoshones."

"I agree there."

"You do?" White Grass patted him. "Good." He halted to observe several boys playing roll the hoop. "I worry. Thinking maybe you no see. Maybe you too young."

"I have grown to like the Blackfeet," Zach confessed.

"We like you. Chief very much like you. Say leave you be. Say let you do as want. Say decide is yours." The warrior locked eyes with Zach. "Very important you savvy. Yes?"

"Yes," Zach said, assuming the keeper referred to the adoption.

"Some maybe want stop. Maybe."

Stop what? Zach wondered, and was going to ask when he was distracted by Bluebird emerging from her lodge and gazing around as if in search of him.

White Grass folded his hands. "He have many arrows. Many, many."

"Who?" Zach asked absently.

"Bird Rattler."

"A warrior can never have too many arrows," Zach said for lack of anything else. Bluebird had missed him and gone back inside.

"You go now," White Grass said. "Remember me."

"I always will." Overjoyed, Zach went to bound off when he thought of something he'd been meaning to ask for some time. "Say, White Grass. I don't mean to pry, but I'm a mite curious. Where did you learn to speak my tongue?"

"Many, many winters past, white man live with Blackfeet. Take Blackfoot wife. Have Blackfoot son. Then he made go when son baby. Much sadness, then, Hackeryking. Much crying and wailing in the village."

"This white man have a name?"

"Yes. I remember well. We good friends, Shake-spear-Mac-a-nair, and me."

It took a moment for the revelation to sink in, and when it did Zach stood and gaped as the old warrior shambled off and was presently lost among the teepees. "Well, I'll be!" he exclaimed. No one had ever told him much about Shakespeare's past. And now that he thought about it, his folks had been left in the dark as well. Was that deliberate? he wondered. Did Uncle Shakespeare have secrets he was trying to hide?

An interruption prevented Zach from delving into the question. He heard a yell and saw Bluebird hurrying to meet him. "I was hoping we could spend more time together," he signed happily.

"You disappeared. Where did you get to?"

"White Grass wanted to see me".

"Was it something important?"

"No."

"He came by our lodge yesterday while you were off with Elk At Dawn and the other boys," Bluebird disclosed. "Father and him whispered together for a long time, and when he went home, father looked sad."

"What were they talking about?"

"I could not hear. Mother shooed me outside so I would not pester them." Bluebird smiled. "But enough of adults and matters that do not concern us. What would you like to do?"

"You pick. I will do whatever you want for the rest of the day."

"Anything I want?"

"Anything."

She held him to his word, and from then until the bottom rim of the blazing sun touched the red horizon they walked and talked and played and had eyes for no one except each other. They hiked out over the prairie, waving when they saw Bird Rattler, Cream Bear, and other men riding off after buffalo. Later they watched youngsters gambol about in the water like frisky otters. They made a complete circuit of the village, not saying a word.

Zachary King would have cause to remember this day, and the others spent with Bluebird, in the not too distant future. But for this one and this one alone his cares and woes evaporated. He was as content as it is humanly possible to be, and his contentment was all the finer because it was part and parcel of that last vestige of innocence a boy enjoys before manhood descends with the weight of an anvil.

Toward evening melancholy filled Zach's soul. His heart was heavy with sorrow he had to struggle to contain. As they neared the lodge, he boldly took her hand in his and felt his heart soar when she didn't try to yank loose. Near the entrance they halted. "I want to thank you for today," he signed.

"There will be many more like this one."

Guilt prompted Zach to release her and half turn toward the sunset. "I hate this," he said aloud.

"What?" Bluebird signed.

"I said I am hungry," Zach signed.

"Men. All they think of is their bellies." Chuckling, Bluebird went in to assist her mother in fixing the evening meal.

As the sun dipped lower and lower, so did Zach's heart. He didn't budge until she came to fetch him. Inside, during supper, he embarrassed her by staring at her so steadfastly her mother signed a remark about his paying more attention to his food, and Elk At Dawn snickered.

The sun had gone and a fire had been lit as a feeble substitute when Zach rose. "Please excuse me," he signed. "I told White Grass I would visit him after we ate."

"Do not be long," the mother signed. "Bird Rattler will want you here when he returns."

Zach stepped to the flap. He paused to look at them: at the industrious mother cleaning up, at the smiling boy sharpening his knife, and at Bluebird, sweet, dear, wonderful Bluebird, who bestowed on him a smile of such dazzling beauty that for a bit his determination faltered. He had to mentally push himself from the lodge. Once out, he didn't look back.

Quickly Zach walked around to the rear. Here, along a strip of grass, the chief kept his most prized horses. Among them was a black bay a lot smaller than the brown stallion, a bay Zach had seen fit to visit regularly the past few days. He'd brought handfuls of sweet grass from near the stream each time, and stroked and petted the animal while it ate.

Now the bay lifted its head but did not shy. Zach rubbed behind its ears, moved to its side, and gripped the mane to swing on top.

"I'm here!"

At the whisper, Zach started and whirled. Abigail Griffen wore a tattered dress, probably the same garment she had worn the day the Piegans snatched her, and a green shawl. From her shoulder hung a full parfleche. Around her waist was strapped a large knife, and in her left hand she held a spare. In her right, a lance. "This is for you," she said, holding out the extra.

Zach took it, wedged the sheath under his belt. "I'll take the lance, too, ma'am, unless you've had more practice with one than me."

She hesitated, then handed it over.

"Pick any horse," Zach said. Clambering onto the bay, he adjusted his grip on the lance and seized the animal's mane.

Abby had picked a paint, a mare.

"Are you ready?"

"I was ready the day I was taken from my Lane."

Zach touched his heels to the bay's flanks and walked the horse westward since the prairie was closer on the west side of the village. Few Blackfeet were abroad. This was the quiet time, when families sat around their fires resting and talking about the events of the day.

"I'm not much of a rider," Abby whispered. "Whatever you do, don't lose me."

"We're in this together from start to finish," Zach pledged. "I won't desert you."

A woman crossed in front of them, her back burdened by firewood. A warrior stood at a nearby lodge offering a prayer, his back to them. A camp dog trotted by, giving them a wide berth.

Soon the plain appeared. Zach angled to the south, toward the Yellowstone. His joy at possibly seeing his parents again temporarily eclipsed his grief at parting from Bluebird. He glanced at Abby and smiled encouragement, then brought the bay to a gallop, eager to put miles between the village and them before daylight.

At that instant a series of harsh yells shattered the serenity. Abby gasped, cried out, "They know already!"

"Ride, then!" Zach coaxed, as behind them the Blackfoot village exploded in bedlam.

Chapter Twenty

Zachary King had no inkling of what had gone wrong. From the uproar he gathered the entire population was falling out to answer the squalls of the yeller, which spurred him into a headlong dash across the prairie. He had to hold the bay in a little in order for Abby to keep up, but they made good time nonetheless. For several minutes they fled unhindered.

"Look!" Abby shouted, pointing rearward.

Torches moved among the lodges. Figures jammed the open spaces. Among them were horses, a lot of horses, and Zach saw warriors mounting animal after animal.

"They'll catch us!" Abby lamented.

"Not if I can help it," Zach said defiantly. There was hope for them if they could lose themselves in the darkness before the Blackfeet organized. He slanted westward again, taking them farther into the comforting veil of darkness. The spirited bay and the paint had not been ridden for several days and relished this chance to gallop like the wind.

Gradually the tumult lessened. Zach checked and believed he spied riders spreading out from the village, bearing to the south. Naturally the Blackfeet counted on them making straight for the river, for the border of Blackfoot country. Had he done so, Abby and he would have been in their clutches within the hour.

The bay took the slope of a basin on the fly, hooves hammering. Zach had to keep one eye on the ground ahead and another on Abby, who flounced awkwardly to the rhythm of the paint but was able to stay on. They flew across the basin and up the other slope.

Here Zach reined up to listen. To the southeast imitation thunder rumbled and warriors yipped, thrilled at the chase. Half a mile away, Zach reckoned.

Abby was trying to keep her paint still. The mare pranced and circled, eager to be off. "We'll never make it," she said forlornly.

"You might try looking at the bright side for a change, ma'am," Zach said. "We'll make it, but we have to keep our heads."

"I'm trying," Abby said. "Lord, how I'm trying. It's not easy after two years, even though escaping is all I've cared about." She rubbed the paint's neck. "Before we go any further I want your promise, son."

"I told you I'd get you to safety."

"No. Something else." Abby's face was in shadow and she seemed to prefer it that way.

"If you make it and I don't—"

"We both will."

"Don't interrupt," Abby said gruffly. "If you make it and I don't, I want your word that you'll try to get word to my Lane. I can't abide the thought of all I've been through, all I'm going through, being for naught."

Zach detected an underlying quaver to her voice. "What is it you want me to tell him?"

"I loved him."

"That's it?"

"And I always did. Always will. There's nothing more that needs to be said ."

Thinking of Bluebird, Zach nodded. "Rest easy. If something happens to you, I won't rest until I track Lane Griffen down and let him know, no matter how long its takes me."

"You've the stature of a boy but the soul of a man. Thank you, Zach King."

"Let's ride."

The night was comfortably cool. Legions of crickets chirped in melodious chorus. For a while a coyote howled in lonely counterpoint but eventually ceased.

Zach was pleased with their progress so far. He bore westward until they had gone over four miles and he judged they were beyond the radius of the search area. Bearing southward, he slowed to a trot to save the horses in case the worst that could happen did.

Abby was too distraught to stay quiet for very long. "There's something else I'd like to say, if you're open to some unsolicited advice."

"Only a fool won't listen to those who know better than him."

"Is that your pa speaking again?"

"My Uncle Shakespeare."

"You're so fortunate," Abby said. "So fortunate." She faced away. "But I wanted to talk about your future, not your family. I saw you, you know."

"Pardon?"

"I saw you with Bluebird."

Zach was thankful the night hid his reaction. "She and I are just friends," he said self-consciously, a trifle peeved the woman had brought the subject up since his personal affairs were none of her business.

"You can't hide true romance from a romantic," Abigail said. "I noticed how the two of you were looking at one another. I saw you holding hands."

"So?"

"Don't waste your life, Zachary."

"I've lost the trail."

"Two years of my life have been spent in captivity. Two years are gone, years I can never replace, never relive." Abby spoke somberly, earnestly. "If I've learned nothing else from my ordeal, it's that time is too damned precious to be wasted. So don't waste yours. Make the best of your life, Zach. Remember that every minute you spend unhappy is a minute you could have spent happy if you seize your life by the reins and guide it where you want to go and not where it takes you. Do you see my point?"

"I think so," Zach said, recalling that White Grass had said something to the same effect. What a peculiar coincidence.

"Too many people drift through this world as if it doesn't matter one whit what they do or where they go. They're wrong, son. Dead wrong. We're not allotted much time as it is. Better, I think, to use it to full advantage."

"I'll remember, ma'am."

"Quit calling me that. You make me feel older than I am. Abby will do fine."

"I'll remember, Abby."

The prairie became broken by intermittent low hills. Sparse trees afforded concealment and Zach threaded a course among them while steadily bearing toward the Yellowstone. On his current heading they would come out miles east of where he had first tangled with the Blackfeet.

Abby became calmer the more distance they covered. She rode better, too, as she and the paint became accustomed to one another.

Zach wished she hadn't mentioned Bluebird. He saw the girl's lovely face in the starry sky, in the rustling grass, in clusters of trees. Try as he might, he couldn't banish her from his thoughts. He fretted he would go on pining after the first love of his life forever.

It was a faint shout that succeeded where Zach's will had not. Stiffening, he swiveled and heard another shout. The Blackfeet had spread farther westward. Perhaps they guessed his tactic and were trying to head him off. To do that they would have to send warriors southwest to get between the river and them.

Suddenly, directly ahead not more than a mile or two, a single rifle shot rang clear.

"That's a signal!" Abby said. "They're in front of us now! How?"

Prairie Blood

Drawing rein, Zach gnawed on his lower lip. He'd made a mistake. They should have galloped all the way to the river instead of pacing their mounts. "A few fast horses must have gotten there ahead of us. By swinging farther west, we'll miss them."

"I pray you're right."

So did Zach. A lowland rife with vegetation was the route he chose to take them another mile. They had to pick their way carefully at times because there was no moon. To their advantage, they were well screened from the surrounding hills.

At the edge of the brush Zach halted to study the lay of the land. To their right, prairie. To their left, hills apparently extending clear to the river. Were there Blackfeet in those hills? he wondered.

"Which way?" Abby asked apprehensively.

"Stay close," Zach advised, swinging southward once more. To reduce the noise they made he walked the horses, the lance across his hips. He would much rather have had a rifle or a bow, but the lance would do. Like all Shoshone boys, he'd spent many hours practicing its use, both from horseback and afoot. He wasn't the equal of a grown warrior but he could hit a man-sized target from ten feet off ten times out of ten.

Katydids called from the trees. An owl answered. A tree frog chimed in, indicating the presence of a spring or a stream.

"This land can be so darned beautiful at times," Abby remarked softly.

Admiring the scenery was the last thing on Zach's mind. They were winding lower along a series of switchbacks. In the distance the Yellowstone materialized, a pale ribbon against the inky backdrop of darkness.

"Look! Do you see it?"

Zach wanted her to keep quiet. A single slip now would result in calamity. He was turning to shush her when the bay's ears shot erect, pointing to the left. A second later he heard the crackle of dry undergrowth and stopped.

Abby, gasping, did the same.

There was movement in the growth flanking the switchback and a rider appeared, a warrior astride a magnificent war horse, a rifle hooked in his left elbow. He was gazing down toward the river. Behind him came another, partially hidden in gloom.

In another moment either of the Blackfeet would turn and spot them. Zach did not bother to formulate a plan. He simply rammed his heels into the bay and charged, leveling the lance as he had heard the old-time knights did theirs in the books his father read to him when he was smaller.

The Blackfeet heard and twisted, the foremost rider bringing his rifle up, the other reaching behind him for an arrow in the quiver on his back.

Zach leaned forward and tucked the lance tight under his arm to absorb the brunt of the impact. He expected to be jolted. The tip of the lance struck the warrior on the side of the chest, slicing through flesh as readily as a knife through lard and unhorsing the Blackfoot. The force of the blow was so slight Zach almost doubted the lance had connected until he saw the man toppling.

Yanking on the bay's mane, Zach swung the animal around the riderless mount. As he did, he straightened, reversed his grip, and hurled the lance at the second warrior from a range of six feet. The Blackfoot was in the act of notching the arrow; he took the lance squarely in the stomach.

In a clatter of hooves Zach was past them and speeding down the switchback. He looked once to make sure Abby was still behind him, then he devoted his full attention to negotiating the hazardous trail. A gulf appeared where part of the ground had buckled. Urging the bay on, he sailed over the cleft, the wind whipping his hair.

Landing heavily, the bay faltered, buckled, nearly went down. Zach had to clamp his legs fast and lock his fingers into the mane to stay on. He brought the horse to a stop and turned just as Abby jumped the gap.

It was obvious she was in trouble in midair. The paint hadn't jumped high enough or far enough. Legs rigid, it hit shy of the rim. Loose dirt slid from under its hooves and it slipped backward.

Abby showed her mettle. She let go and shoved off, vaulting at the edge, her hands grasping for purchase.

At the same instant Zach leaped from the bay and dashed to the edge. He saw her fingers digging desperately for a hold and dived, closing his hands on her wrists. She was too heavy for him to hold for long. But the seconds of leverage he gave her were all she needed to brace her knees, dig in her toes, and heave herself over the top.

They clung to one another, Zack shaken by the close call, Abby trembling uncontrollably. From below rose thuds and whinnies of torment as the paint tumbled down the slope.

"We have to keep going," Zach admonished. In confirmation of his point, one of the Blackfeet cut loose with ear-splitting screeches to draw others. "We'll ride double from here on out."

The bay stood panting as they mounted. Zach felt Abby's arms slip around his waist, felt her press against his back. He continued lower, moving as fast as the terrain permitted. He hoped the land would flatten once they reached bottom but found a confusing maze of gullies and hillocks blocked in spots by downed trees. Picking his way through was an annoyingly slow process. He could imagine the Blackfeet closing in from all directions.

An hour passed. The gullies gave way to knolls, and before long Zach was on a high point a quarter of a mile from the Yellowstone.

Horsemen moved below.

Zach cut back, into timber. Again he bore westward, avoiding clearings where possible. He had to shake the Blackfeet for good, yet the only way he could think of entailed great risk.

The timber ended, mesquite taking its place. Zach reined up, lending an ear to what the breeze had to tell him, which in this instance was nothing at all. The screeching had long since died, perhaps the screecher also.

"Why have we stopped?" Abby whispered.

"I have a plan." Zach pointed. "I'm afraid

we've got to cross the river."

"Do you know where it's safe?"

"No. We'll just have to pick a likely spot and say our prayers before we try."

"We'll be sitting ducks if the Blackfeet spot us."

"I know. But it's our only hope. By morning this area will be swarming with them. South of the Yellowstone is Sioux country, and they might think twice before venturing over yonder."

"If you think it's best," Abby declared. "You've gotten us farther than I ever thought we'd get, so do what you have to. And one more thing."

"Ma'am?"

"In case something happens, I want you to know you're more man than most men I know. You'll make your pa proud when you grow up."

Zach rode toward the pale ribbon, stopping often to scour the landscape. The bay was tuckered out and plodded at times. A line of willows and cottonwoods was all that separated them from the gurgling water when Zach heard the ringing crack of a hoof striking a rock somewhere to the left. He gained the sanctuary of the trees and halted.

Five riders moved along the river's edge from east to west, their outlines stark black against the rippling surface. All had lances or bows.

Stroking the bay so it wouldn't nicker, Zach waited with baited breath for the Blackfeet to ride from sight. Beyond them the Yellowstone gurgled softly. He had no idea how deep the river was at that point, nor could he accurately judge the distance to the opposite shore. Both would have been nice to know. Had there been time, he would have checked. But he had to cross before the Blackfeet discovered them, so he would just have to chance it.

The five warriors stopped. Zach gripped the hilt of his knife, prepared to slash his way through if the Blackfeet had spotted the bay. They seemed to be peering across the Yellowstone, although why they should do so mystified him. Presently the foremost warrior barked a single word and the entire party rode on.

"Get set," Zach whispered to Abby. He listened to the dull clop of hooves, and when they died, he nudged the bay across the flat strip of rocky shoreline. Abby's arms constricted around his waist and she breathed in shallow puffs as if fearing the Blackfeet would hear her.

Zach looked right and left. Nothing else moved along the river but there might be warriors hidden in the brush. Dreading an outcry or the report of a rifle, he came to the water. The bay stopped and had to be goaded before it slowly entered.

To Zach's anxious mind, the slight splashing the horse caused sounded like the roar of a waterfall. He felt the animal tense up under him and he didn't blame it. The water was too murky to see under the surface. An unseen hole or cleft could result in a bad fall or a broken leg.

The bay halted of its own accord, nervously bobbing its head. Zach smacked his legs against its sides to prod it on. The current didn't look very strong and he saw no evidence of rapids or whirlpools. Gradually the water level rose, first to the bay's ankles, then to its hocks, then to its belly. The lower half of Zach's moccasins were soon soaked

Twenty feet farther the bay stopped again, ears pricked toward the south shore. Zach looked but saw no cause for alarm. He had to drive his heels into the animal's flanks repeatedly before it would move, and when it advanced it did so skittishly, seemingly fearful of whatever lay ahead.

They were about at the midway point when shouts broke out on the north side of the Yellowstone. The rattle of hooves attended the shouts.

Glancing around, Zach spied another search party heading in the same direction as the first. They were forty yards to the east and very close to the water. Too close, Zach thought. All one of the warriors had to do was turn his head and he would see them.

"Bend low," Zach cautioned, doing so as he drew rein. Abby shifted her weight on top of him, and pressed together they watched the Blackfeet approach.

"It's Cream Bear!" she said fearfully.

The lead warrior did appear to have Cream Bear's build, but Zach couldn't be sure if it was or it wasn't. The Blackfeet went by without slowing. Once they were gone, he finished crossing, rode a quarter of a mile onto the prairie, then swung westward.

"We did it!" Abby said in amazement, giving him a squeeze. "Or I should say, you did it."

"We're not out of the woods yet," Zach said.

"Some of the varmints might have crossed to this side."

For the rest of the night they trotted westward, both of them so on edge they started at any unfamiliar or loud noise. Zach was mighty tired by the time the eastern sky brightened with the advent of sunrise. His gaze had seldom wandered from the north side of the Yellowstone but he had seen no trace of their pursuers.

Now, with daylight so near, Zach remarked, "We should hole up and rest a while."

"Don't stop on my account. I can go on all day if need be."

"I'm not thinking of us. It's the horse that needs a break, unless you like the notion of walking clear to the Rockies."

"We'll stop."

A large tract of thick woodland where the river curved was the site Zach selected. He had ridden a dozen yards into the dense undergrowth before he realized something was wrong. No birds were singing, no small animals were present. And on taking a deep breath he smelled the faint odor of wood smoke.

"They're here!" Zach declared, lifting the reins to wheel the bay. He was much too slow. From out of the brush on both sides figures in buckskins pounced, some grabbing hold of the bay, others seizing Zach and Abby and pulling them off.

Zach heard Abby cry out. He got his fingers around the hilt of his knife as brawny arms swept him to the ground. Like a striking snake he whipped the blade overhead to strike and then froze in disbelief on seeing the curly black beard covering the lower half of the face above him.

"Hold on there, small coon! Don't be stickin' old Miles. We don't mean you no harm. We just didn't want your horse to run off or make a fuss. Truth is, we took you for a young Injun at first. Thought maybe you were one of the Blackfeet we saw prowlin' the other side of the river a while ago."

"You're white!" Zach blurted.

"As a sheet," Miles jested.

Zach gawked at the other four men. "You're all trappers!" he deduced.

"And not no company men, neither," Miles said proudly. "We're all free as tumbleweed." He gave Zach a friendly clap on the shoulder. "So what say you put that pigsticker away and come chaw with the booshway of our outfit. We'll be wantin' to know all about you."

"This lady is Abby. I'm Zachary King, son of Nate King. Maybe some of you have heard—" Zach began, then stopped. They were looking at him as if he was some sort of creature not seen every day.

"King, you say?" Miles said, sounding astounded. "It's true, I reckon. This sure enough is a damned small world."

"I don't understand."

"You will, soon enough," Miles promised.

A dozen yards brought them to the edge of a wide clearing where other trappers were engaged in various tasks. The frontiersmen glanced up, their surprise at seeing a white woman so profound many of them were utterly dumfounded.

311

Zach barely noticed them. He was dumfounded himself on seeing a white-haired figure propped on a saddle near a low fire. Racing over, Zach sank to one knee and touched the mountain man's arm. "Uncle Shakespeare? Are you all right?"

Shakespeare McNair opened his eyes and blinked. "Zach? That you son, or am I dreaming again?"

"It's me. Oh Lord, I'm glad to see you!" Zach went to give the older man a hug but Shakespeare weakly raised a hand, stopping him.

"Better not yet. I'm a mite sore from the operation still."

Zach was going to ask what McNair meant when a smothered squeal diverted his gaze to the middle of the clearing where Abigail Griffen was hurling herself into the outstretched arms of a dazed trapper. He heard her sob, saw tears pour down her face. "Who—?" he wondered aloud.

"Lane Griffen is the gent's name," Shakespeare said. "And If I had to hazard a guess, I'd bet that woman is the wife he feared he'd lost."

"She is," Zach confirmed, his elation knowing no bounds. He wanted to leap up and whoop for joy. Everything had turned out just fine, better than he had dared to hope, almost as if the hand of Providence had guided them. "Where are ma and pa?

"I thought maybe you could tell me," Shakespeare said. "We were separated during the storm and I haven't seen hide nor hair of them since."

"They could be dead, then."

"Don't jump to conclusions, son. It's bad for the disposition." Shakespeare smiled frailly. "Besides, we both know your pa is a survivor. If it's humanly possible he'll track us down."

Zach observed Abby and Lane embracing and kissing, heedless of the other trappers, and an odd sort of heavy sensation filled his chest. "I hope you're right," he said softly. "Lord, I truly do."

Chapter Twenty-one

Indian lives were governed by rituals. There were rituals for greeting the new day, rituals to go through before going on buffalo surrounds, rituals to perform before marriage, rituals to heal. And there were rituals done before going on the warpath.

The Pawnees held theirs the night before the war party departed for Sioux country. A grand feast attended by all was followed by a dance in which the warriors going on the raid participated. Mimicking the deeds of valor they hoped to achieve in battle, they held mock fights, counting imaginary coup. The women and children were caught up in the martial spirit and encouraged their favorites on.

Nate King was left to his own devices. Those who supported Mole On The Nose shunned him. Those who backed White Calf were involved in the festivities. He sat on the side, in the shadow of a lodge bordering the central area of the village where the ceremony was being held, and watched the dance unfold. It was a lot like the dances of the Shoshones and held no great interest for him. He was preoccupied with visions of escape, pondering various ways of doing so once the war party left the village far behind. There was no doubt the medicine man would keep a close eye on him. But it was a long journey to Sioux land, and eventually the Pawnees were bound to relax their vigilance.

At the moment a number of warriors, shamming the part of Sioux, cowered before the onslaught of Pawnee attackers. White Calf was among the latter, dispatching enemies with mock glee that hinted at the sadistic savagery he would resort to in real warfare.

Nate had to admit that the medicine man was different from most he'd met. The majority were healers, plain and simple. Some mended the sick, invoked spirits, and presided over tribal functions. White Calf did all those things and did the others one better; he was also a warrior. Occasionally medicine men took part in combat, usually when their village was set upon by enemies. It was rare for one to actively seek coup as White Calf was doing.

But then, Nate reflected, the others lacked White Calf's secret motive. By establishing himself as a warrior of note, White Calf doubled the prestige he already enjoyed as medicine man. All to further his fervent ambition to be the most powerful man in the whole Pawnee nation.

Glory mongers, as Shakespeare liked to call them, were a lot alike, whether white or red. They craved influence over all else. They always thought of themselves first. And everyone else was a means to their end.

Nate sighed and stared at the ground. He was sick to death of staying with the Pawnees and hankered to be out seeking his family. Angrily jabbing a finger into the dirt, he saw a shadow fall across his legs and glanced up.

Standing a few feet off was the young woman saved from the black bear. She wore an expression of utter dread. The finest of buckskin dresses covered her full figure, and she had washed and braided her hair.

"Hello," Nate signed, trying to recollect her name. It came to him so he added, "It is a pleasure to see you again, Black Buffalo Woman."

The frightened Pawnee smiled, a twisted curling of her cheery lips that more resembled a grimace. "Yes, Sky Walker. I am pleased to see you."

Nate doubted as much. He thought she was just being polite and would turn and leave, so he was taken aback when she strode forward and knelt submissively in front of him.

"I am ready."

"For what?"

"For tonight."

At a loss, Nate leaned against the lodge and

signed, "You must forgive me. I have no idea what you are talking about."

"You did not tell White Calf that you wanted a woman for the night? You did not order him to have me sent to you?"

Controlling his budding temper with difficulty, Nate stared at the medicine man, now disemboweling a dead 'Sioux'. "He sent you?"

"Yes. He said those like yourself who come from above the clouds are fond of our women. He said that since you favored me by sparing me from the bear, I had a duty to present myself to you so that you might do as you please with me."

There had been a time when Nate King might have accepted the offer. That was before Winona, before he met the woman he loved more than life itself and vowed to be her man for as long they both lived.

Plenty of trappers had more than one wife. Some had two or three Indian wives, others had a single Indian wife and a white wife back in the settlements. Still others were married but no one would know it from their sexual shenanigans.

Nate King was not party to the goings-on. He had been raised in a puritanical household by a strict father and molded to believe love between a man and woman was special, a unique pairing that must be preserved at all costs and never violated by unfaithfulness.

In the years since Nate had taken Winona as his bride in a simple Shoshone ceremony, he had never dishonored the memory of that

special event. He had remained true to her trust.
And on those few occasions when other women
had offered themselves to him, he had declined.

Nate looked at Black Buffalo Woman, at the
swell of her bosom under her dress, and signed,
"You do me great honor with your offer but I
cannot accept."

"Do I displease you?"

"No."

"Am I too ugly? Too plain?"

"You are a very lovely woman."

"I have washed and put on a new dress just
for you. I have put mint in my hair and sucked
on sweet berries."

"You smell very fragrant."

"Should there be anything else I can do to
make myself more appealing to you, let me
know and it will be done."

The woman's frantic attitude puzzled Nate.
He figured she would be glad he had declined.
Yet she acted as if her very life depended on his
acceptance of her offer. "Black Buffalo Woman, you are as pretty a woman as I have ever
seen. Any warrior here would be thrilled to
stand under a buffalo robe with you. Go mingle with your people and find the man of your
choice."

"It must be you," she insisted.

"Why?"

Black Buffalo Woman hesitated.

"Our words are strictly between us," Nate
signed. "No one is paying attention. They are
all too involved with the dance."

"He will know," she signed, holding her hands
close to her waist so no one except him could
see.

"Who?"

"I cannot say. He will bring bad medicine down on my father and mother if I talk about him behind his back. He is very powerful."

The word explained everything. Nate looked at White Calf, who had scalped the 'dead' warrior and was holding a mock trophy aloft in triumph. He moved his hands close to his own waist to prevent anyone else from reading them, and signed, "I know who you mean. Question. You are very scared of him?"

The young woman trembled.

"There is no need to tell me. I can see for myself." Nate leaned closer to her. "Do you believe I am who he claims? The truth, please."

"I did not think so at first. Then you saved me, killing the great bear. Now I know you are."

"And if that is so, am I not more powerful than he who sent you?"

"You are mightier than a hundred like him. He has told us so himself, many times."

"Then why do you fear? You are under my protection, as I have already proven. If he hurts you or threatens to hurt you, I will punish him severely."

Black Buffalo Woman gazed at him in wonder. "Why do you do this for me?"

"Because I want you to see that he does not speak on my behalf. He does not know what is in my mind or my heart. Only I can say how I truly think and feel. Let your family and friends know this."

"He will be unhappy when he hears we did not spend the night together."

"He will be even more unhappy if he touches you or your family. This I, Sky Walker, vow."

The gratitude in the young woman's eyes as she rose gave Nate a warm feeling deep inside. He reached out, touched her fingers. Instead of flinching, she responded to his squeeze. Then, shy as a doe, she scampered into the midst of the crowd.

Near the fire, White Calf danced in fierce abandon, unaware of the thwarting of his plan.

Nate unconsciously put his hand on his flintlock. It reminded him of the attempt on his life and he scanned the faces of the Pawnees to see if any betrayed the intense hatred of one who might be inclined to try and split his skull before the night was through. He hadn't relaxed since the attack, despite the medicine man's assurances that no one else would dare try to kill him.

True to White Calf's prediction, the sole survivor had refused to divulge the identify of whoever put him up to it. Rumor had it the Bear Society had sheathed their claws after the thwarted try and stopped spreading malicious tales about Nate.

One mystery had been cleared up, however, at least to Nate's satisfaction. Shortly after the attempt, he'd learned of four warriors who owned guns. They all possessed small amounts of black powder and lead balls. They all knew how to properly load a pistol. And three of the four were members of the Bear Society.

The dance wound down. The people began to scatter to their lodges. White Calf, flanked by warriors who would be leaving on the morrow, came over to Nate. "I am surprised to see you still here, Sky Walker," he signed. "I arranged for you to have companionship tonight."

"When I want companionship," Nate responded, "I will request it."

"She must not have been attractive enough. I am sorry. I assumed she would be since you came to her aid at the river. But never fear. I will find another when we return from our raid."

Nate had an urge to grab the medicine man by the front of the shirt and shake the stuffing out of the him. But he dared not, since it would jeopardize his prospects of escaping. "That will be fine," he signed. "Remember though that Black Buffalo Woman is special to me and I do not want her touched in any way."

"Ahh. You are saving her for later. I should have guessed. It will be done."

Nate stood and changed the subject before his anger made him do something he would regret. "Do we leave at dawn?"

"We do. Twenty warriors go with us. Within three sleeps we will be in Sioux country. Within six sleeps we will be where the Sioux like to camp during the Heat Moon." White Calf rubbed his hands in glee. "We will strike terror into their hearts. And when we return our people will sing our praises."

Nate allowed himself to be led toward the medicine man's dwelling. Singly and in pairs the attending warriors veered off to their own lodges. Soon only Nate and White Calf were left.

"Will you sleep outside again?"

"I will," Nate signed. "That reminds me. Is the bear hide ready? I would like to use it tonight."

"The final scraping was done today. I have it inside." White Calf stooped and entered.

Moving to the spot where he customarily slept, Nate gave the roll of bedding a kick that sent it tumbling off. The lice–infested blankets made him itch all over every time he looked at them. He would be glad to have the clean hide in which to bundle himself.

Nate heard the medicine man moving about within. Stretching, he rubbed a stiff spot low on his back, then gazed at the river, which reminded him of the storm and the rain–swollen Yellowstone. He thought of his family, of Shakespeare, and prayed they were still alive.

The movement in the lodge had stopped. Nate heard rustling, then several odd grunts. He turned toward the entrance just as two warriors locked in mortal combat rolled outside. For a moment he stood riveted with surprise, watching Red Rock throttle the life from White Calf

No one wanted the medicine man dead more than Nate did. But White Calf was the sole reason Nate hadn't been rubbed out. And White Calf's raid was Nate's sole hope of salvation. So, belatedly, Nate took a step and leaped.

Red Rock had the instincts of a panther. Glancing up in the nick of time, he released the medicine man and ducked aside, drawing his knife. Nate drew his own and feinted, thinking to force the warrior into overextending himself but Red Rock was too smart for the ruse.

Nate circled, awaiting an opening. He saw that White Calf wasn't moving, saw blood on the medicine man's mouth. His lapse of attention almost cost him dearly. Red Rock lunged, blade spearing at Nate's heart. Parrying, Nate skipped to the left and swung at the warrior's hamstring but slippery as an eel Red Rock evaded the blow.

Anxious to find out if his sole hope for freedom lived, Nate went for the flintlock. Red Rock must have been expecting him to because the warrior's knife got there first, nicking the back of his hand as the pistol cleared the belt. The sting of pain made him drop it as blood trickled over his wrist.

Red Rock laughed lightly, a dry, hateful, mocking laugh that expressed more than words ever could why he had violated tribal taboo and attacked them. He had been humiliated time and again. He had seen his ambush fail. He had endured having the Bear Society insulted, his own status mocked. And it had driven him over the edge.

Nate deflected a lightning thrust, tried to stab the Pawnee's groin and in turn lost some fringe off the sleeve of his shirt.

Shifting his weight from foot to foot, Nate attempted to keep his antagonist off balance. Like weaving snakes they thrust and retreated and thrust again. Nate drew blood when he creased the warrior's thigh.

The village lay quiet under the stars. Most had retired or were in the process. The dogs were still, the horses dozing. None would have suspected another dance of death was taking place, one decidedly more lethal than the mock acting done earlier.

A simple shout would have brought assistance. Nate could have yelled and warriors would rush to the scene. But he didn't. This was between Red Rock and himself, the inevitable result of the blind hatred bred in the warrior's breast by the differences in their skin color. This was the time to finish it, once and for all.

Nate suddenly took a step and kicked, down low. The Pawnee hopped to avoid it and Nate grabbed Red Rock's knife arm at the same moment he slammed his shoulder into the warrior's midriff. Together they crashed to the earth, Nate on top, exerting all his strength as he tried to pin Red Rock's arm while he lanced his butcher knife at the Pawnee's stomach.

Red Rock caught Nate's wrist, stopping the blade inches from his skin. Chest to chest they toiled, each to gain the upper hand. Nate made no headway. To gain distance, he rammed a knee into the warrior's leg and when Red Rock recoiled, he shoved free, then swept upright.

The Pawnee did the same, his blade close to his chest, his face glistening with sweat.

Nate moved to the right. Red Rock moved to the left. Nate stabbed high and the warrior's knife clanged against his. Pivoting in a blur, Nate tried again, low this time.

Like an oversized jackrabbit Red Rock leaped high into the air. The knife cleaved the space under him and as he came down he tried to cut Nate's hand off at the wrist. Nate barely jerked his arm back in time.

The warrior grinned, either to taunt Nate or

to show he was confident he would prevail or both. He unleashed a flurry of strikes that Nate deflected or dodged. And it was then, while both were totally engrossed in their vicious clash, that White Calf groaned loudly.

Either one of them might have looked but it was the Pawnee who automatically glanced at the medicine man, and it was the Pawnee who paid for his folly by having his stomach sheared into by nine inches of cold, hard steel.

Red Rock's features reflected incredulity as his body melted into wax of its own accord. He clawed at Nate's face, missed, and seized Nate's shoulder. By a titanic effort he tried to stay erect, to raise his knife. He weakened so rapidly, he was on the ground before he could.

Nate wrenched his blade out and wiped it off on the Pawnee's leggings. "You should have left well enough alone," he said, "Less than twelve hours from now I would have been out of your hair for good."

Red Rock spoke softly in his own tongue. He began to convulse, his arms and legs twitching. Blood frothed his lips, dribbled over his chin. Without making another sound, he closed his eyes and died.

Suddenly tired, Nate sat down. He felt eyes on him, heard footsteps, and sighing, looked up.

"You saved me," White Calf signed.

"I saved both of us."

"He was waiting for you, I think, and I happened to go into the lodge first. Had I not bumped into him while searching for the bear hide he would have cut you down as you entered." The medicine man laughed with sadistic pleasure. "Now the second most powerful threat to me is gone, and without the support of Red Rock, Mole On The Nose will soon lose his influence. The people will say all of his medicine is gone. *I* will be the one they look up to."

Nate stared at the knife in his hand. One stroke was all it would take. One stroke and he would do the Pawnees the biggest favor any white man had ever done them, maybe the biggest anyone had ever done them. Sadly he stuck the knife in his sheath.

"I must go spread the news," White Calf signed. "When the people hear, no one will dare defy me again." Sneering at the corpse, he hurried off.

Sometimes life was too ridiculous for words, Nate reflected. Rising, he took a breath and entered the lodge. The bear hide was near the entrance, where it must have dropped when the two Pawnees tangled. He carried it out, shook it vigorously, then walked behind the lodge and spread it out. Voices came to him on the wind. Criers were going around the village informing the Pawnees. He laid down on his back, wrapped the bear pelt around him, and tried to fall asleep.

The uproar made rest impossible. From every corner of the village the Pawnees flocked, many with torches, lighting up the area around the medicine man's lodge as if it were daylight. Their chatter went on for hours.

Nate had almost drifted off when the ground crunched under the pressure of dozens of feet.

He cracked an eyelid to find Pawnees filing past. Gripping the pistol, he moved it to the edge of the hide, but there was no need to shoot. They weren't there to exact revenge. They gazed on him with varying degrees of awe and fear, whispering amongst themselves. The parade went on and on.

It was past midnight when the village quieted. The body was removed. White Calf came to sign goodnight, so cheerful it was sickening, then went in.

Nate propped his head in his hands, listening to a bullfrog croak. A cough made him aware of two warriors nearby, guards posted by the medicine man to guarantee no one bothered him before morning.

Excitement kept Nate awake now, excitement born of the first glimmer of hope since the whirlwind. One thing was certain. No matter the outcome, he wasn't coming back to the Pawnee village. He would regain his cherished freedom or he would perish, and if that was his fate he would die defying his captors with his last breath.

He would die as a man should.

Chapter Twenty-two

Practically all tribes went on the warpath periodically. Some did so more often than others because warfare was the yardstick by which the warriors measured their manhood; they needed to count coup to advance in tribal standing. Other tribes raided for plunder, for horses and guns and whatnot. Others, pacifists by nature, resorted to war only to avenge an attack.

The tactics employed were the same: locate an enemy encampment, wait for a suitable moment, then swarm into the unsuspecting village slaughtering with savage abandon or sneak in and make off with the property desired.

There were two means of reaching enemy territory, either on foot or on horseback. Some tribes, like the Apaches and those allied in the

Blackfoot Confederacy, preferred the first way. Others, like the Pawnees, used either, depending on how far they had to travel.

On this raid they rode, with White Calf in the lead and the nineteen men who had volunteered to go along spread out in a ragged line in his wake. All wore breechcloths and moccasins and little else. Most had painted their bodies with splashes of red or yellow. Some had symbols on their chests or on their mounts. The most common was a likeness of the human hand, which stood for foes killed in personal combat. One brave was armed with a rifle, the rest with bows or lances. War clubs and tomahawks were abundant. And every man carried a knife.

Nate King rode alongside the medicine man, his bear hide tied behind him. It was midday, and they were six hours out from the village. Shimmering grassland surrounded them, broken by rare islands of trees. Antelope were a common sight, fleet animals that bounded off in prodigious leaps at speeds no horse could ever match. Hawks wheeled on the air currents. Every so often scattered groups of buffaloes were seen.

White Calf waxed eloquent, jawing on and on in his tongue. Nate noticed that the warriors hung on every word. Whether they did so out of loyalty or fear, he couldn't say.

That evening the war party camped in a hollow. A small fire was built. The best hunters headed into the grass and returned an hour later with enough rabbits to fill everyone. Chunks of raw meat were impaled on arrows, then roasted over the open flames.

Nate tucked himself into his bear hide early and tried to sleep. Excitement made him restless. It was the middle of the night before he dozed off.

The next day was a repeat of the first, and the three days that followed. Toward the middle of the fifth afternoon the Pawnees bunched up and became markedly more vigilant.

"Are we close to Sioux country?" Nate asked the medicine man.

"We are in Sioux country," White Calf revealed. "And we must stay alert in case we are seen. If an alarm is given, we would be set upon by every warrior in the tribe. They would hem us in, cut us off, rub us out."

"Maybe we should travel at night."

"That is taboo."

Nor would most other Indians do it, thanks to a widespread superstitious dread of being killed after dark. Many tribes believed that the soul of a man slain at night would be unable to reach the next side. Others held that the bodies of such men were tainted, to be denied proper burial or whatever means was used to dispose of the dead.

"You should send out scouts," Nate suggested.

"I know what to do," White Calf signed in juvenile irritation. "I have led war parties before." At barked orders from him, three warriors left the main group, one riding a quarter of a mile to the right, another an equal distance to the left, while the third rode well in advance.

"Satisfied?" White Calf signed.

Shortly thereafter they came on an Indian road. Well worn by frequent use, it was eight feet wide and ran from north to south. The Pawnees were quite agitated by the discovery since it meant they were in the heart of Sioux land. They immediately swung to the northwest, into the prairie, and shunned all roads from then on.

That night they made a cold camp. Nate sat with his back propped on his folded hide, watching the stars appear. By them he could orient his position in relation to the Yellowstone River.

White Calf strolled over, a blanket around his shoulders. Sitting, he signed, "Tomorrow we will reach the village. The morning after we strike. I pray your good medicine will bring us success."

"I will do what I can but there is only so much I can do," Nate signed. "I will be one against many." He didn't point out that he intended to slip away under cover of the battle and leave the Pawnees to fend for themselves. "You will be greatly outnumbered."

"But we will have surprise on our side," White Calf said, "and that is the same as having five times as many men. We will slay the Sioux as they run from their lodges, while they are still sluggish from sleep. If they cannot organize resistance they will bend before us like limbs bending in the wind, then break when the confusion is at its highest. In a panic they will try to run but we will rub them out as they do."

Nate had never been one to regard wholesale slaughter as anything other than the rank butchery it was. "You will count many coup," he signed noncommittally.

"And capture many horses, for the Sioux are rich in them," White Calf signed greedily. "But that is not all."

"What more?"

"There is one other thing we must do, and here your help would be of great benefit, Sky Walker. You can pick one without blemish, one who will be pleasing to Tirawa."

"Pick a horse?"

"No. A maiden."

An invisible icy finger scraped Nate's spine. "You want me to select the next sacrifice?"

"If you would." White Calf signed. "For who should know better than one sent by Tirawa how to please him?" The Pawnee chuckled. "There will be many beautiful women to choose from. While we keep the men occupied, find one who is perfect." He smacked his lips like someone who had just tasted a delicious morsel. "If we rout the warriors and have the time, maybe I will find a maiden for myself. I have not lived with a woman in eight or nine winters and it would be nice to have a warm, young body to keep me warm on cold nights."

"And then you would sacrifice her when you tire of her?" Nate asked.

The medicine man acted indignant. "You test me, Sky Walker. We both know only pure maidens may be sacrificed or bad medicine will result. Our crops would wither, our river dry up, our young be born dead." He idly rubbed his belly. "No, when I tire of them I offer to trade them off. Or, if they have given me trouble, I send them home."

"Back across the prairie alone? That is the same as sending them to their deaths."

"Life is hard."

Disgusted, Nate unrolled the bear hide and spread it out as a signal he wanted privacy in order to sleep. But the medicine man had more on his mind.

"I have been meaning to ask, Sky Walker. How much longer will you remain among us?"

As short a time as possible, Nate reflected. Hands flowing, he signed, "I have not decided yet."

The medicine man looked around, verifying none of the other warriors were paying attention. "It might be best if you were to return to the clouds before we return to our village."

"You want me to go?"

"I always knew you would not stay with us forever." White Calf's mouth curled in an odd sort of smile. "You have other tribes to visit, other medicine men to honor with your presence."

Sarcasm dripped from every gesture. Nate, confused, signed, "You will let me go? Just like that?"

"Were you to stay, mighty one, sooner or later you might make a mistake, might forget yourself and do something that would give the people cause to believe you are less than I have claimed. And if they should decide you are not a sky walker, but instead are an ordinary lowly white man, they would tear both of us apart with their bare hands for daring to deceive them."

Nate was flabbergasted. Was the medicine man saying he'd known all along Nate was a trapper? How could that be, unless White Calf had been putting on an act the whole time? If so, it meant the Pawnee had been using him in ways he hadn't even imagined. Suddenly he saw White Calf in a whole new, chilling, light, saw him as deviltry made flesh. He'd already learned the medicine man would do anything to gain more power over the Pawnees, but this newest revelation exposed the full wicked extent of White Calf's sadistic, conniving, cruel nature.

"I see the look in your eyes," White Calf signed. "I can guess your questions." He bent forward. "Right this moment you want to know my innermost thoughts more than you have ever wanted to know anything. You want me to speak with a straight tongue, to confirm your suspicions. But I will not, great Sky Walker. You must decide for your own self whether I am more or less than I have seemed. You must decide whether I am the sly simpleton you have taken me for or the man who will one day lead the Pawnees to the greatness they deserve."

With that, the medicine man stood and rejoined his fellows, leaving Nate to piece together the truth from the events as they had unfolded. He remembered how fearful White Calf had acted at their first meeting, and then later how White Calf abruptly changed and treated him so special. Had that been a sham, a ruse on White Calf's part to make him think the medicine man really did regard him as a being from above the clouds? Had White Calf used him to bring the power struggle with Mole On The Nose and Red Rock to a head?

Had White Calf set him up as bait, knowing Red Rock would try to prove he wasn't a sky walker?

There were so many unanswered aspects, Nate couldn't decide for sure. He couldn't see any one person being so deviously malevolent. And yet, there was no denying there was more to the medicine man than met the eye.

Something else occurred to Nate. If White Calf had used him to trick the whole tribe, the medicine man wouldn't care for anyone else to find out. White Calf might not be content to let him go his own way. Dead men, after all, kept secrets much better than live ones.

Nate draped a hand on the flintlock. It had always puzzled him that White Calf let him keep his weapons. Maybe now he knew why. The medicine man had wanted him to be able to defend himself since it wouldn't do for the mighty Sky Walker to be slain by mere warriors.

A combination of unease sparked by the new insight into White Calf and excitement over being so close to regaining his freedom made it difficult for Nate to drift off. His sleep was so short, he hardly felt rested when he was awakened by several of the Pawnees moving about before daylight.

This day was different from the rest. The warriors were as alert as prowling wolves, their weapons always in hand. A river appeared to the northwest. The war party promptly hastened into the undergrowth bordering it. They stuck to the heaviest cover from then on, stopping once early in the afternoon to water their mounts at a sheltered inlet.

It was here that Nate remembered to pose a question he had been meaning to ask since leaving the Pawnee village. "You told me we are raiding the Sioux," he signed to the medicine man, "but you did not say which branch of the Sioux it will be. Is it the Oglalas? The Brules? The Hunkpapas?"

"We raid the Minneconjous."

Soon the Pawnees were strung out in single file, advancing as soundlessly as they could. Nate rode third from the front, behind White Calf. Sunset was still an hour off when the lead rider reined up, and a second later Nate found why. He heard the merry titter of female laughter, the yell of children playing.

A single scout was sent ahead on foot. On his return he reported they were half a mile from a huge Minneconjou camp. A hundred yards from the heavy brush in which they hid was a pool in which the Minneconjou women washed clothes and youngsters swam.

White Calf issued whispered commands. The horses were herded into a makeshift pen formed by a wall of branches. The warriors crept to where they could see the pool. Beyond, scores of lodges had been set up in traditional order. There were not many Minneconjou warriors in evidence, leading Nate to wonder if most were off on a raid or out hunting buffalo.

It so happened that a small stream fed into the river a few dozen yards from where the Pawnees were concealed. The mouth of the stream was situated at such an angle from the village that it couldn't be seen, affording a degree of privacy, and in the waist-deep water Minneconjou women were accustomed to bathing.

The Pawnees gazed hungrily on the seven young women disporting themselves in the water. Naked bodies glistening, the women dived and swam and splashed one another, all the while chattering endlessly on. Nate saw White Calf eye the youngest of the bunch, then lick his lips.

The sun dipped to the horizon. The women dressed, joining an exodus into the village. Naturally the children dallied, wringing every last second of fun they could out of the day.

During the quiet twilight period a large group of warriors galloped home from the north. The Minneconjous scattered to their lodges, from which wafted cooking smoke mixed with the tantalizing odors of food. Nate's stomach grumbled but would get no relief. That night the Pawnees went hungry.

The war party slept in relays, with a third of the men slumbering at a time. Nate was the only one allowed to sleep the whole night through, but he couldn't. He tried and tried, finally giving up and stealthily moving to the picket line. As luck would have it, he squeezed between a pair of tall bushes and came on the medicine man.

"You cannot find rest either, Sky Walker?" White Calf signed, then continued before Nate could answer. "I do not blame you. Neither can I. Tomorrow is the day that will shape my whole future, the day I have been working toward for a very long time. And it is an important day for you, as well."

Nate stared at the darkened teepees.

"Have you ever gambled, Sky Walker?"

"Yes," Nate answered the unexpected query.

"Ever played with dice?"

"Yes," Nate signed again. The Shoshones had a game they were inordinately fond of that involved the use of buffalo-bone dice. So, he figured, did the Pawnees.

"Have you ever thought that our lives are a lot like games of chance? We pin our hopes on a roll of the dice, never knowing what fate will bring us. Yet the uncertainty never stops us from risking all we have in the hope of gaining more." White Calf paused. "Why is that?"

"There is no joy without effort, no excitement without risk."

"Well said. But there is more to it, I think. We are all gamblers at heart, whether we admit so or not, for life itself is a gamble, the biggest one we take." White Calf nodded at the lodges. "Some of us will die there. That is certain. Yet knowing this does not stop us from carrying out our attack."

"Because in our hearts most of us do not think we can die," Nate signed. "We believe death always happens to others, never to ourselves."

"Do you believe this, Sky Walker?"

"No. Our time may come at any moment. None of us is favored more by fate than others."

"You are wrong. Tirawa has favorites. I am living proof, since I am one." White Calf indicated the murky mouth of the stream. "That reminds me. Did you see those women bathing? The young one is my favorite. Should you see her tomorrow, take her captive."

"Is she to be your wife or a sacrifice?"

"My wife. Like Tirawa, I prefer women who have never laid with men, and she looks young enough to be a virgin." He indulged in his habit of smacking his lips. "I will drink her dry."

The medicine man left to make sure those who were supposed to be awake weren't dozing. Nate leaned against a tree and checked his pistol. He took a sharpening stone from his possibles bag to hone his knife and tomahawk, trying not to think of the uses they would be put to before the new day was done.

An hour before sunrise the Pawnees mounted their horses, then crossed the river at its narrowest, shallowest point. They rode to the east, taking cover in a dry wash that opened out fifty feet from the lodges. Now the sun would be at their backs when they attacked, giving them an extra slight advantage.

Bows were notched with arrows. Lances and shields were made ready. Tomahawks and war clubs were wedged loosely under breechcloths so as to be handy when needed.

None of the Pawnees spoke. They all knew what to do. Some would head straight for the clusters of Minneconjou horses, to drive the animals off. Others would rove among the lodges, slaying warriors as fast as they appeared. Still others would seek captives, either women or children, preferably young boys who would be reared as Pawnees.

Anxious eyes were fixed on the eastern sky. The black of night gave way to the dark blue of predawn, and among the teepees there was movement as women who were early risers walked to the river for water.

White Calf exhorted the members of his war party in soft tones, then raised his lance overhead and applied his heels to his horse. In a tight mass the warriors swept out of the wash and down on the unsuspecting village, giving voice to piercing war whoops along the way.

Nate had hoped to be able to escape the Pawnees long before this moment came, but had never been able to. There had always been warriors nearby, always someone watching over him or the horses. In moments, though, the Pawnees would be too busy to give him any thought, and he planned to veer off and cut through the village to the open plain and safety. The only hitch were the Sioux. They would slay him as readily as they would the Pawnees, and if he was taken alive they would torture him for days.

A pair of women heading for the river were the first Minneconjous to spot the attackers. Screaming in warning, they turned to run back but were downed by Pawnee arrows before they had gone three steps.

The war party split, Nate staying close to the medicine man's mount for the moment. The rumbling of hooves nearly drowned out the shouts breaking out in the lodges nearest the point of attack. He spied a sleepy Minneconjou warrior framed in the opening of a lodge an instant before an arrow imbedded itself in the warrior's throat. Another warrior rushed into the open trying to nock an arrow to his bow string and was run down by a Pawnee who speared him through the chest.

More yells added to the din. Horses were whinnying, small children wailing.

The Pawnees were ruthlessly efficient. They weaved among the lodges dispensing death with seasoned skill, their arrows accounting for a score of casualties among the Sioux before half the defenders quite knew what was happening.

Some of the Minneconjou women had set up cooking pots outside their lodges. The Pawnees upended every one, took burning brands from the cook fires, and set teepees ablaze. Fanned by the strong northwesterly breeze, the flames often leaped from lodge to lodge or crackled across open spaces to ignite another one. Thick columns of choking smoke soon spread outward, blotting out entire sections of the village.

In the meantime, the battle raged.

So far Nate had not needed to resort to his pistol. An arrow had whizzed over his head, but otherwise none of the Sioux had tried to rub him out.

Only two Pawnee warriors were with Nate and White Calf when they rounded a lodge and encountered a small knot of Minneconjous, men and women. The Pawnees closed, stabbing and slashing in unbridled ferocity, transforming the small open area into a milling swirl of confusion.

It was now or never, Nate reflected, slowing. Working the reins, he angled to the right, galloped past a smoldering lodge, and nearly collided with a Sioux on horseback, a tall man with a barrel chest. The Minneconjou held a bow. Nate saw him lift it, saw the arrow being drawn back to the man's cheek. In a twinkling Nate leveled the pistol and fired.

The ball ripped into the Minneconjou's right eye, the impact snapping his head back and knocking him off.

Nate didn't wait to verify the brave was dead. Jamming the flintlock under his belt, he turned to the left, passed several lodges on the fly, then was brought up short by a wall of smoke.

Changing direction again, Nate sought some sign of the prairie. He spotted Minneconjou women and children fleeing to the west, spotted Sioux and Pawnees locked in life and death struggles. An opening between two lodges on his left seemed the best path to take, so he galloped through it only to behold another Pawnee grappling with a raven-haired woman, striving to pull her up onto his horse. Nearby an elderly woman lay, her skull cracked wide.

Nate was wheeling his horse to seek another avenue out of the village when he realized the Pawnee was White Calf. He assumed the medicine man had found the young maiden from the river until the woman's lovely face, contorted in grim defiance, was lifted in profile. For a moment he thought he was imagining things, that he'd gotten more smoke into his eyes than he'd thought. Then the tussling pair shifted and he had a good look at her features. A keg of black powder seemed to explode inside his head. The world spun, or his brain did.

It couldn't be, and yet it was! It was impossible, yet there she stood!

Winona!

Chapter Twenty-three

No sight is guaranteed to arouse the wrath of a man in love more than the sight of his beloved in peril. In the masculine chest beats the heart of a protector, as ingrained in the male nature as stubbornness and pride. So powerful is this urge that many an errant coward has found his courage on the field of romantic valor.

Nate King was certainly no coward. Time and again he'd proven his bravery against vicious men and feral beasts. So he needed no added incentive when he saw the woman he adored being forcibly hauled onto the horse of the man he despised the most of all the men in the world; he vented a Shoshone war whoop and charged, waving his tomahawk aloft.

White Calf looked up in consternation. Blatant amazement overcame him when he saw who was bearing down on him like an avenging fury. He recovered quickly, firming his hold on the woman's waist as he broke into a gallop and fled.

For Winona King's part, she was no less astounded. She had about resigned herself to not seeing her family again for a long time, if ever. They had no idea where to look for her, and should they dare penetrate Lakota country they faced certain death if discovered. Plus she had the added worry of her baby. Once it was born, she would be tied to the Minneconjou village until the infant was big enough and strong enough to endure the rigors of a lengthy journey. That might be a year off, maybe longer.

Winona's despair had known no bounds. For the past week she had cried herself to sleep, convinced her future was as bleak as the southwestern desert. She had prayed to Apo, the Shoshone Father on high, and to her husband's god, the Lord of Heaven and Earth. But deep down she had never expected her prayers to be answered.

The night before had been typical. Winona had retired early, badly in need of rest after another trying day. Her discomfort was growing. She had a hard time getting around. The littlest exertion left her exhausted. Having Butterfly to help around the lodge was of tremendous benefit.

Then came the morning, and as usual Winona had been tossing and turning, her legs laced with cramps, the baby trying to widen her navel from the inside with its kicks.

The first screams from the east had made Winona sit up and listen. There had been shouts, gunshots, the uproar of a village under attack, sounds she knew all too well.

Butterfly, ever a heavy sleeper, hadn't responded to Winona's cries. Winona had to push herself erect and wobble over to nudge the elderly woman. Together they had stood near the doorway, debating in sign whether to stay or flee.

The burning lodges decided them; to be trapped in one would be a horrible end. Butterfly had held the flap while Winona stooped and went out. They had only taken a few steps when the pounding of hooves behind them heralded the arrival of a somber, merciless enemy, a Pawnee warrior who had brought a war club smashing down on Butterfly's upturned head before she could lift a hand to defend herself.

Winona had tried to run but in her condition it was hopeless. She had glanced over her shoulder, expecting the same fate as the kindly Minneconjou. Instead she had been grabbed, then pulled onto the Pawnee's mount even though she fought like a wildcat.

On hearing the war whoop she had looked around in startled surprise. On seeing the source she had felt her heart swell with love even as her mind filled with disbelief. Nate's reappearance was too sudden, too unexpected. How could Nate be in Sioux country when she had last seen him near the Yellowstone? And what was he doing there in the middle of a Pawnee attack?

Logic fought with reality and lost. Winona automatically reached for him, longing to clasp him close, but the Pawnee bore her away, deeper into the village. She tried to land a punch but she was on her side, facing the horse's neck. She couldn't kick the Pawnee for the same reason. Helpless, she clasped her stomach and hoped the baby wouldn't be harmed by the hard jostling.

Nate saw his wife being swept off and gave chase, oblivious to all else. He only had eyes for her. The Pawnees and Sioux meant nothing to him; it was as if they didn't exist. The burning lodges, the terrified women and children, might as well have been phantasms. But they weren't, as Nate found out the hard way when a screeching woman darted directly in front of his horse and he had to haul on the reins to avoid her. As he swerved, another obstacle presented itself, a much more serious one, a Sioux warrior with a long forelock and a lance upraised to throw.

Having already used his pistol, Nate had to rely on the tomahawk, which was usually a close combat weapon but could be thrown with fair accuracy if a man knew how. Since first acquiring his, Nate had idled away many an hour tossing it at targets and had perfected a near flawless toss. So on seeing the warrior dash out into the open, Nate arced his right arm in a fluid motion that sent the tomahawk flying end over end.

The Minneconjou with the forelock started to whip his throwing arm forward when the keen edge of the tomahawk bit into his forehead above the nose, cleaving the flesh and the bone underneath as if both were so much butter.

Nate went around the falling body. He saw that White Calf had gained ground on him so he didn't even try to reclaim the tomahawk. Winona came first. Nothing else mattered.

The medicine man had witnessed the Minneconjou's death. He lashed his war horse with his quirt, attempting to go faster. A child ran in his path and he ran the boy down without a second thought. He had to get away. Once safe, he would try to figure out why the bearded one had turned on him.

A large cloud of gray smoke blotted out the lodges to the left. White Calf was going to bypass it until an idea struck him. Smirking at his own cleverness, he changed direction, plunging *into* the smoke.

Nate saw, and cursed. Seconds later he entered the cloud at the exact same spot and instantly was unable to see farther than the end of his arm. A towering triangular mass loomed out of the gloom. He turned the horse, narrowly missing the teepee. Another and another appeared. Each time Nate swerved past them with inches to spare.

White Calf had disappeared. Frantically, fruitlessly, Nate probed the smoke. If he lost them now he would never see Winona again. He tried listening for hoofbeats but the general bedlam made it impossible. Although he breathed shallow, his lungs began to burn, his eyes to smart.

Suddenly the drifting gray veil thinned and Nate saw a rider. Angling to intercept, he drew his butcher knife. As his mount burst into fresh air he realized the rider was a Sioux, not a

Pawnee, an elderly man who shouted orders to the panicked Minneconjous. A chief, Nate figured, and would have left the man alone had the Sioux not spied him and lifted a lance.

Nate flew past, his arm lashed out, flicked once. A crimson slash blossomed across the chief's throat, from ear to ear. The Minneconjou stiffened as blood gushed and a stupid expression came over his face.

Nate saw no more because he was flying toward another rider barely visible through the lodges. He pursued, trying to make headway in the midst of the pandemonium, being careful not to collide with fleeing women and children and to stay well shy of armed Sioux warriors. By this time a stream of Minneconjous and animals flowed westward, women driving their prized mares before them with fear-struck children at their sides and yapping dogs in attendance. Warriors ran to and fro, still largely unorganized, clashing here and there with Pawnees.

Nate glimpsed the prairie, watched the rider he was after clear the last lodge. His pulse quickened when he recognized the medicine man and saw Winona trying to free herself. He came to a clear avenue between the lodges and gave the horse its head. This proved a costly error.

From out of nowhere came another rider, this time a Minneconjou armed with a tomahawk. The warrior's horse plowed into Nate's, the shock bowling both animals over.

Nate leaped clear with a hair breadth to spare, rolling as he hit. He pushed erect, spun. The Minneconjou was on him before he could raise the knife. He leaped backward and the tomahawk fanned his face. Shifting on a heel, he speared his blade at the warrior's midsection but missed.

Meanwhile White Calf was getting farther away. That thought goaded Nate into gambling his life on his reflexes. He feinted, deliberately exposing his chest but keeping his left arm close to his waist. The Sioux took the bait and swiped at Nate's ribs. Nate twisted, seized the warrior's wrist, then buried his knife between the man's ribs.

There was no fear in this Minneconjou, no weakness at all. Mortally stricken, he nevertheless wrenched on his arm while clawing at the knife hilt. Slowly his eyes became vacant and he slumped earthward.

Nate turned toward the horses. His had sustained a broken leg, the shattered bone jutting through its skin, and was thrashing on the ground in pain. The Sioux's had regained its feet but was too shaken to run off. He ran to it and vaulted onto its back. Grabbing the reins, he lit out after the Pawnee medicine man who by now was a scarecrow figure in the distance. He wondered how his wife was holding up, and mentally vowed to make the Pawnee suffer the agony of the damned if she was harmed.

Winona, to this point, was doing well. She'd been scratched and bruised and her stomach was queasy from the motion of the horse, but she'd been spared serious harm. Try as she might to break loose, she couldn't, so she had given up the effort to conserve her strength. Since she couldn't see the village, she had no idea whether Nate still pursued them. The strident screams and angry shouts, rapidly dwindling, gave the impression of wholesale slaughter taking place, and she feared greatly for his life.

Winona wondered why the Pawnee had stolen her when there were so many younger women in the village. And in her state! She guessed that in all the excitement he simply hadn't noticed. She was wrong, though.

White Calf had indeed seen that she was pregnant and been about to pass her in his search for the maiden from the river, or any maiden, for that matter. Time was pressing, since soon the Minneconjous would rally. He'd about made up his mind to forego finding a woman when Winona's strikingly beautiful features caught his eye. A shrewd judge of men and women, he'd detected a vibrant lust for life in the way she moved, the way she carried herself. She was special. And being pregnant was a bonus, not a detriment. The child, if a boy, could be reared as White Calf's own son. If a girl, later in life she would fetch a handsome dowry when she was married off, provided he didn't grow tired of the mother and cast her aside first. So, acting on the spur of the moment, White Calf had snatched the woman.

Looking back, the medicine man saw no trace of the mighty Sky Walker. He congratulated himself on having outwitted his enemies and scoured the plain for fellow Pawnees. To the southeast a large herd of stolen horses raised clouds of dust. He saw his men on the outskirts, goading the animals on. He also saw a bunch of

Minneconjous on their heels.

To the east a thin strip of vegetation rimmed a gully. White Calf galloped under slender cottonwoods, then paused. The grassy slope inclined gently. He rode to the bottom and headed northward, pleased at the turn of events. The Minneconjous would concentrate on the other Pawnees, leaving him alone.

Winona heard her captor laugh lightly. Twisting her head, she saw him clearly for the first time and inwardly flinched at the cruelty dancing in his eyes. Something told her she'd have been better off with the Sioux. She tried to twist further, to look for Nate, but her belly stopped her.

Had she been able to turn, Winona would not have spotted him. Nate King had seen the medicine man gain the gully but had elected to swing wide of it and ride parallel to the strip of vegetation, just out of earshot. He pushed the Sioux war horse to its limits, confident he could outdistance the Pawnee who was burdened by Winona's weight.

In a mile the gully curved westward. Nate reined up at the bend and screened his eyes with a palm so he could scour its length to the south. The medicine man had yet to appear. Dismounting in the high grass, he hurried to a willow and tied the horse. Then he went over the rim to a narrow shelf eroded by rain. Here he laid flat, the bloody butcher knife in front of him.

Presently the gully echoed to the thud of hooves. Nate coiled, one hand gripping the edge of the shelf. The Pawnee rode into view,

Winona still over the horse. White Calf halted at the bend to look back.

Nate dug his toes into the soil for added purchase. Like a mountain lion poised to spring, he glued his eyes to the medicine man as White Calf advanced. He wished he could alert Winona so she'd know what he was about to do and could brace herself. Then the paint trotted under the shelf and he sprang.

The Pawnee would have been taken completely unawares if not for Nate's shadow passing over him. He glanced up, eyes widening, and elevated his war club, deflecting Nate's knife a heartbeat before Nate slammed into him. They tumbled to the slope, just missing Winona. Both landed on their shoulders and rose, a yard apart.

Nate would rather have had his tomahawk. A knife against a war club was an unequal contest since the war club was bigger and longer. With the aim of ending the fight swiftly, he stabbed at the medicine man's stomach.

White Calf was no slouch as a warrior. He swatted the blade aside, then countered with a blow that would have crushed Nate's knee to bony splinters had Nate not jerked his leg aside.

Winona, seizing the opportunity, slid off the paint, grasping the reins as she did so it couldn't flee. She glanced down at her feet, found a small stone, and picked it up.

Nate was pressing his enemy, slashing repeatedly, endeavoring to break through White Calf's guard. The Pawnee retreated a few feet, then refused to be budged, his war club flashing in an intricate web of defense that prevented Nate from scoring. Evenly matched, they swung, countered, swung again.

White Calf's wrath mounted with every miss. He held the club in two hands, flailing like a madman, lips curled in a bestial sneer. The white man ducked under a high swing, skipped aside from a low swing. It was like fighting an agile wolverine, only more vexing.

The war club whisked past Nate's shoulder. He tried to seize the handle, but failed. A desperate tactic was called for if he wanted to prevail. Bounding backward, he flipped the knife in his hand, reversing his grip so he could throw it as he had thrown the tomahawk The blade cut the air almost too fast for the eye to follow, yet not fast enough.

Instinctively, White Calf had brought the war club in front of his chest to protect himself. The knife hit the haft a few inches above his fingers and glanced off, falling at his feet. Now the only one armed, he roared a challenge and went on the offensive with a vengeance.

Nate backpedaled. He didn't dare try to block blows with his forearms or the war club would splinter his bones like so much dry kindling. Prancing right and left, he saved himself time and again from having his head smashed to a pulp.

Then the unexpected reared its ugly head. Nate's left heel slipped on slick grass. His leg shot out from under him and he fell on his back. He tried to roll but bumped a boulder. Looking up, he saw White Calf loom above him, the club tilted at the sky. He couldn't evade the next swing and knew it.

Winona saw his predicament. She took a step and hurled the stone, throwing her entire weight into the act.

White Calf, tingling with blood lust, bunched his shoulders for the killing stroke. He felt something shear into his eye, felt blood spurt. Pain rocked him on his heels. Summoning his willpower, he swung anyway, but the delay had cost him.

Nate shoved on the boulder, catapulting himself to the left as the war club descended. It clipped him, but not hard enough to do real damage. He kicked, ramming the medicine man's shin, sweeping White Calf's leg out from under him.

The Pawnee fell onto his back, then quickly scrambled to one knee, trying to keep his good eye fixed on his adversary. He saw the boulder but not Sky Walker.

Nate had skipped to the left. Jumping in close, he slammed his knee into White Calf's face. Cartilage crunched as the nose shattered and White Calf crashed onto his back again. The Pawnee tried to rise, wildly swinging his club. Nate kicked, catching White Calf on the elbow, numbing the medicine man's arm. White Calf gamely tried to wield the club one-handed but Nate delivered a devastating punch to the jaw that stunned him.

"That was for all those maidens," Nate said, tearing the club from the Pawnee's grasp and flinging it down the gully. He bunched his fist, raised White Calf's head off the ground. "This is for my wife." He punched the medicine man full in the mouth.

White Calf uttered a sputtering gasp, clawed at empty air, and went limp.

Nate pivoted, saw his butcher knife. Retrieving it, he stepped to the Pawnee and touched the tip of the blade to White Calf's throat. "This ends it, you son of a bitch!" His blood boiling, he went to sink the knife in when a soft voice ripped through him like a bolt of lightning.

"Husband."

Whirling, Nate stood frozen, drinking in the loveliness of the woman he was proud to call his mate. She had tears in her eyes and her lips trembled. He tried to speak but his vocal chords were paralyzed.

"I have missed you so," Winona said huskily, her heart near bursting with joy such as she had never experienced. She lifted her hands and began to move toward him but he reached her first, taking her into his strong, muscular arms and pressing her close to his broad chest. Winona wanted to tell him that she loved him, that there was no one else in all creation for her, but the words wouldn't come. Inside her a floodgate opened. Burying her face in his shirt, she did that which she rarely did; she cried, emptying herself of all her pent-up emotions, her accumulated grief and horror and, yes, her love.

Nate was shocked. He couldn't recall Winona ever crying before. He held her close, her body quaking gently, and fought back his own tears. Inside his head he seemed to hear surf pounding on a rocky shore, and in his chest there was an intense itching sensation, neither of which made any sense.

A long time they stood there, neither moving or speaking but saying more in their simple embrace than many couples said in a lifetime of empty chatter.

The nickering of the horse brought Nate to himself. He coughed, stroked Winona's hair, and leaned back. "We have to get out of here before the Minneconjous come looking for you."

"There is so much I have to tell you," Winona said, tenderly touching his cheek.

"Tonight, and every night thereafter." Nate embraced her, lowering his lips to hers, giving her the sort of kiss a woman would remember the rest of her life. They broke for air and he gazed affectionately into her eyes, expecting to see his love mirrored there. In place of love he saw terror, and too late he realized she was looking past him, not at him.

A tremendous blow landed on Nate's right shoulder, driving him to his knees. Swiveling, through a haze of torment he saw White Calf, one eye socket filled with blood, the other eye dilated in murderous madness. The Pawnee was slowly raising the war club for another blow.

"This is for me!" Nate bellowed, and drove his knife into the medicine man's stomach, sheering upward into the vital organs under the ribs.

White Calf released his club, clutched at his abdomen, and tottered. He swung his dilated eye from Nate to Winona and back again, and it was clear he wanted to say something. His lips moved, spewing a dry croak laced with red spittle. He stumbled, fell against the boulder, then sank onto his side, fingers twitching convulsively. When they stopped moving he was dead.

"You knew him?" Winona asked.

Nate nodded. "It's a long story." He moved to the horse and offered her his hand. "I'll give you a boost."

Winona took a step, then halted, her features locked in astonishment. "No!" she said. "It can't be!"

Thinking she was hurt, Nate took her arm. "What is it? The baby?"

"Yes."

"Oh, Lord! And us without a doctor or a midwife. How bad do you reckon it is?"

"Get me a broken limb, a stout stick, anything" Winona urged. "Hurry!"

"A stick? What good will that do?" Nate responded, confused. Then he recalled that Shoshone women gave birth by squatting and leaning on whatever was convenient, whether it be a branch or a lance or a rock the right size. "You mean now?" he said, thunderstruck.

"Now."

"Can't you hold it in?"

Winona hitched at her dress. "A woman has little control over the time or the place." She eased down. "All that bouncing and the fight have brought it on sooner than I expected."

"We're only a mile or two from the Sioux camp. What if they find us?"

"Then they can watch."

Nate just looked at her, and Winona grinned. He grinned, too, loving her more at that moment than he ever had, more than he had ever thought it possible to love another human being. He might have stood there forever, entranced, had she not gestured impatiently.

"Are you going to help or must I do it all myself?"

Chapter Twenty-four

The trappers had their packs in order and were stowing their gear in their canoes. Everyone had a job to do except Shakespeare McNair, who sat with his back against a tree stump and poked at the fire. A scowl creased his lips when he saw Lane and Abby strolling hand in hand by the river. They reminded him of two others, and the hurt was too awful to bear. To himself he quoted softly, "Alas, poor Yorick! I knew him, Horatio. A fellow of infinite jest, of most excellent fancy. He hath borne me on his back a thousand times, and now how abhorred in my imagination it is." His voice broke and he couldn't go on.

Just then a commotion broke out at the east side of the clearing. Loud voices mingled with laughter, and through the trees several trap-

pers came, guiding a pair of newcomers who
led a single horse.

Shakespeare stared, and stared. For one of
the few times ever he was stupefied beyond
measure.

The newcomers walked straight over and regarded him with twinkling eyes.

"What do you suppose he is doing?" Winona
asked.

"Sitting there catching mosquitoes in his
mouth, I reckon," Nate answered. "Although
I could be wrong. Shakespeare fanatics are a
peculiar bunch."

McNair so forgot himself, he put both hands
on the ground and was going to stand. They
stopped him, one on either side.

"Don't you dare," Nate said. "Knorr told us."

"One hundred and seventy-eight stitches,"
Winona said. "And I thought I had a rough
time."

"You're alive!" Shakespeare exclaimed. "Dear
God in Heaven, you're alive!" He hugged them
both and bowed his head, and for ten minutes
the trappers kept a respectful distance. Finally
Shakespeare wiped his eyes and straightened.
"Forgive this old coon," he said gruffly. "My
years are catching up with me."

"Why do men always think they are being
weak when they cry?" Winona asked. "You try
to act like you have hearts of stone when the
truth is that your hearts are as soft as ours."

Shakespeare smiled. "The differences between men and women are too deep to fathom,
fair lady, and I hope they always are."

"Oh?"

"It gives us something to ponder when we can't sleep at night." Shakespeare nodded at the bundle cradled in her left arm. "New buckskin, I see."

"I killed the deer a week ago," Nate said.

"Can't help but notice the way it's wriggling and cooing. Might I take a gander?"

Winona parted the folds, revealing the smooth face of the tiny infant. "Meet Evelyn King."

"Evelyn?"

"Remind me to fill you in sometime," Nate responded.

Winona carefully passed the baby to Shakespeare, who placed the precious swaddled wonder in his lap. "I will hereupon confess I am in love," he quoted. "Happy the parents of so fair a child."

"I cannot wait to get back and show her off," Winona said proudly. "I think she is the image of her father."

"Insult Evelyn like that again and I'll keep her for myself," Shakespeare threatened. Imitating a pigeon, he tickled the child's chin.

"Back to normal," Nate commented. Sighing, he sat cross-legged and saw another woman near the Yellowstone. A white woman, no less! He wondered whether she knew what she was letting herself in for.

The baby tried to grasp the bottom of Shakespeare's beard. "Look at this," he said. "Living proof they can't wait to get their hooks into a man. I always knew they started young."

The mention brought Zach to Nate's mind, and he asked, "Did you see any sign after the storm? Any on your way here?"

"Just a band of Blackfeet," Shakespeare misconstrued. "But these were a newfangled breed. Instead of shooting you, they talk you half to death."

"They were the only ones you saw?"

"Yep," Shakespeare replied, and was mystified by the acute sorrow that came over his friends. For only a moment, though. "Tarnation. You haven't heard the whole story yet, have you?"

"About the bear? Yes."

"To hell with the grizzly! I—" Shakespeare began, but did not go on. Two trappers who had gone off hunting earlier were at that moment returning, and behind them bobbed the tousled head of the Kings' firstborn. "It's a good thing I'm the one holding little Evelyn," he remarked.

"Why do you say that?" Winona asked.

"I'd hate for her to get squished to death when all of you get to smothering one another."

Nate voiced a bitter, dry laugh. "As usual you don't make any blamed sense whatsoever."

"Do tell," Shakespeare said. He commenced counting, out loud. Winona and Nate exchanged glances and regarded him as if he was touched in the head. The howl of delight came when he reached seven.

"*Ma! Pa!*"

The whole camp turned out to witness the reunion of the King family. Shakespeare was grateful the Blackfeet were long gone or the whole party would have been rubbed out. The rejoicing was so loud, a flock of sparrows clear across the Yellowstone was startled into flight.

Even Evelyn gave a little jump. McNair smiled at the sweet, innocent babe, and touched the tiny tip of her nose with a calloused finger. "You're lucky, little one. You have two of the best parents in the world. And if they live long enough, they'll watch over you and help steer you through this maze we call a life. And maybe, just maybe, when you come out at the other end, you'll be able to deal with this old world of ours on its own terms and be none the worse for wear." Settling back, he rested a hand on the thick book beside him, winked at the infant, and said, "Anyone ever told you the story of Romeo and Juliet?"

WILDERNESS

GIANT SPECIAL EDITION:
SEASON OF THE WARRIOR

By David Thompson

Tough mountain men, proud Indians, and an America that was wild and free—authentic frontier adventure during America's Black Powder Days.

The savage, unmapped territory west of the Mississippi presents constant challenges to anyone who dares to venture into it. And when a group of English travelers journey into the Rockies, they have no defense against the fierce Indians, deadly beasts, and hostile elements. If Nate and his friend Shakespeare McNair can't save them, the young adventurers will suffer unimaginable pain before facing certain death.

_3449-2 $4.50 US/$5.50 CAN

WILDERNESS

By David Thompson

Tough mountain men, proud Indians, and an America that was wild and free—authentic frontier adventure set in America's Black Powder Days.

#12: Apache Blood. When Nate and his family travel to the southern Rockies, bloodthirsty Apache warriors kidnap his wife and son. With the help of his friend Shakespeare McNair, Nate will save his loved ones—or pay the ultimate price.

__3374-7 $3.50 US/$4.50 CAN

#13: Mountain Manhunt. When Nate frees Solomon Cain from an Indian death trap, the apparently innocent man repays Nate's kindness by leaving him stranded in the wilds. Only with the help of a Ute brave can Nate set right the mistake he has made.

__3396-8 $3.50 US/$4.50 CAN

#14: Tenderfoot. To protect their families, Nate King and other settlers have taught their sons the skills that will help them survive. But young Zach King is still a tenderfoot when vicious Indians capture his father. If Zach hasn't learned his lessons well, Nate's only hope will be a quick death.

__3422-0 $3.50 US/$4.50 CAN

WILDERNESS
The epic struggle for survival in America's untamed West.

#17: Trapper's Blood. In the wild Rockies, any man who dares to challenge the brutal land has to act as judge, jury, and executioner against his enemies. And when trappers start turning up dead, their bodies horribly mutilated, Nate and his friends vow to hunt down the merciless killers. Taking the law into their own hands, they soon find that one hasty decision can make them as guilty as the murderers they want to stop.

_3566-9 $3.50 US/$4.50 CAN

#16: Blood Truce. Under constant threat of Indian attack, a handful of white trappers and traders live short, violent lives, painfully aware that their next breath could be their last. So when a deadly dispute between rival Indian tribes explodes into a bloody war, Nate has to make peace between enemies—or he and his young family will be the first to lose their scalps.

_3525-1 $3.50 US/$4.50 CAN

#15: Winterkill. Any greenhorn unlucky enough to get stranded in a wilderness blizzard faces a brutal death. But when Nate takes in a pair of strangers who have lost their way in the snow, his kindness is repaid with vile treachery. If King isn't careful, he and his young family will not live to see another spring.

_3487-5 $3.50 US/$4.50 CAN

Jake
McMasters

Follow Clay Taggart as he hunts the murdering S.O.B.s who left him for dead—and sends them to hell!

#1: Hangman's Knot. Strung up and left to die, Taggart is seconds away from death when he is cut down by a ragtag band of Apaches. Disappointed to find Taggart alive, the warriors debate whether to kill him immediately or to ransom him off. They are hungry enough to eat him, but they think he might be worth more on the hoof. He is. Soon the white desperado and the desperate Apaches form an alliance that will turn the Arizona desert red with blood.

_3535-9 $3.99 US/$4.99 CAN

#2: Warpath. Twelve S.O.B.s were the only reason Taggart had for living. Together with the desperate Apache warriors who'd saved him from death, he'd have his revenge. One by one, he'd hunt the yellowbellies down. One by one, he'd make them wish they'd never drawn a breath. One by one, he'd leave their guts and bones scorching under the brutal desert sun.

_3575-8 $3.99 US/$4.99 CAN

LEISURE BOOKS
ATTN: Order Department
276 5th Avenue, New York, NY 10001

Please add $1.50 for shipping and handling for the first book and $.35 for each book thereafter. PA., N.Y.S. and N.Y.C. residents, please add appropriate sales tax. No cash, stamps, or C.O.D.s. All orders shipped within 6 weeks via postal service book rate. Canadian orders require $2.00 extra postage and must be paid in U.S. dollars through a U.S. banking facility.

Name_____

Address_____

City _____ State_____ Zip_____

I have enclosed $____in payment for the checked book(s).

Payment <u>must</u> accompany all orders.□ Please send a free catalog.